Ruthless Saint

DESANTIS MAFIA
BOOK ONE

S. MASSERY

Editing by Studio ENP

Cover Design by TRC Designs

For Ari

Introduction & Warning

Hello dear reader!

PLEASE NOTE: some things happen to our heroine that readers may find distressing, including sexual assault.

We first meet Amelie Page in the Fallen Royals series (although it isn't necessary to read those before this story). She was the classic mean girl at her high school, Emery-Rose Elite. And her hero is her perfect foil.

I hope you enjoy Amelie's journey now as she takes the spotlight!

Playlist

Messed Up — Little Hurt

False God — Ryan Hurd

Sweet Little Lies — bülow

I'm So Mad At Him — Kesly Karter

Gone — Blake Rose

can't look back — Machine Gun Kelly

Spaces — Jaymes Young

Four — The Wrecks

Give In to Me — Garrett Hedlund & Leighton Meester

Slow Dancing in a Burning Room — John Mayer

Prologue

Today started with a wedding.

Mine, to be exact. I had the perfect dress, a lace veil that covered my face, something borrowed, and something blue. Pearls strangled my neck.

I didn't picture my life like this.

And I know what you're thinking. Blah, blah, Amelie. Everyone says that. That's true to an extent. Everyone does complain that their lives are miserable and they have no control.

They don't know real helplessness.

Your every move planned down to the minute.

Where to be, when to speak, what to say.

While dread held my body hostage, my family was eager. They had been awaiting this day for years. Our house was filled with never-ending talk about the alliances they were forging. The steps forward we were taking.

Steps forward meant power. Respect.

Power required money—of which we had plenty.

It was the respect part that dear old Dad was always

chasing after, and perhaps that's why he never was able to fully grasp it.

That, plus one other important factor—respect could seem a lot like fear.

Therein laid the trap: his eldest daughter was a hostage. And not just that...

A bargaining chip.

There was the dress and the veil and the stupid sapphire earrings that made my lobes ache. The walk down the aisle, toward a man I had done my best to understand. The eldest DeSantis brother. The one with the most to lose—and the most to gain, depending on the outcome of our union. We'd been in orbit for a while, and today we were on a collision course.

But my entire world rotated on its axis that day.

My life was planned from my sixteenth birthday onward, like the second hand of a clock. Onward; drearily, relentlessly forward.

But my wedding?

Instead of a kiss on my lips, it ended with blood splattered across my veil.

And that... well, that's where our story begins.

CHAPTER 1
Amelie

I learned of my impending marriage on my sixteenth birthday. We were at our summer home in southern France. Most summers were spent lounging around, enjoying the warm air that felt distinctly different from the United States. The buzz of foreign language, of time moving slowly, of happy, tired families outside our door.

But my birthday always tended to be a wickedly lavish celebration. Sometimes a friend would be flown out for the week, sometimes a whole plane full. Sixteen was supposed to be special. *Sweet.*

Instead of a friend flying in from Rose Hill, New York... it was a man and his sons who crossed the border from Italy.

Jameson DeSantis had grown close to my father. It seemed that they were only staying in Sanremo for a vacation and nothing more. A summer ancestral home, a bit like ours, if we hadn't purchased ours four years prior. He walked into the courtyard like he owned the place, kissed my mother on the cheek, and took my hand. His lips skated across my knuckles, and revulsion was my first gut instinct. Then annoyance.

His sons—three of them, all in a row—had appraised me.

I think they found newly sixteen-year-old me lacking.

I found them lacking, as well, of any sort of manners and charm. They were wild boys, honed to a fine edge like a chef's knife. The sharpness of them would've scared me if I had known any better. But there was an absence of everything that would've made them appealing. All except one.

Wilder DeSantis came forward and mirrored his father's actions, kissing my knuckles. His breath seemed to sink under my skin and into my blood.

"You're my future wife," he said.

I didn't know what he meant, but I soon found out. The door of my cage slammed closed, and I hadn't even noticed the bars being constructed.

"Amelie," my mother calls now, jarring me from my thoughts. "Here."

I take the sapphire earrings and test their weight in my palm, then slide them on. Everything is expensive. Everything is lavish. They've wasted no expense on their eldest daughter. The stones are heavy in my ears, the pain a dull ache. I can deal with it for a minute, then an hour, then an evening.

That's how you swallow a sword: one inch at a time.

"Your dress," Mom urges.

My sister sits in the corner, scrolling through her phone. We're in the DeSantis skyscraper in Manhattan, too high up for escape. I think that's part of it—they like their women trapped.

If I had the urge to flee, I wouldn't make it two floors before someone caught me.

My father is a few floors below us, probably at the bar on the seventeenth. He's much more celebratory than us. Mom seems solemn.

"You're strong," she whispers, holding my shoulders for a moment. "You can do this."

But why?

That question has been answered in a variety of different ways over the years, but nothing hits home like the truth will. It's the only reason I keep asking: I'm desperate for someone to be honest with me. I know it has to do with our business in Manhattan, my parents' late-night arguments. It's been going on for years, so much so that it's become normal.

What they did to put us in this position—that's the mystery.

She helps me navigate into the dress, then turns me to close the buttons. It takes precious time, and I have to press my palms against the wall to avoid being shoved around. The dress is tight, like a corset, and it flares out at my hips.

It gives me curves I wish didn't exist.

"Mom," I say softly. "Why is this happening?"

She pauses, then finishes the buttons. "You like Wilder."

"I like Wilder the same way I like pizza," I retort. "It's nice, I'd give it up if it was the one thing I could eat for the rest of my life."

My sister snorts. "Great analogy."

"Lucy," Mom hisses.

I straighten. "Just another hour or two, Lux. Then you'll never have to see me again."

"Don't call her that," Mom says.

Different names for different occasions—but calling Lucy *Lux* might be the straw that breaks the camel's back. She's the rebellious child. The one who gets away with murder while I am strapped with responsibility.

Lucy stands, stashing her phone in her dress pocket. "It's okay, Ames. Mom's just on the verge of losing her only daughter."

Hurt flashes across Mom's face, and she turns to my sister. "You are still my daughter."

Lucy shrugs. "News to me."

Someone knocks on the door, interrupting whatever

response my mother had. Mom opens it a crack, then pushes it wider. All that's missing is my veil, but it's clutched in Lucy's hand. A young DeSantis boy stands in the hall, flushed bright pink. He's got to be no older than eight or nine.

"They're ready," he says.

Mom nods. "We are, as well. Come, Amelie. It's time."

Lucy puts the veil in my hair, pinning it into place with two pearl-studded clips. "I'm going to get a tattoo of your face on my arm after this," she whispers. "So I'll never forget you."

I roll my eyes. "I'm not dying."

Her expression drops. "You may as well be."

I may as well be. Yes, that's true.

Mom shepherds us into the elevator, then a car. I imagine all the things Wilder and I will have to talk about. We barely had a chance to converse at the rehearsal dinner last night, and then he was whisked away by his brothers.

But we have the rest of our lives to talk... and do other things.

Maybe we'll even fall in love.

"You've got this," Lucy whispers.

She takes my hand. Mom rides in the front with the driver, and our car pulls out of the garage in a line of others.

"I wish your friends could be here for you," she adds.

I close my eyes and concentrate on the warm French summers. The mosaic tile above the kitchen sink, the smell of rain. Happy things.

Not a wedding in the small chapel just outside the city, closer to Rose Hill than Manhattan. Not what will happen after.

CHAPTER 2
Amelie

What no one tells you about war is that it's discussed beforehand. Prior to the first shot being fired, there are meetings. Drinks. Political bullshit.

There are plans and promises.

Handshakes and smiles.

Meanwhile, each side plots to stab each other in the back.

"We had a deal," my father yells. He's livid, the embodiment of fire. Red face, explosive movements. All he needed was a bit of oxygen to get going, and now he rages.

Jameson DeSantis stands with his hands in his pockets, not at all rising to my father's level of pissed. He's one of those quietly scary men, anyway. Dad's all shouting and steam pouring out of his ears. When he's upset, the whole world knows it.

Jameson is the viper.

"I didn't say the deal was off," Jameson replies. He finally moves, but it's toward me.

I start when his hand comes out of his pocket, extending a handkerchief. I take it and curl it into my fist.

"Your son—"

"Michael," my mom snaps at her husband. She hovers behind him. "That's enough."

Dad blinks, the steam essentially sucked out of him. It leaves him deflated.

"Let's discuss this downstairs," Jameson offers. "Give your daughter a moment. Our guests are currently being transported to our estate, and we should join them."

As soon as the three of them are gone, I stand. The handkerchief is cool in my fingers, and I'm half-tempted to use it. Too bad a DeSantis gift always has strings attached. This one might not cost me much, but I cannot let myself slacken. Or worse, get used to their kindness.

The room I'm in has two wide windows, the gauzy curtains closed against the sun. There's a bathroom attached. We were to be married outside, by a cluster of giant trees, but the heat drove us into the chapel. And now I'm in the building next door, on the second floor.

I would've used this room to take photos with Wilder. It's set up as such, with soft light and open spaces. They would've arranged the train of my dress just so. And yet now, when I think about what might've been, my imagination has stained us all red.

I hardly remember the trip up here, but someone carried me. A hand cupped the back of my head, pressing it to their chest. I do remember the scratch of their boutonniere against my cheek, but I was nearly out of it.

Still... my mind can't erase the gunshot. How different it sounded from what I expected. How much louder it seemed.

Abruptly, I wheel around and take in the rest of the room.

Now that I'm alone, the silence creeps in, pulling along what happened only minutes ago.

One minute there was a crack, and the next, my chest and face were coated in warm liquid. The wet veil stuck to my skin.

My eyes closed. I'm not ashamed to admit the reflex.

Something hit my front, and I snapped my eyes open. My hands came up automatically, grabbing on to firm shoulders I had never touched before. For all of our engagement, I'd never laid a hand on Wilder. It didn't seem right, even when he asked if he could kiss me.

He held my hands half a dozen times. He did kiss me, just once. But how is it that I can only have two points of contact with the man I'm marrying? The man I *was* marrying. We didn't finish. We didn't trade vows.

My almost-husband slid to the floor and took me with him. There was no way I was going to hold him up, not alone, but my grip didn't loosen. We crumpled to the floor together.

It took too many seconds to realize he was bleeding.

That no one had let off a firework in the middle of the church.

Something—someone—crashed into me from the side, knocking me away from my fiancé. Another crack.

Screaming.

My head bounced off the marble steps, and everything went gray.

Not black, really, although I wish I had lost consciousness. I wish I could forget the way I zeroed in on Wilder's pale face.

He was losing blood.

I jerk, shaking free the memory, and cross to the bathroom.

The dress is off-white. Not exactly cream. Not starched white, like fallen snow. Off-white. Just a shade to the left, closer to mud.

My only thought when I agreed to wear it was that the endless row of buttons might delay my future husband from consummating our wedding night.

It isn't that I never pictured sex with Wilder. I did. Sometimes it was all I could think about. But I didn't want that choice taken away from me. The *expectation* was to finalize our marriage through that type of union—something Mom often reminded me.

I'm not a virgin, but that doesn't mean my choice mattered any less. And so… the buttons.

But now, I'm alone and desperate to get it off.

A soldier doesn't need armor when there's no one else in the room.

I flick on the light. It's belated: I've been standing in the dark for a minute.

I'm in shock, that's all, I reassure myself.

And then I meet my own eyes and gasp.

Someone took the veil off my head. I remember that much. It was swept back, and a thumb ran along my cheekbone. There's evidence on my face: droplets of blood on my skin, fine as mist, and a smear.

I dip the cloth under the faucet and rub at it. There's more blood on my dress—I guess it's not just off-white anymore—but I can't focus on that.

It's in my hair, too. In the braids that wind around my head like a crown. Spread across my chest, collarbone. The necklace.

Wilder is dead. I know he is.

Jameson DeSantis is one of the most powerful Mafia lords I've ever seen in action. Not that I've seen too many… On a deeper level, I understand why Wilder would be a target. He was most likely going to take over for his father in a few years—but that was never confirmed. Not to me, at least.

I close my eyes again and lean on the counter.

If his family wasn't a bigger mystery than I knew what to do with, I might've looked forward to the wedding. He was pleasant. Charming, even. A stark contrast from the family I knew was lurking around him. His brothers scared me. It didn't take much longer than the initial meeting for me to realize they had darkness in them that Wilder seemed to lack.

But I saw our marriage for what it was.

"Don't be stupid," I tell my reflection.

His death hasn't sunk in.

The arrangement has been set in stone for three years. I'm nineteen and terrified of what comes next, because our whole lives hinged upon the protection of the DeSantis family.

DeSantis—what a joke of a last name. Saints, they are not.

The door opens and shuts quickly.

Lucy rushes me. "Oh my god. Mom and Dad told me to stay where I was, but then they were herding everyone back to the DeSantis estate, and I knew you weren't there. Everyone scattered. The gunman—"

I hold up my hand. "I can't do this, Lucy. Not right now."

She bites her lip.

We haven't always gotten along. Lucy grew up with our grandparents in the next town over. She was allowed back when she turned seventeen and showed, in the words of my parents, *considerable improvement*. Mom often said that a troubled past required more hands-on rearing.

I didn't know what that meant.

I still don't, actually.

All I know is that my sister and I aren't as close as we should be for two girls who share DNA, but it stemmed from a childhood apart. I'll give her credit: she's been trying.

She stops just short of me, running her gaze up and down my body.

"I should've brought you clothes."

I continue scrubbing at my face. "Where would you even have found clothes?"

She's silent, then, "Maybe you should wash your hair."

"I will when I get home." I pause.

Shit.

It's unlikely that I'm going home. Not at this point.

They'll herd us this way and that in an attempt to keep us safe.

Safe.

Yet they couldn't manage to keep Wilder alive...

And then another thought hits me: if Wilder is dead, what happens to us?

"There's a man outside the door," she whispers. "He's acting like a guard. I'm pretty sure he was one of the ushers."

"Did they catch the person who did it?" So much for not wanting to talk about it.

She shakes her head. "It looked like it came from above us. The choir section, maybe? But I don't think they found who it was. They were yelling at us to stay down, stay in our rows, but so many people started running. There were DeSantis guys rushing around with guns. I lost sight of you..." Lucy grabs my hand. "Who brought you up here? Were Mom and Dad here, too? They tried to stop me..."

"No one could stop you," I tease.

She shrugs. "You'd be surprised."

Impulsively, I wrap her in a hug. She stiffens in my arms—I've never been the affectionate type—and then relaxes. "Mom and Dad were up here yelling at Jameson," I whisper. "I don't know what's going to happen." To our family. To me.

In high school, I was perfect. Captain of the cheer team, a body guys drooled over and girls envied. I was popular, infamous, and a little cruel. I had to be ruthless to get to the top, and that seemed to be the only way to keep my parents happy.

I spent most of the first semester of my senior year in Paris. Upon my return, it was like a weight was lifted off the senior class. We did it. Schools had accepted us, and all that stood between our class and a party-filled summer were a few lousy finals. Meanwhile, iron had settled in my stomach.

Marriage was just around the corner at that point.

"What do you think's going to happen now that Wilder—"

She breaks off.

I forgot she knew him, too. Dinners at our house in France and their Italian villa, visits to Rose Hill and their Manhattan skyscraper. Did we know that every visit took us one step closer to my wedding day?

Not back then.

As I said: war isn't just about the first shot. Many pieces have to line up first, and my parents know how to play the board. Sometimes I wish they had taught me the game, too. I knew I was going to flounder as a Mafia wife.

The thought turns my stomach.

The door opens, and my mother sticks her head in. "Lucy! Dear heavens, we've been looking everywhere for you."

My sister takes my hand. "I've been keeping Ames company. She's being guarded, did you see?"

"I'm well aware. Come on. Both of you."

Mom hurries us down the eerily quiet hall. The people who were buzzing around pre-wedding are gone. Only DeSantis men remain, scanning the area like the shooter might return. Who knows—maybe they will.

We pile into a waiting SUV, and as soon as the doors close, my bubble of surrealism pops.

We were shot at.

Wilder is almost certainly dead.

My hands shake, and cold creeps in. I fist the skirt of my blood-soaked dress. I caught him as he fell and lowered him to the floor before someone knocked into me. My head pounds, and the way my temple hit the stair bursts to the forefront of my mind.

"Mom?" Lucy calls. "Something's wrong."

"I'm f-f-fine." My teeth chatter. Not fine.

Lucy pulls me into her side, wrapping her arm around me.

"It was so scary," she whispers, "but Luca saved you while Aiden went after the shooter. Can you imagine?"

"Well, honey, he had good reason," Mom quips. "Without Amelie, then one of them would have to marry you. And we all know what a handful you've threatened to be."

If there's one thing Lucy has been vocal about over the years, it's that she won't be 'strapped down' by marriage. I never mentioned that her fantasy of escaping fate was thanks to me. If I threw that tantrum, it would be her with the engagement ring on her finger.

One of us had to do it, was what my mother told me one night, years ago. And Lucy... she beat me to the punch. To the refusal.

It's fine.

How can they be so calm? How is Mom always put together? I'm falling apart at the seams.

Lucy scoffs. "Don't pretend you didn't have a choice, Mom. You and Dad are basically sacrificing Ames—"

Mom reaches back and smacks Lucy. "Do not say that."

My sister raises her hand to her cheek.

The violence isn't surprising. It wasn't a hard slap—just a reminder.

"We're here," the driver says, clearing his throat. The iron gates swing open to admit us, and he navigates down a paved driveway to the front of the house.

Lucy bolts from the car and disappears up the front steps. Why she's so eager to get away from us is anyone's guess. But maybe Mom's handling hurt her worse than I thought. She didn't grow up with that, I'd imagine.

The driver climbs out, too, but stops just outside my door with his back to the glass. Waiting. Keeping me inside. The estate is buzzing with people. Guests from the party, extra security. An empty police cruiser sits off to the side.

"Mom?"

She twists around and meets my gaze.

"What's going to happen to me?" I can't stop shivering, and I twist my fingers tighter into my dress.

"You heard your father. The deal will be honored," she says. "Just stay here."

The deal.

Unwillingly, my mind turns to Wilder's two younger brothers. Aiden cleans up the family's messes. He goes where ordinary people can't—scratch that, he goes where ordinary people know damn well to avoid. He finds people who are desperate to remain hidden.

I don't know much about him, just because I haven't spoken more than three sentences to him the entire time I've known the DeSantis family. I do know he's a savage man, prone to rage.

And Luca...

The youngest. There were rumors about him whispered behind their backs. That he wasn't really his father's son. A bastard raised as Jameson's own.

It set him apart—whether the rumors could be believed or not is another story—and made him different.

Angrier.

Colder.

Wilder was the perfect front. Charming and charismatic. Aiden is lethal, and Luca... ruthless.

The car door opens, and Luca DeSantis himself leans into the opening.

He extends his hand, a scowl marring his otherwise handsome face. "Come with me."

CHAPTER 3
Luca

I didn't have violence on my radar today, which is fucking stupid.

Later, Aiden will chew me out for my slow reaction. But I've spent the last two years working behind the scenes. I smooth things over with our men, keep the construction business afloat. Father didn't trust the task to be delegated—or he didn't want me sticking my head where it didn't belong, and this kept me busy.

Either way, I've been using my words a lot more than my fists lately.

My brother paces in front of me, trying to contain his fury. He had raced after the shooter while I ran to Amelie. Wilder's pretty fiancée had grabbed him by the lapels, shock and blood splattered across her face. The dainty lace veil was practically soaked in it.

Another gunshot went off, and I leapt at her.

Her head hit the stair, even though I tried to cushion her landing. Wilder slumped away from us, and mass chaos took over once people realized what was happening.

I carried her across the lawn and up the stairs, to a quiet

room. She was dazed, her eyes unfocused, and I left her there. And now I'm here, in Aiden's room, wondering if he's going to do something stupid.

"It had to be the Wests," he says. "They've been coming at us for years. It's about time they did something bold. They deserve to be strung up like pigs—the whole lot of them."

"It could be them," I allow. "We don't know."

"Like hell we don't know!" he yells.

I raise my hands. "Easy. I'm not your enemy."

Enemy I may not be—but I can't seem to swallow what just happened. Wilder was loaded on a stretcher and taken to the closest hospital. Dad sat with him in the ambulance, holding his limp hand. It just happened too fast.

"Luca."

I jerk.

Aiden pauses in front of me. "The Page girl. They wanted her dead, too."

I can't accept that. "How can you be so sure?"

He shakes his head, his expression crawling with disgust. "There was a bullet hole in the steps only a foot from where you knocked her down."

Fuck.

"Good thing I was there," I mutter drily.

Aiden drags me to my feet by the front of my shirt. "*Good thing* the shooter was distracted—or else you'd be in the ambulance next to Wilder."

I shove him away from me and carefully straighten my shirt. I grab my jacket from the back of the chair I slung it over and put it on. "You have a plan to find who did this."

He eyes me. "I do."

My thoughts once again turn to Amelie. The way her slumped body felt against mine. I never allowed myself to think of her. For the sake of my sanity, it was better that way. She was pretty and captivating, but she wasn't mine.

But maybe she could be. The chess pieces have arranged themselves for a neat little checkmate, if only I play this right.

"Luca," Aiden says suddenly. "Now isn't the time to be soft."

Father will jump on board. Amelie and Wilder's marriage was going to secure not only a hefty donation to our business, but the Page support, too. They have their own empire, and if we want to play hardball against the Wests, we need them.

The arrangement is actively slipping away.

I narrow my eyes. "When have I ever been soft, brother? I have a plan to save our family, and you are going to avenge it. We're both playing our roles."

He exhales and turns away, accepting my words.

His phone rings, and he puts it on speaker.

"Wilder died in the ambulance." Dad doesn't sound particularly hurt about it, but that's his way. That's life. He's lost so much, he's become a master at compartmentalizing it. And this isn't a surprise—the surprise is that he was alive when they loaded him up. The blood spreading across his chest... He continues, "I'm headed back. Where are the Pages?"

I straighten. "I'll find them."

Father grunts. "Keep that girl away from everyone else. You and I will talk when I return."

CHAPTER 4

Amelie

Luca doesn't ask me twice.

I glare at him, but he ignores it and lunges for me, wrapping long fingers around my wrist and yanking. Out I come, the dress tangling around my feet.

His grip is bruising.

I barely have time to get my feet under me, then we're off, bypassing the front entrance and going around to the back. My heel catches on a loose stone, and I barely stay upright.

The hem of my dress drags behind me. It was once a train, but someone half-heartedly pinned it up. I don't remember when that happened, or who did it. Most of the day has blended into a blurry mess.

When I walked down the aisle, one of Wilder's little cousins carried the train. The pool of satin swept behind me. My mother made a show of checking the kid's fingers, making sure they were clean.

I shake off the thought before it can continue. Luca still has ahold of me, and he moves quickly enough that my arm is stretched out in front of me. I have to keep grabbing at my skirts with my free hand so my shoes won't catch.

Around back, there's a smaller building. A guest house stationed by the pool.

"Here," he says, motioning for me to enter.

Dread seeps through the numb disbelief. I can't go in there. He can't lock me away and take advantage. What does he even want from me?

I plant my hands on the frame. "No."

He huffs behind me. "Seriously?"

"Tell me what the hell we're doing—"

"You need to stay here for your safety," he says.

His hands grip my hips, pulling me back toward him. The movement is unexpected, and I don't have time to hold on to the door. His arms bind around my torso, trapping my upper arms to my sides.

"Stop. Struggling."

I stomp on his foot, throwing myself backward.

I don't know him—I'm definitely not going to make getting kidnapped easy on him. And would it kill him to say *please*?

He lurches, and for a second, I think I'm going to hit the ground. I wouldn't blame him for dropping me. But his grip solidifies, and he lifts me off my feet. He carries me like that into the guest house and sets me down.

I whirl around, ready to lash out, but he just smirks at me.

Infuriating man.

White walls. Dark oak furniture.

Bleak and uninteresting, just like him.

There's a rack by the window with a few hangers on it, and a plastic sheath that probably held his tux. There's a bedroom through a wide opening, the French doors open.

The couch and television are paltry compared to the main house. This is for guests or people not staying long. Of course he'd try to keep me here.

"How dare you—"

"You're a target," he says. "So just... stop."

I blink and follow him into the bedroom.

He already lost his tie, but now he shucks off his jacket. It lands on the bed in a heap. His fingers work at his shirt buttons, then peels that off, too.

I gape. "You're undressing in front of me?"

"And you're covered in blood." He tosses me a shirt and shorts from the dresser and disappears into the closet. When he reemerges, I'm in the exact same spot and he's changed into a fresh shirt.

"To get out of..." He looks me up and down, the corners of his lips inching farther down.

I follow his gaze. There's blood soaked into the bottom of my dress, splattered up the front of it. Red-hot mortification works its way up my throat. I'm covered in his brother's blood.

It's sprayed across my chest, too. I already took care of my face, but the *rest of me—*

"Oh god." My stomach twists. "Get it off me."

I reach behind me and scrabble at the buttons.

Stupid fucking buttons.

For a second, I forget that he's not the DeSantis brother I should be alone with. Today was going to go a lot different.

I was resigned to my fate, but this just seems cruel.

He doesn't move.

"Luca," I prod. "Unbutton me."

He... still doesn't move.

I'm going to go crazy, or my arms are going to dislocate because of the awkward angle. I bow my head. "Please."

That snaps him out of it. "Never thought I'd hear you say that word."

I grunt, about to face him, but his hand on my bare shoulder stops me.

I freeze.

His fingers work at the buttons with quick efficiency, and

I sigh in relief when it loosens. I can breathe again. His finger grazes my skin, just over the edge of my slip.

Goosebumps run down my arms.

"That should be sufficient." He backs away.

Holding his clothes to my chest with one hand and my dress up with the other, I tentatively glance back over my shoulder.

"Thank you," I say.

"Don't thank me, Amelie. This wedding got my brother killed."

He leaves without another word.

I slam the door behind him, my stomach somersaulting. I shove the dress down, struggling for a split second to get it over my hips. There's a tearing noise, but I put it out of my mind. It can burn for all I care. In fact, it would probably be better for it to be destroyed.

What an ugly dress—fitting for the occasion.

I stand in my shift for half a second, contemplating what to do. I could be in shock. My limbs tingle like I just finished a marathon. Everything hurts.

I go to the bathroom and tear off the shift, turning on the shower. Before the steam can cover the mirror, I eye my naked body. There's a bruise forming on my hip, and I recall a flash before someone knocked me to the floor.

Luca.

I step under the scalding-hot water. It might be enough to wash away the blood, but it won't carry away the trauma.

Tears form in my eyes.

It happened too fast for my mind to track.

Crack. Blood. Falling.

I pull at the pins in my hair and yank out the sapphire earrings. Something borrowed and blue—well, they can go straight to Hell. I let them fall to the shower floor. Once my hair is loose, I dunk my head under the stream.

And if I cry a little, at least no one will know.

There's a lump behind my ear. My head hit the altar pretty good, and if this and the bruise are my only injuries... I'm lucky.

After I shower, the smell of Luca's soaps wafting over me, I put on his clothes. Then there's really nothing left to do except wait.

I check every drawer and scope out his nearly empty closet, but this is clearly not where he lives. He's a guest as much as I'm an imposter. After going through all the cabinets in the mini kitchen, I flop onto the bed just to test its softness.

As soon as I land, I regret it. Too comfortable.

My eyes keep leaking, too. An unfortunate side effect of... well, witnessing a murder?

Almost being killed myself.

Every once in a while, I scrub at my face to clear away the tears. Pesky things keep coming back.

"Sleeping?" Luca stands in the entry of the bedroom, arms folded.

I make sure my face is dry before I sit up. "You think I could sleep after what just happened? I'm not that cold-hearted."

He shrugs. "Your parents are waiting for us in the kitchen."

Nervous energy coils in my belly. I stand. "Is he really dead?"

His gaze runs up and down my body, then locks on to my eyes. "Yes."

"Who wanted him—?" I could only voice it once, apparently. My throat closes.

"Who didn't?" He sweeps his arm, beckoning me to go ahead of him. "We have a long list of enemies."

"Were they trying to kill me, too?"

"You're procrastinating."

"Wouldn't you?" I mutter. "Mom said they were going to honor the deal—whatever that means."

He lifts one shoulder. "Guess you'll find out. Either way, there isn't anything you can do about it."

Well... isn't that the worst bit of news I've heard all day?

CHAPTER 5

Amelie

There's no one in my corner.

I knew that on the surface level, but it's finally sinking in. It hits me when my parents both turn to me expectantly after the news is delivered. Like I should just roll over and accept my new fate.

There's more to this wedding than I expected. I don't know why it takes me by surprise. I suppose my parents are better secret-keepers than I gave them credit for. There's a contract hanging on the end of my name. A donation to the DeSantis cause. Wilder was the one who was involved in politics. The one who would've taken the leverage of marrying me, plus the money, and twisted it into a strategy for his campaign.

God knows what he would've run for. I wasn't privy to that information.

But my parents and Jameson DeSantis must've come up with a new arrangement. There's clearly a war coming, and they want the support of the Page empire.

Why, *why* did Dad have to stick his nose where it doesn't belong? We would've been perfectly happy in Rose Hill. But he wanted more. He pushed his company into Manhattan, making deals with all sorts of people. The good and the bad.

But as Page Printing, Inc. expanded, it seemed to attract the wrong sort of people. For protection, the DeSantises would back them. It's a symbiotic relationship, although I think I'm a casualty in this.

I pieced this together slowly over the last three years, but the whole plan didn't click together until today.

The point?

They're all waiting for my answer.

About whether I'll marry *him*.

Luca DeSantis stands by the wall, his gaze on me. Part of me wonders if he's as interested in my answer as our families. If he has anything riding on this.

For the first time, I focus completely on him.

Wilder knew what he was getting into—and I knew the kind of marriage I was walking into when I agreed to it. I told him I needed to go slow—I was not going to rush into an actual relationship with him. Those things took time.

My feelings for him were complicated. I knew him as much as I could, but there was always something missing. A layer I expected to peel back after the wedding. He held more family secrets than I could fathom, and it scared me.

I knew what the rumors whispered. *Mafia*. Deep and dark. And I was going to walk into that blindly. Partially blind, maybe. I had time to swallow my fate with Wilder. Time to learn the pieces he gave me.

Luca is a complete mystery.

Little stones fall into my stomach the longer I watch him.

"Amelie," Mom says, "can I have a moment?"

I follow her down the hallway, and she presses me to the wall with one finger on my collarbone.

"What is wrong with you?" she snaps. "If you don't do this..."

Their livelihood and their lives. It's this or broker a deal with someone else. The Wests? Jameson DeSantis might not take too kindly to us reneging on the deal. And then we'd be killed... probably by Aiden. Because that's how our world works now. We got involved with them, and there's no turning back.

Maybe Dad shouldn't have made the decisions he did to need the DeSantis family's protection in the first place.

"Luca, though?"

"Aiden is gone," she says. "It's only Luca left. I know you've spent the last three years talking to Wilder. I'm sorry. But this is how it's going to go."

"Maybe I could just take a few days..."

Screaming rings from outside the house.

I automatically grab my mother, dragging her to the floor. My heart jumps into my throat.

Luca sweeps into the hall, followed closely by his father and mine. My sister rushes along behind them. Luca grips my arm just above my elbow, prying me away from Mom. I fight him for a second, until I realize the screams are getting louder.

Coming closer.

"What's happening?" I ask him.

"Aiden will handle it."

"Mom just said Aiden *left*." I fight him, although I'm not sure why. Instinct is to go against him.

"Stop resisting me," Luca barks.

We go down a flight of stairs in the middle of the room, into the wine cellar. Jameson shuts the hatch, and it isn't until we're all gathered in a tight circle that I realize another man has joined us.

I swallow.

The judge from Brooklyn has a carefully blank expression. Maybe he's paid not to give a fuck—or maybe he's a relative.

It's hard to tell when half of the city's population seems to be Italian.

"Here?" Luca asks his father in a dry voice. He's still got a grip on my arm.

"Good as any." Jameson glances up, his brow crinkling.

The noises are muffled now. They've all stopped screaming, but a siren reaches my ears. The police cruiser in the driveway, maybe? Help on the way?

And why were they screaming?

There were wedding guests upstairs. Jameson's brothers and sisters, cousins. Nieces and nephews. Even some of my family had made the trip, although most were under the impression that this was a love marriage. And they weren't very pleased with the idea of a nineteen-year-old getting married, let's just say that.

If this thing goes sideways, I'll have no one.

Let's be real, though. I'm already there. Didn't we just agree that no one was in my corner? It's true—I felt the absence of their caring at sixteen, when Jameson marched his sons into our French villa and the agreement was made known to me.

"What is that, Jameson?" Mom asks. "You promised us protection."

He says nothing. Perhaps there's nothing to say to that. His son is dead, after all. If he couldn't keep him safe, who's to stop someone from killing me? Or Lucy? Or any of us.

"We don't claim to be body armor," Luca says to her. "Our protection is a security system. The promise of force if you meet resistance." His gaze flicks to Dad. "That's what you wanted, wasn't it?"

My dad shifts on his feet, turning to the judge. "You brought the license?"

I narrow my eyes, hating everything about this. I'm being backed into the option *they* want—not me. They're waiting for me to agree with them, but I don't have a choice in this. I never did. The illusion fades away, and I can't hide the hurt from my expression.

Dad eyes me. I've never seen this look in his eyes before—fierce and sad. "We're not doing the whole ceremony. Just sign the papers."

And that would seal the deal.

A simple signature.

'Til death do us part, minus the kiss.

"Fine," I whisper.

I scan the papers and take the pen from the judge, scrawling my name.

Bile climbs up my throat. I'm signing my life away, really, but I try not to think about it. We were raised Catholic, and marriage means forever.

Luca signs.

"I now pronounce you man and wife," the judge says.

Dad exhales, the invisible weight of worry lifting off him. He's been stressed for the past year, worrying about any little thing getting in the way of this union. But to see him visibly relieved twists my stomach.

I suppress my grimace.

And Luca? He takes a step toward me, then another. His hand slips around the base of my neck. I stay perfectly still, shoving away the urge to shiver.

I try to decipher his expression, but then there's no more time. He slams his lips against mine. I remain rigid, suddenly crushed to him. His lips are firm and soft, unmoving. This isn't a kiss of passion—it's a show.

It's also a long, hard look at my fate.

He forces his tongue into my mouth, and I taste the whiskey he must've drunk before retrieving me. I bite the tip of his tongue, and the hot, metallic taste of blood greets me.

He breaks away and grins. It's not for me, though. It's directed over my head, to where our family stands.

"Get them out of here," Jameson orders over the sudden pepper of more gunfire.

His son nods. His hand is still around my neck, and his thumb moves the tiniest fraction against my skin. Chills skitter down my back. I don't know whether to lean into it or shrink away.

An ounce of fear oozes up my spine, but it's sluggish. It hasn't caught up to my racing heart or frozen brain.

Luca doesn't remove his hand like I expect. He uses it to guide me out, the pressure even—and, in a weird way, reassuring. I don't know how to react to a situation filled with firearms and violence, but he does.

He's dealt with this sort of thing before. He knows how to survive it.

"See you on the other side," he calls to his father.

We go up a different set of stairs, into a long, narrow hallway. A man with a huge gun stands at the opening, peering out.

"Report," Luca demands.

The man straightens. "After some of our men retaliated, the Wests are pushing back."

Luca stares at him for a moment, and a silent conversation takes place between them.

The guard breaks first. "We have two cars waiting."

He tosses Luca a set of keys and the other to the judge, who had followed close behind us.

"You know where to take her," Jameson says.

But *I* don't know where we're going. My breath stalls in my chest.

"Don't think about what happened out there," Luca says to me under his breath. "Don't think about any of it. Just get ready to move."

I open my mouth, then shut it again.

Don't think about it? That's his advice?

I probably still have his brother's blood stained on my skin, yet he's telling me to stop thinking about it.

"Amelie."

I meet his gaze.

"Stay here a moment. I'll be right back." He pushes me against the wall and waits for my nod. I'm loath to resist it, but the fear is winning out.

If ever I had a question about whether I'd pick fight or flight—I now know my route. The third option: freeze.

So, I do. I stay even as my parents slip past me, the judge leading them out. My sister squeezes my hand, then she's gone, too.

Jameson pauses next to me, but he doesn't look down. He just says, "Be adaptable, Amelie. And if anything, you just need to survive the next forty-eight hours."

Cold, cold man. He grew through the ranks of the DeSantis Mafia—I'd be willing to bet he's seen his fair share of bloodshed.

I tilt my head, appraising him. Too late for me to ask anything, though, because he disappears down the steps, into the courtyard. The cars' engines turning over reaches my ears.

The guard and I stand silently. I open my mouth a few times but think better of my questions.

"Amelie." Luca reappears.

There's a gun in his hand that I don't think he had a minute ago.

Was he out killing people?

"Let's go," he urges.

I… can't move.

My bones are jelly.

He holds out his hand, a sympathetic expression flickering over his face. It's quickly replaced with the familiar scowl.

To take it or not?

I thought I was prepared for this life. Wilder and danger and men making lethal decisions. But the truth of the matter is that I'm scared shitless. I'm drowning in fear.

"I can't." I back into the house. "Definitely not."

I turn and run. I can't help it. Everything closes in on me: the hallway narrows, my chest hurts. My vision flickers.

Oh god.

Someone catches me before I crumple. I didn't even realize I'd stopped.

There's a strange ringing in my ears.

"You're hyperventilating," Luca says in my ear. "Breathe."

I can't. It's too much. Black spots overtake my vision. The last thing I see is the ceiling—and Luca's face.

CHAPTER 6
Luca

Amelie Page.

My wife.

There's no ring on our fingers, and besides a kiss, nothing physical ties us together. Well, a piece of paper does.

But mentally? She doesn't give a shit about me. We're strangers.

The twinge in my chest is odd. Wilder and I weren't particularly close. He was a few years older, always busy learning the business and being a general pain in the ass. He was gearing up to jump into politics—something I definitely don't give a shit about. There aren't that many brotherly moments I can look back on with fondness. There were bouts of dealing with his anger, fighting about girls, him thinking he had some sort of control over me because he was the oldest. He and I were polar opposites.

Not just in looks or actions, but because of my mother. I was an outsider, as much as Aiden tried to convince me otherwise.

Still, Wilder is dead and gone. Besides the twinge, I don't feel anything.

Maybe relief—but maybe that's due to the fact that I successfully spirited Amelie away from New York. It wasn't too difficult to get her on the plane. She seemed a bit out of it, honestly, and leaned most of her weight on me. We accessed the jet from a private entrance, and the pilot didn't comment when I scooped Amelie up and carried her into the cabin.

She settled quickly, not even asking where we're going. I offered her a tiny bottle of Fireball—which might've been cruel of me—but she tossed it back without so much as wincing and closed her eyes. She hasn't moved since. At one point, I covered her with a blanket.

The rest of the flight I settle back, dividing my time between checking emails and watching her sleep.

We're going home.

It feels weird to call it that, because I haven't spent a lot of time in Northern Italy. My mother was born here. She left a house to me when she passed away, but I couldn't leave New York City for too long.

Now I have an excuse.

The time passes quickly. We travel forward in time, through the night, and I manage to get some rest before the pilot wakes me.

"We're starting our descent in a few minutes," he informs me.

I nod and return my attention to Amelie, wondering when she'll wake up. Her sleep isn't normal—it's the exhaustion that follows an adrenaline rush. My sympathy is sudden and strong. She didn't ask for any of this.

It's not her fault her parents are dumb fucks.

I stare at her until the plane touches down, and my new wife groans. She blinks, rubbing at her face.

She isn't pretty. Her hair is a wild tangle of waves—

whereas prior to today, I'd never seen it anything other than pin-straight—and there's drool crusted in the corner of her lip. She's in my clothes. No, she isn't pretty like Wilder used to taunt, used like a whip against my skin. She's goddamn beautiful.

And mine.

She liked Wilder. Maybe even deluded herself into loving him once upon a time. He would return from meeting her and give us details of their outings. Aiden didn't care, but I had to work harder for my indifference.

Maybe that's why Wilder always divulged—he could see that it got to me.

According to Wilder, their conversations were superficial. She never divulged her hopes and fears, and he didn't ask. They weren't part of the equation. Who cared if she wanted to finish college or get a job? She'd be too busy carrying the heir.

I choke back my laugh at the irony. Now she's married to the bastard son. The condolence prize.

I won't rule this family. I've barely been allowed to touch it. Aiden... he'll struggle, and I'll help him. Aiden and I are close. Almost the same age, just a few months off.

Amelie's eyes flutter shut, then open again.

Not willing to face reality, perhaps.

"Where are we?" she murmurs.

Her bags—at least three of them, judging from the grunting and back-and-forth of the driver who took us to the plane hangar in New York—are locked away below with mine. We're not going stateside until the coast is clear.

Dad's orders.

In New York City, a war has bloomed out of the cease-fire. The Wests destroyed the city's peace by killing Wilder. It's a bold move. One that hasn't been tried in the last few decades. It's sure to rock the foundation of New York's underground... but again, I won't have a part in it.

I'll be keeping Amelie alive—because we promised her family safety, and that meant leaving the country.

"Luca," Amelie presses.

I push up the window shade, exposing the countryside shrouded in twilight. She'll be familiar with this airport—she's flown into it many times. It's a small one for private planes, set on French soil, but only ten minutes from Italy.

She inhales slightly, nostrils flaring, and I nod to myself. She recognized it faster than I would've guessed. Now she pulls back and glances around, and I wait for it to click.

"This is my parents' jet," she says slowly.

The plane parks by a hangar, and she unbuckles, standing on shaky legs. I need to figure out what to do with her. Marriage is so outside the scope of anything I expected, but I can't deny that I'm feeling a bit... possessive.

"Why are we here?" she asks.

I shrug. "We've been removed from the playing board."

She raises her eyebrow. "Did you steal our pilot, too?"

I don't answer. Her feistiness is a pleasant surprise. She wanted Wilder to like her, and I think she succeeded by making herself demure.

I know better, though. I see through that mask—and I'm going to rip it off.

CHAPTER 7
Amelie

Jameson shipped us off so we're not liabilities, and because we've become useless.

Dad and I used to play chess, but we haven't sat at a board together in a long time. High school dramatics got in the way. The rush of being the best, of having attention centered on me, was too heady. And then I learned I was going to be married to a stranger, and my attitude soured.

My bad.

But can they blame me?

I almost wish I could go back to those days of sitting across from Dad, studying the pieces. Sometimes he was quiet, but most times he'd offer advice. The reason behind moves, chess theory. I soaked it all up back then.

I fear I've forgotten most of it.

The drive into Sanremo is short, winding through mountains—sometimes literally, blanketed in darkness as we pass through tunnels—coming into the city from the west. I ignore the tingling that zips through my body at Luca behind the wheel. He doesn't pay me much attention, even when I'm ogling him. In the back of my mind, I'm wondering how the hell I slept so long. Maybe he drugged me.

If I remember correctly, there's a turnoff of this main road that will lead to the villa Jameson DeSantis owns. We didn't go there too often—just once or twice each summer—but it tugs at my memory.

Instead, Luca carries on straight. I don't realize we must've passed the road until we enter the city limits, and the houses crowd closer to the road.

"Where are we going?"

He scowls. "You think I live on my father's property? I made my own way in the world."

I chew on that. Honestly? I did think he coasted along on his father's coattails. It would have been easy enough for him to do it. His father provided a lot, and Luca was present at the DeSantis estate when my family visited.

Never mind the bastard rumors—clearly Jameson took him in, raised him as his own.

The streets get narrower, more winding. My eyebrows hike up the farther we get into the city. It was built into the side of rolling hills, each house stacked up higher than the one in front of it. Each one has a view of the ocean—and their neighbors' yards. Privacy here would be a luxury.

Several sharp turns later, the car slows.

He hits a button, and a garage door to our left slides open. The garage seems to be built into a hill. Above it stretches the house and a glass-walled yard.

He kills the engine in the garage, and the door rumbles shut behind us. I follow him through a laundry room and upstairs, onto the first level of the house. One wall is made almost entirely of windows, giving us an uninhibited view of the city and ocean in the distance. The yard has a small pool tucked in the corner by the glass fence.

Whoever decorated this first floor had a good eye for

details. Furniture breaks up the open space into different sections. A set of couches faces each other with a rug and coffee table, and a television mounted to the wall. A dining table toward the back—and another one outside. The kitchen is sectioned off in a U shape, but there's an opening that creates a breakfast bar area. Three stools are tucked under it.

The whole space has a clean, very *Italian villa* vibe. I'm surprised that I like it so much.

"You own this?"

He nods, going to a side table and rifling through a few pieces of mail left for him. "Ricardo will grab your bags."

I squint at him. We didn't pass anyone. I didn't notice anyone follow us from the airport, either. And yet, a second later, a large man appears with two bags.

Wait.

"Huh?"

Luca watches me.

Ricardo disappears up another set of stairs, then returns a minute later. We watch in silence as he comes back up with a third bag, plus a smaller black suitcase—clearly Luca's.

"Where did you get those?" Because I certainly didn't pack *three bags* worth of stuff.

When I left, I assumed I would be going back home—at least to get my things. My room needed to be boxed up, my clothes sorted. Had I been procrastinating those chores? Absolutely.

I didn't want to leave. I'd delay it if I could.

But my mother must've known...

Luca just cocks his head, like I'm an object in the museum that confuses him.

I rush up the stairs and stop dead. There is no hallway, just... one room. One large room. Thick curtains hang from the four bedposts. Two plush chairs are stationed by the floor-to-ceiling windows. The glass walls are on sliders, and a wide balcony promises good views.

I turn away from it.

My bags are by the closet.

I drag one down and unzip it, flipping through the clothes. Nothing I would've picked for myself. Nothing familiar—just clothes I kept stuffed away, ignoring my mother's pleas for me to wear them.

"Shit, shit, shit." Foreign country, foreign husband, foreign clothes.

I go to the next bag, tossing clothes out. A pile grows around me. Everything is horrible. And then...

I pull out a long strip of lace, my face crinkling. I hold it up and try to figure out what it is. It takes a second to click.

My mother packed lingerie for me.

"Wow." Luca laughs. "I didn't know you were such a temptress."

I shove it down. "Shut up."

He stops next to me and stares down. My eyes are level with his thigh from my position on the floor, but I tilt back to check his expression. I figure it'll either be thunderous at the mess I'm making or his usual scowl.

Instead, he seems curious. "What's wrong?"

The switch is unsettling, so I squint at the piles of clothes. I'm untethered, but I can't say that. I can't say anything I'm thinking. "Nothing."

"Okay."

I didn't expect that response. Most people pry. *Surely something is wrong, Amelie*. But him...

I rub at my eyes. When I look up again, he's gone.

An hour later, I've sorted through the clothes and put them into three piles: acceptable, trash, and maybe. After careful consideration, the lingerie ended up in the maybe pile.

The trash pile is quite a bit bigger than the other two combined.

What was my mother thinking?

Europe has been a second home for my family as long as I can remember. But now that I'm here without them, I'm lost. I miss Lucy and my bed. I miss the traffic of the city. Hell, my thoughts even linger on how Mom would knock on my bedroom door in the mornings. Rainy days cast my room in shades of grey, and she'd occasionally surprise me with a mug of tea.

I curl up in one of the chairs in the corner and stare out the window. The sun is shining, and the world continues to move on as if I hadn't married a freaking stranger. Not a nice one, either.

Someone tried to kill me.

Every time I close my eyes, Wilder's pale face is all I see. The smell of blood is so thick in my nostrils, I can't breathe.

This is probably a panic attack.

I slide off the chair and onto the floor, pressing my forehead to the cold tile.

"Hey," Luca whispers, his hands wrapping around my shoulders.

I flinch. He's quieter than a ghost, that one.

He ignores it and lifts me into his arms. He doesn't even grunt with effort. I'm cradled like a child, gasping for air, and wholly unprepared for his lips to touch my temple.

Holy shit.

"Your sister called you Ames," he says. "Do you prefer that to Amelie?"

I focus on his words. He's talking about my sister.

Wilder called me Ames, too. They were the only ones. I don't mention that my stomach did somersaults when he did, because it felt forbidden. We weren't married—we weren't touching. We just existed side by side, and he did what he could to soften the blow of being chained to him forever.

Not to mention his talks of etiquette. Being proper.

Wilder once accused me of being an air-headed party girl. That was after he came to Rose Hill to see me, but I had already been drinking with my friends. Those two worlds weren't supposed to collide, and I'd cringed seeing him in my home town.

He left, and the next morning his words sliced into me. He stood on the walkway, a good six feet away from me. The shame in his eyes hurt, but I wasn't his yet.

The box with the engagement ring sat untouched on my desk. I was still desperately trying to get my ex-boyfriend, Caleb, to love me, to sweep me away to some far-off island so I wouldn't have to marry Wilder.

I was seventeen and anxious for the rest of my life to begin.

For the anchor to attach itself to me and drag me beneath the waves.

That's how I felt around Wilder sometimes. Like the rest of my life could be hopeless if I didn't do exactly what he said. If I wasn't *perfect* for him.

Luca's grip tightens on me, and I curl my head under his chin. It's the best way I can think to avoid his gaze.

"Sometimes I prefer Amelie," I manage.

He sits on the bed, resting me in his lap. It's oddly comforting, being held like this. I didn't grow up with a lot of physical affection. But it triggers another memory: his body hitting mine, knocking me down. He carried me across the lawn and up the stairs of the building next to the chapel, setting me down on a chair. He knelt beside me and brushed his thumb across my cheekbone, then left.

"You were hyperventilating. Again."

How do I tell him I hate this? Every moment of it. I don't

hate *him* because I don't know him. And I can't hate Wilder because he's dead.

So where does that leave me?

I struggle to get off him. He holds tight for a moment, then releases me.

I shoot to my feet. "It's a lot to process. Did you bring me here to rub it in?"

"Is that what you think of me?"

"I don't know you." I cross my arms, tempted to stomp my foot. "And you can honestly say you're okay with being married to a complete stra—"

"Yes." He stands and comes toward me.

I back away quickly, unsure of what to make of his expression. Dark like thunderclouds, but maybe there's a bit of sunlight in him, too.

"I see you, Amelie. All of you."

I put my hand on his chest, trying to stop his pursuit. Little embers of fear rain down, hot on my skin. Fear burns like no other.

It's no use. He backs me against the wall and cages me in. "It's just you and me, so you have to decide what you can live with. Can you handle this? Our life together?"

I lift my chin to meet his eyes.

I need to decide. Fear or... something else. I could embrace this.

When he doesn't do anything else, I hesitate. There are too many emotions running through me, but the worst is a new, odd sense of comfort. Like the words coming out of his mouth are true, and not just lies to get me to be a good little wife and spread my legs.

"Are you afraid?" he asks.

Slowly, I shake my head. He can kiss me or strangle me—that doesn't scare me. It angers me. Fear of the unknown scares me. I'm terrified of what I'll become. And that's the worst of it all, because I have no control over that.

He leans down until our lips are millimeters apart.

I close my eyes and brace myself.

This is it. He's going to kiss me again.

"Fear keeps us alive," he whispers. "It's a good instinct."

And then, nothing.

I open my eyes slowly, looking around.

He's gone.

CHAPTER 8
Luca

At the end of the street is a small restaurant. They're famous to the locals, but it's a hole-in-the-wall spot, generally kept out of the travel guides. I walk around the building and slip in through the back door. This kitchen is nothing like the commercial stuff they have in Manhattan. It looks more like the kitchen I have at home, with the addition of two more ovens.

A woman stands at the butcher block island, kneading dough. Her wild dark hair is caught back in a green bandana. It's warm in here, and sweat dots her brow. I watch her work the dough for a moment, digging the heels of her hands into it, rolling it slightly. It folds easily. Over and over, until she has it just right.

It joins a pile of them.

When I was a child, I would be on a stool next to her with my own little projects. I can't remember how many times we'd experiment with flavors or herbs, folding in seeds or cheese. After, we'd sit at an empty table and tear chunks off. Some tasted great—others, not so much.

Just remembering it brings a smile to my face. The kitchen

smells of the same herbs and spices, of butter and toasting bread.

I rap my knuckles on the doorframe, and she nearly jumps out of her skin.

She gasps, bringing her hand to her chest.

"Luca, dear boy. You scared me," my aunt says in Italian. My mother's sister is the only connection I have to her side of the family, and I don't see her nearly as much as I should.

Just another reason to be happy I'm back in Sanremo.

"Sorry," I reply. "It was an unexpected trip."

She waves away my apology, coming forward and cupping my jaw. She pulls me down, kissing both my cheeks. I grin and snatch her hand before she can retreat, bringing her into a hug.

"I missed you, *zia*."

She tuts. "Antonio will be here soon for our preparation. In the meantime, help me lay these loaves to rest."

I can't stop smiling as I stand opposite her and carefully cover each loaf. I follow her lead, feeling more like a kid than ever before. Father has a way of implying we should've been mature even when we weren't. The only time I had a true *childhood* were my summers here.

That was the deal they'd struck, if Jameson was to welcome me into his house.

I can't imagine what he would've been like at my age, fighting for his rank.

"How is New York?" she finally asks. She's been chewing on the words for a while, rolling them around her mouth until she decided to spit them out. She hates the States. Hates my father for tearing me away from them and killing my mother.

He didn't *really* kill her. Paloma will say my mother died of a broken heart.

That much I believe to be true. Summers weren't enough for her, but she was forbidden from coming with me. I came back for the funeral, which took place on my eighteenth birthday.

The fucking irony.

After that birthday, I would've been a legal adult. I could've stayed with her, learned more of our history, built a life in this quiet town.

But she'd died, and I'd stayed in America.

My attention skates around the kitchen. It's exactly the same as it was. There's something about this town. At its heart, it doesn't change. Even when the hotels go up, and things seem to chug toward modernism.

"I got married," I tell her.

She snorts. "Always a comedian."

"No, really." I frown. "It was last minute. She was supposed to marry Wilder."

"Your brother backed out so you stepped in?" She narrows her eyes. "Or did you steal the bride away, Luca?"

"Wilder was killed." It hurts worse to say it to her, because she's removed from the situation. Telling her is like telling a stranger my elder brother died. It crystalizes. I can't meet her gaze. "He was actually on the altar when he got shot. I think the gunman would've tried to take out Amelie, too. Ruin the deal between our families. But I just couldn't let that happen."

She circles the island and takes my hands. Hers are dry and smooth, strong from decades of work. "You love this girl? Amelie?"

I scoff. "I don't know her, *zia*. Maybe I could love her someday, but it's a duty. She was brought into the family because her parents demanded certain protections." Whether they deserve such protection is unknown.

She sighs. "Antonio and I had an arranged marriage. I hated him at first, but he eventually won me over. Sometimes fate likes to mess with us, to create a struggle, so we appreciate the end."

We're both silent for a moment. I like Antonio. He used to be a fisherman before arthritis made hauling lines impossible. He's almost ten years older than Paloma, with weathered dark-brown skin and green sea-glass eyes. They make you feel like he can examine your soul with one glance.

But he's kind, too. He treats my aunt with tenderness, helps her now around this restaurant that's been handed down her side of the family for generations. Back when I would hang out with her, my mother would be the one on the front lines —pouring drinks and laughing with customers, delivering their food. She was the life of this place.

"Where is this girl?" she asks.

I raise my eyebrow. "Amelie? I left her at Mom's."

She smacks the back of my hand. "You took an American girl away from her family after her fiancé was killed in front of her, brought her to a foreign country, then *abandoned* her? Bring her here at once."

"You wouldn't like her," I say immediately.

"Bullshit," she grumbles. She turns away, wiping a rag across the wood. "If she was your girlfriend? Maybe. But this is your wife. Of course I'll try to like her."

Try.

I crack a smile. "Okay. I'll bring her by for dinner."

She calls my name when I'm almost out the door, worry etched in her features. "Did you give her a ring?"

I freeze. "A ring?"

She swears at me in Italian, and I shake my head. I didn't get Amelie a ring—didn't know it was needed until five minutes before we signed the marriage license. I wonder if we'll ever have a normal wedding... once we like each other, perhaps we can entertain that idea.

Look at me, talking with surety. *If* we ever like each other...

"I didn't," I say.

She scoffs and works the ring off her own finger—not the little band, but the engagement ring that must've been in her family for decades. It features a large round diamond in the center, supported and framed by smaller diamonds around it. The metal weaves between the smaller diamonds, creating a rope-like effect. And the stones continue halfway down the thick band on either side. It's probably worth a fortune.

A lump forms in my throat. "You're still using it."

She smiles and touches the simple band of twisted white gold left on her ring finger. "That gets in the way when I knead the dough, and this band is all I need. If your mother had married, it would've gone to her. And then to you."

Her eyes fill with tears, but she bats away my concern.

"It's yours. Don't make a fuss."

I nod slowly. "Thank you. I don't know how to repay—"

"Bring her," Paloma says. "Let me meet your new wife and give her a proper Italian welcome."

"I will." I dip my head and slip outside, back up the steps.

A little way down the street, someone whistles to me.

I pause and find the man. He leans over the half-wall fence of the house above the road, grinning down at me.

"Long time, DeSantis," he calls.

"Matteo," I answer. "To what do I owe this pleasure?"

"My good graces." He comes around, trotting down the ceramic steps until he's on street level. "You know we're due a call when you come into town."

I grimace. "Is that so? I'm not here for trouble."

"You're here for something," he points out.

He's grown since the last time I saw him. It's been almost a year, and the patchy stubble on his young face has filled out. He seems sturdier, less sharp angles of a gangly kid and more like a fighting man. I note all of this with a sweep of my gaze, keeping it as subtle as I can.

"A honeymoon," I finally say. "Just visiting my aunt."

He sighs. "You look good, DeSantis. It makes me wonder if the Costas shouldn't take a little trip to visit New York. There seems to be plenty to go around."

"There isn't." I force myself not to cross my arms.

His brow lowers. "No? You take and take and then when you're tired of the hard work, you come crawling back here. That's always the way of it. And the people in this town are sick of you."

"Sick of me, Matteo, or my last name?"

"Be careful," he warns. "Don't think your lack of family loyalty will win you any favors around here. The opposite, perhaps." But then he perks up. "Honeymoon, you said. You have a pretty wife in your bed?"

Nowhere near my bed. "Does your brother want to see me, then? Or shall you just give him my regards?"

He smirks. "How about this? You come in with me, and I'll have Santiago go fetch your woman. We'll have lunch."

"You will do no such thing," I growl.

A hand lands on my shoulder, and I silently curse myself for my tunnel vision. I grab it and twist. The man yells, doubling over to relieve the sudden pressure. I glance around, and dread tightens my chest. I'm surrounded.

Aiden taught me to fight at a young age. I was a fast learner because I had to be—that's the only way you survive in our world.

I shove the man into one of the others and snap my foot out, connecting with one's stomach. He lets out a sharp exhale and falls back. They come in closer now, pummeling me. One's knuckles catch my cheek, and it cuts against my teeth. Blood fills my mouth.

I spit, blocking where I can, but there are too many of them. I doubt even Aiden would've been able to fend them off. No, scratch that. He'd be strapped with guns and would just fucking kill them all. Consequences be damned.

A whistle cuts through the noise of their grunts, and everything stops.

At what point did I fall to my knees? Hands pull me upright, and I blink through the sweat and blood to see Matteo approaching. The bastard is clean. Hell, most of them look untouched.

I'm furious at myself for this surprise attack.

"This is a warning," Matteo says. "Next time, we'll get your wife involved. Maybe take a finger for each time you ignore our ways."

Next time.

They'll die before they touch her.

I just have to be more prepared.

They drop me, and I fall to my side. They disappear like dust carried away by the wind. It's only after I'm alone that I slowly push myself upright. Pain lances through me, more vivid than I would've expected. Still, I can walk. The right side of my face has its own heartbeat, but my ribs seem okay. Maybe bruised.

My eye is swelling shut, and the taste of blood is heavy on my tongue.

Just get home.

CHAPTER 9

Amelie

I am annoyed at myself.

For being weak. For being selfish. For being hungry.

It's the last one that drives me back downstairs and into the kitchen. It takes me a minute to decide on a meal—limited by what's in the fridge, really. It's surprisingly full. Ricardo must be more than someone to get the bags. Hired help for collecting groceries, too?

At least he didn't put flower petals on the bed for us. *That would've been awkward.*

I've managed to get most of the meal put together when the garage door rumbles below my feet. I made enough for two people—grudgingly—and now I'm glad I did. If only to offer an apology to Luca.

He says he sees me, but that's what I need to apologize for: I don't think he does. He probably gets the same picture everyone else does. Cheerleader and popular girl, the one who has all the answers. She sometimes comes off as weak, but that's just one slight character flaw. Everyone has those.

The door opens, and Luca strides in.

I gasp, drawing his attention sharply toward me.

He's bloody, bruised. One of his eyes is swelling shut, and it's a kaleidoscope of reds and purples.

I'm sure there's more damage than just his face. The closer I watch him, the more concern edges out my discomfort. He strides toward me.

I can't stop staring.

I open my mouth, then abruptly close it.

"Don't ask me questions about that side of my life," Wilder used to say. "I won't be able to tell you."

I don't know if I'm allowed to ask Luca. I certainly don't know if he'll tell me. No one ever tells me anything. Not my parents, certainly never Wilder. They thought I was something fragile to be locked away.

"It smells good," Luca says gruffly. He rounds the counter and gingerly sits on one of the stools.

I move back to the stove, directly in front of him, and eye him warily.

"Breakfast sandwich," I reply. "I made two..."

He nods slowly.

I pluck the English muffins from the toaster and place them on two plates, carefully sliding the eggs and cheese onto them. Then the bacon, and avocado simply because it was available. I set his in front of him and pick mine up where I stand.

We eat in silence, and I keep one eye on him. Like he might teeter off the stool at any moment—even though I know that's a lie.

I finish before him and grab one of the dishcloths, soaking it in water. He watches me with hawk eyes as I come around and stop next to him. He swivels toward me.

You can do this.

I step between his legs and raise the cloth, dabbing it along his face. "This should probably be iced to prevent the swelling," I whisper. "I'll..."

He catches my wrist before I can leave and draws me back into him. His hand slides along my jaw, and we meet in the middle. Our lips slam together. He licks the seam of my mouth, parting it, and our tongues tangle. I swear, I've never felt fireworks before—but there's a bottle rocket bouncing around my brain now.

We're fused together.

I can't kiss him. The thought is unwanted but strong. Kissing is intimate, but I can't seem to stop. My first mistake.

I wrap my arms around his shoulders, and his hand leaves my jaw. He stands, then lifts me.

I'm no stranger to sex. In fact, I'd say I probably enjoy it too much. He pushes me against the wall and moves to my throat.

"Fuck," I groan, tilting my head to give him better access.

His erection strains against his jeans. I reach between us and palm him, grinning when he thrusts in my hand.

I didn't feel the tension boiling between us until this moment. The lust is unmistakable, a hot and heady sensation.

"Fuck me," I moan. "Luca."

He groans, tearing himself away. "Get naked."

My feet hit the floor, and I put one hand on his chest. He backs up a step, eyeing me.

I wink and slowly pull my top over my head, dropping it beside me. His gaze is hungry when I move to unhook my bra, sliding it off.

He steps forward, but I keep him back.

This is my show.

I'm not certain I like him, but a little sex never hurt anyone.

Famous last words.

I shimmy out of my pants, turning to give him a view of my ass. I smirk to myself, risking a glance over my shoulder.

He's already lost his shirt, and now he steps forward, kneeling behind me.

My mouth dries. "What—"

He grips my hips and drags me back, biting my ass cheek.

I let out a shriek of surprise—but what's more surprising is the rush of wetness at my core. He kisses the spot, then nips it again. I grab on to the counter and bow my head, unsure why I'm enjoying this so much. I was expecting... normal.

More of the same.

But this is so much different.

He reaches around and finds my clit.

"Luca," I say.

My legs are going to give out, but he doesn't seem to mind. And then—*oh god*. His tongue plunges into me and my brain shorts.

His hand digs into my hip, stabilizing me as he tongue-fucks me. And his finger on my clit is almost overwhelming. I come without warning, clenching around him.

He pulls out of me abruptly, but his finger doesn't stop moving on my clit. I squeeze my eyes shut and try to stop the whimpering erupting from my throat.

"Hold tight," he warns, then thrusts into me.

His grip is bruising, and he yanks me back to meet him. He stretches me, hitting a deep spot inside me. I'm already strung tight from my orgasm, but I'm greedy. I need more.

"Harder," I grit out.

He fists my hair, almost dragging me upright. I reach back and scratch my nails along his ass and thigh. His tempo increases, and his finger returns to my clit.

"You like it rough?" he asks in my ear, then chases it with a nip.

I groan, my eyes fluttering shut.

"Dirty little wife."

This is too much. *Wife?* Now? "Luca, I can't—"

"You fucking agreed to this," he growls.

I push back on him, but he's everywhere. Invading every one of my senses. I struggle. "I didn't *agree*, you bastard."

He slides out and hits the back of my knee with his own. We both go down. He pushes me forward, face to the floor. I try to kick him, but he easily blocks it. He pins my legs together, between his, and I grunt in frustration. He captures both of my wrists, holding them together at the small of my back. He wraps something around them, effectively binding me.

"Beautiful wife," he murmurs.

I wriggle, but I have no leverage.

And I'm scared out of my wits. He could do anything to me. He never even took his jeans off—the rough fabric brushes my legs. And yet, part of me is intrigued. It's the curiosity that will get me into trouble.

"Get off me, Luca," I demand.

He tsks. "You only panicked when I called you wife. Is that right?"

"N-no—"

"Do not lie to me."

His finger slides into me, and I press my lips together.

"What's a just punishment, wife? For every lie, I'll rip an orgasm from your body. Even when you beg me to stop. Even when your body breaks. Your mind must break first." He's silent for a moment, but his finger doesn't stop moving.

Fear bleeds through me, and I struggle. He's got me perfectly exposed. I hate the vulnerability—that he's taking advantage. That of all the things he could've done, *this* is one of them.

My mind goes back to the buttons on my wedding dress.

I knew, even then, that sex would be used as a weapon against me. That I was meant to be fucked, impregnated, and left. I didn't blame Wilder for it—I *hated* him for it. I wanted love. Luca is wrong, though. I've been mentally preparing myself for this type of war for years.

"I won't forgive you for this," I whisper.

He leans forward and brushes the hair from my face. "Do I scare you, wife?"

I glare at him from the corner of my eye. "Yes."

He withdraws, and I push my forehead into the floor. Ice seeps into my body from the cool tiles, but it doesn't help. I'm already frozen.

"Why you?" he asks.

I go still. "What?"

"Why *you*, Amelie Page, and not your sister? Why does a parent ever choose one child over another?"

Ouch. But he's aiming to hurt me, and I can't let that show. "I suppose I should ignore the fact that I went from marrying the DeSantis heir to *you*." I roll my eyes, knowing he can't see it. "You're worse than him."

He chuckles and slaps my ass.

I jolt. "What the fuck was that for?" I yell.

His fingers massage the spot, then dip into me again.

"Just testing a theory," he says.

He rises off me, and I turn my head in time for him to drop his jeans and kick them away.

I flip onto my back and wince. My arms are still bound behind me, but I manage to push myself into a sitting position. His erection is thick and long, glistening at the tip with precum. He's already been inside me, but I still tense.

He's too beautiful naked. Dark hair, abs, and a cut line of muscle straight to his cock.

I navigate to my knees and go toward him.

"Amelie—"

He quiets when I take him in my mouth. My hands will be no help, so I use all the skills I have. I take him in until I gag, and tears spring into my eyes. He doesn't move while I suck him off, he just sharply exhales. He cups the back of my head, sliding himself deeper inside. I swirl my tongue around. White stars burst at the edges of my vision as he gets more into it.

I abruptly sit back on my heels.

A quick glance up shows me he's burning with the desire to take my mouth. His eye looks worse than before. It's an ugly purple, swollen almost all the way shut. But he pays it no mind, so I ignore it, too.

I lean back farther and spread my legs. "You want to fuck the truth out of me, Luca? The least you can do is look me in the eye while you do it."

This is how I will survive—by pushing back.

He nods, joining me on the floor.

Who would've thought we'd have sex for the first time here? I could've guessed a bed, a couch, a wall...

Luca undoes my restraints and guides me back. He tosses the belt he used aside. I rub my wrists, glaring at the offending length of leather. He grips the backs of my thighs and slides the head of his cock up and down my slit.

I groan, my eyes fluttering. That feels good—too good.

He slides home. "You're soaked."

"Because you gave me an orgasm and a half," I reply.

He frowns and inches deeper. I gasp, lifting on my elbows, and grab the back of his neck. I pull him down over me and wrap my legs around his hips. His gaze bores into me, and I don't look away. I can't.

He automatically takes on a slower pace, until he's inching in and out of me. Every thrust makes me full-body tremble.

We hover inches apart.

Something inside me unlocks. Cracks, really. He's my husband. I've got to accept that. Whatever I thought I might have with Wilder died with him. Luca and I... we might be able to forge something different.

"Tell me a truth," he says in a low voice. He leans to the

side and cups my breast, pinching my nipple between his fingers.

Little zaps of pleasure shoot through me, and it couples with the way he fills me.

I remember picking out my dress like armor. Of imagining the cage closing in on me. Hopelessness and anger and no answers or reasons.

And Luca wants a truth from me.

"I'm glad he died," I say.

It's the only truth I have to give.

Luca thrusts into me hard enough to split me in half, once, twice, three times. I come on a hoarse cry, digging my nails into his back, and he follows a second later.

CHAPTER 10

Amelie

He offers me his hands and helps me to my feet.

The aftermath of sex has never made me feel quite as awkward as I feel right now. It was an explosion of our emotions, of anger and too much truth, if we're being honest.

I told him I was *glad* his brother died.

What kind of person even thinks that?

"Go clean up," he says softly. "I'll pick up this..."

I glance around. Early afternoon sunlight streams through the glass doors. Our plates are still on the counter, his breakfast sandwich half-eaten. Funny to think I wanted to do something nice for him... now I'm feeling particularly stabby.

The scalding-hot water in the shower does little to lighten my mood. I ache all over, and it's only after I'm out, staring at myself in the mirror, do I realize he managed to leave a trail of hickeys down my neck.

Before the sex, I would imagine.

My stomach flips. He didn't use a condom, which isn't the end of the world. I have a birth control implant in my arm. I touch it now, just to make sure I haven't lost it. My mother scheduled an appointment for it to be removed a month before the wedding. Fortunately for me—and a *fuck you* to her—I'm a legal adult. The doctor couldn't disclose if it was removed or not.

So I lied about it.

Anyway, pregnancy fears notwithstanding, he better be clean. If he's not...

I shudder.

In the bedroom, I choose an outfit that won't give him any ideas: a black tank top and leather jacket, and black jeans. The definition of badass, in my humble opinion. All I'm missing is the brass knuckles. My mother would have a heart attack if she saw me.

Luca comes up as I'm slipping on silver earrings. He does a quick double take, then smirks. "Dressed for war, wife?"

I shrug.

"We have dinner plans. I can show you the city before, if you'd like."

I squint, then nod. Sure, he can show me around the city—and frighten away any of the nice people. If we're going to be here for any length of time (and it's seeming like a good possibility, since I'm sure he owns this place), then I should get to know the locals on my own. Our neighbors, at the very least.

He closes the bathroom door, and the water turns on a second later. I grab my boots and trot downstairs. Once I'm laced up, I go down through the garage. There's a door off to the side, and I close it gently behind me. I don't know why I'm sneaking—Luca is in the shower. He can't hear.

I just... want to explore on my own.

And get my thoughts in order.

My ass still stings, and if I think about the pleasure mixed with the fear...

Stop it.

I'd never had sex like that before. All-consuming. Sex, yes. Good sex, even. But that...

"Mrs. DeSantis," someone calls.

I whirl around.

Ricardo comes up from the street, meeting me in the short driveway. "Mr. DeSantis asked me to accompany you if you left the property."

"Please don't call me Mrs. DeSantis," I say. "I'm just going to explore. He said it was okay that I went alone."

He shakes his head. "I sincerely doubt that, miss."

I tilt my head. I never got around to asking Luca—our conversation got off track quickly. "Why do you say that?"

Ricardo glances away. I don't think he's allowed to spill DeSantis secrets—even to a new member of the family.

I nod slowly. "Okay, fine. You can accompany me."

Relief overtakes his expression. "Thank you."

I gesture for him to walk with me. "How do you know Luca?"

"Ah." He grins. "He's a relative on his mother's side."

I bite back the curiosity and go for aloofness instead. "She passed away, I heard."

"Yes, miss."

"I'm sorry for your family's loss." I catch Ricardo's eye, hoping he hears the sincerity. Death sucks, and if she raised Luca to be at all in her image, she was probably a matriarch.

"And yours," he says softly. "I only met Wilder a few times, but he seemed well-loved."

I'm glad he died. I cringe. "He... was. He had a lot of stress, sometimes it came out on those around him."

Like his brothers.

And maybe eventually it would've come out on me.

"It's funny, my sister never liked him." I shrug. "She only met him at the engagement party, and then again at the rehearsal dinner. She seemed..."

Lucy was firm in her dislike, but she hid it extraordinarily well. It only came out once. After that, she tucked it away like it didn't bother her.

"Where are we going?" I ask. We've been on a street that's grown steadily steeper downhill, and every so often the ocean is visible.

"There's a market down here. It should be opening back up soon."

Most things close for a long lunch, and I would imagine we're on the tail end of it. The streets are silent, almost sleepy. I take a deep breath. We quickly fall into silence. I use this time to consider what I know about Luca.

He only tagged along with Wilder and Jameson occasionally, with Aiden. They paid me very little heed, even on their estate here in Sanremo. Aiden was always whispered to be a hit man with a volatile temper. With Wilder gone, I expect the second son will have to step into some big shoes to fill. And Luca... well, he was raised by Jameson.

What else is there?

All in all, I know next to nothing.

I turn to speculation. Luca was the one who knocked me to the altar floor after Wilder was shot. He might've even saved my life. And he carried me away from the danger.

He's possessive, with no problem getting married to a stranger and dragging her halfway across the world. He likes to call me *wife*. He's got anger issues, if his threat about orgasms and lies is real.

I press my lips together, annoyed that my thoughts have found their way back to the sex. He didn't kiss me after that first time, and it's better that way. Sex is fine—it's kissing that's the real issue.

Right. No more kissing.

"Here," Ricardo says.

A whole street has been shut down for this tiny market.

Rows of stands dot the sidewalks, and there are a lot of people milling about. *This* is where everyone is.

A band plays farther down, loud music that seems to vibrate in my chest.

I close my eyes and soak it in—the noises, the smells of sauce and meat, drying herbs, the warmth on my skin—and then smile.

Okay.

"Let's go," I say.

He follows, ever the diligent shadow. We wind between tables, and he's patient when I stop and lift little baubles. Some of the people pay me no mind, but others try to engage in rapid-fire Italian.

Ricardo often steps in to translate. I give the table owners weak smiles, unable to buy a damn thing. I should've brought money, or my purse. Hell, even my phone.

Good one, Ames.

Someone calls Ricardo's name. I'm busy running my fingers over crystal pendants, and he barks a short, "Stay." Then he's gone.

"American?" the woman asks.

I look up and smile. "Unfortunately."

She chuckles. "What brings you here?"

"A honeymoon."

Her gaze sweeps past me, to Ricardo. "I didn't know he was engaged."

I grimace, and her eyes widen.

"Um, sorry," I backpedal. "I'm not married to him. Do you know Luca DeSantis?"

Her smile fades. "It's best if you moved along. Good day, dear."

She turns away from me abruptly, and I take a quick step back. Then another. The sudden dismissal stings.

I glance around for Ricardo, but he's out of view.

And I can't *stay*, so I go. I don't stop at any of the other stalls, I just keep moving my feet. Ricardo might catch up with me, or I can figure out my own way home.

Stupid.

I don't know why I thought Luca was well-liked in this city. Or why I guessed his name carried the same weight it does in New York. Back home, it opens doors. The only doors it won't open are West-owned or run companies, and frankly? They're easy to avoid.

I emerge on the other side of the market. I walk farther down. I'm not sure why I'm trying to catch my bearings, because this whole neighborhood is unfamiliar. We took trips down to the beach a few times, ate with Wilder and Jameson at a restaurant overlooking the harbor, but wandering by myself is an anomaly.

Someone calls out to me in Italian. I glance over at the man leaning against one of the buildings and shake my head.

He switches to English. "Aren't you a pretty one?"

I straighten and purse my lips. How many times have I been catcalled in my life? Too many. But this one has already drawn a reaction from me, and swift anger floods my body.

I stalk away from him, refusing to give him another second of attention.

Men like him were always hanging around Dad when I was younger. Lucy and I were untouchable, but that didn't mean they couldn't look at us.

Or talk at us.

And boy, did they always have something to say.

"Pretty girl," he says behind me, "in such a hurry to leave. Where are you going?"

I ignore the goosebumps breaking out along my arms.

When my friends and I went into the city, I always had something to protect myself: pepper spray or a knife, keys I could put between my clenched fingers like claws. And here I am with not even my phone. Nothing to save me.

Stupid.

I take a turn, risking a glance over my shoulder. The man walks casually, his hands in his pockets, and his attention goes everywhere except in my direction.

Trepidation floods my body. I pick up my pace, taking another corner too sharply, back toward the market. Make a circle, end up where I started. Crowds are dangerous, but they can also be safe. Ricardo will be searching for me.

I skid to a halt.

Dead end.

I pivot, going down another side street. Someone's whistling, but the rest of the town seems asleep, everyone absent. They're herding me. In the back of my mind, I know this might be sexual assault 101, but I can't see a way out of this.

I can't be that far away from the market.

A deep-seated worry is batting its wings in my chest. The fear that I'm lost.

"I always like this game," the man says, suddenly close behind me. His accent is thick.

I jump and whirl around.

He seems just a bit younger than Luca. Dark eyes, a neatly trimmed beard. He's not dressed badly, either. Not like a vagrant.

He smiles at me. For the first time, I wonder how many other girls he's done this to. Backed into a corner.

I force myself to speak. "What game?"

"Cat and mouse." He inspects his fingernails. "Why don't you smile? You'd fair better."

I keep my face blank. Not today, asshole.

He suddenly lifts his chin, his attention going to the connecting street.

Drifting on the wind is the whistling that caught my attention earlier.

A new man arrives. The whistling cuts off, and he licks his lips. His expression is hungry.

"Who's this, Matteo?" he asks.

"A new friend." Matteo, then. A ringleader? Or the dutiful sheepdog about to bow out for its master?

My muscles lock, but I can't make myself look away from them. Any minute now, I'll run. Sprint to safety. I just need to...

Rough hands of a third person grab my shoulders from behind, and I can't help it. I let out a loud yelp.

Matteo laughs.

I kick out, but he easily moves out of the way. Fear spurs on my adrenaline, and I claw at the one holding me, flinging myself out of his grip.

And right into the whistler.

He shoves me at the wall and grips my jaw. His fingers dig into my cheeks. His dark eyes bore into mine, but I hesitate at the pain.

What are you doing, Amelie?

Fight.

I lash out, a wild scream tearing from my throat. The heel of my palm connects with his throat. My knee hits something soft, and I get another kick in before he releases me, staggering away.

But it's three against one—there's no chance this will be a fair fight.

The one who grabbed me from behind comes closer.

"We just want to play," he says in a low voice. It's followed by a string of Italian that I don't understand. He snatches at my wrist.

"Let go of me!" I yell. If I'm loud enough, maybe someone will come. Someone can rescue me.

He still has my wrist.

I shove him away, and he goes. Easily, with a smile.

I frown, turning slowly.

The fear will strangle me if I let it, but my brain can't seem to stop trying to find an escape route. They're spread out, and their attention is solely focused on me.

"You're the DeSantis girl." Matteo draws my attention to him. "Luca's."

My cheeks burn. My chest aches, and knots form in my stomach. They haven't hurt me, but they will. "And what if I'm not?"

The whistler darts forward, lifting a strand of hair. I push him back, baring my teeth. Cat and mouse—I'll show *them* I'm not a mouse.

"You stink of him," Matteo says. "And your husband ignored our invitation to lunch."

I raise my chin. "You beat him—the same way this is going, then? Three against one?"

His two lackeys laugh.

"Did he come crawling home to you?" Matteo asks, sauntering closer. "I hope it stoked his anger, because we've been dying for a fight."

Oh, no.

"Bait, then?" I manage.

He tugs at my jacket, exposing my tank top. His gaze lingers on my chest. "You're a smart one. Too bad you lost your guard in the crowd, because we would've enjoyed breaking his jaw. But yours will do." He smirks at my petrified expression. "Maybe we'll see how well your mouth works before we ruin it. You must suck dick decent enough to capture Luca's attention."

My skin crawls, but I can't move.

His hand goes to the top of his pants.

I'm going to be sick.

"Matteo," someone calls. "She's with me."

They wheel away from me.

Luca stands at the mouth of the alley with an insane grin. If I had to guess, Matteo was right: it *did* stoke his anger—and this has fanned the flames into an inferno.

One of Matteo's guys pulls out a knife.

Blood spraying across my face haunts my memories, and I send a silent prayer into the universe that I won't know that feeling again. The two lackeys advance toward Luca.

Luca smirks. "I do love a fair fight."

Matteo, though... he steps toward me and grabs my jaw, yanking me into his side. I shriek like a banshee and flail, batting at him.

He releases me with a grunt, shoving me into the wall.

Pop. Pop. Pop.

I flinch, covering my head. The noise of gunshots rattle in my brain, around and around. My ears ring. Someone just fired a gun, and I can't seem to make my muscles cooperate. My whole body shakes, teeth clacking together. I can't feel my fingers.

Luca better not be dead.

With that thought, I peek out from my ball.

He's not dead. He stands over the two fallen lackeys and unflinchingly squeezes the trigger again. If they weren't gone, they are now.

Matteo stands a few feet from me, his eyes narrowed. "Killing me would bring war on your family. On more than one front—can you afford that?"

Luca laughs. "You don't have the connections to bring a coordinated assault against us." He stops right in front of Matteo. The handgun is loose in his grip at his side—and maybe that's why I don't see the final shot coming.

He barely raises it and fires it into Matteo's knee.

The latter screams, falling to the side, and Luca kicks him. Again and again, he pounds into Matteo's ribs, his legs.

"Luca," I scream.

He takes one look at me, and the chill in his eyes vanishes.

How does he do that? Flip a switch, cold to hot, like it's nothing?

"You're shaking." He crouches in front of me and cups my cheek.

"You killed them to save me..." I don't understand. I'm nothing. No one. Not to him, not to my family, not to *his* family. But he just risked war, and he doesn't even seem upset about it.

So, I do something very un-Amelie-like.

I burst into tears.

CHAPTER 11
Luca

"I've got you." I scoop her up. I don't have much experience dealing with crying women.

With killing, and men, and shoving our emotions away… I can handle that. Amelie didn't even cry after someone shot at her. The fact that she's sobbing in my arms right now is a sign that things have gone too far.

Her arms wind around my neck, and she holds on for dear life. She won't stop trembling, even after we get onto the wider street and the sun touches our backs. Her chin rests on my shoulder. Every so often, she releases her grip to swipe at her face.

I hug her tighter, and some of the fury eases back. I should've killed Matteo. He was the instigator. Knowing him, he had eyes on my place. And of course, *of course* she slipped out while I showered. One moment I left her alone…

Ricardo called me as I was getting dressed, informed me that he'd *lost her*. Seemed calm despite the fury I was going to be unleashing on him. I'd never got ready so fast, and I grabbed my gun at the last moment. With the Costas out…

Well, let's just say I'm glad I didn't have to try and fight them off again.

Still, this incident is going to bring hell down on my family unless we smooth things over. We'll have to play the move I was hoping to avoid.

A sigh racks through her body.

I press my lips to her temple, but I wonder if the action is soothing to her or just irritating.

My only role models for a healthy marriage are Paloma and Antonio, and I didn't see them nearly enough for any of their advice to stick.

"Did you kill him?" she whispers.

We're nearing the top of the alley, and my thighs burn. It's steep, and steeper still when carrying someone.

Him being Matteo. The others were definitely dead—no mistaking that. I finished the job by putting a bullet into each of their brains.

"No."

"Why not?" she asks.

I shrug. "Didn't want to make things worse."

She blinks up at me. "Where are we going?"

"I didn't feel like returning just yet. We've got some time to kill before dinner, and I'd like us far away from here." We're headed toward the water.

Paloma owns a boat, and she's often tried to get me to go on it. Now seems like a good time, even if we only stay tied to the dock.

"You can put me down."

"Why?" I tighten my grip.

She exhales. "Because I'm perfectly capable of walking."

"Just because you can doesn't mean you have to." I let a rare smile out. "Besides, you can't run away again."

"I didn't run away," she says. "I just... needed air."

I shake my head. "You could've gone onto the patio if you

needed air. You didn't have to go wandering alone in a foreign city—and *no*, I don't care how many times your parents have taken you to the beach or my father's estate. This is different."

She winces. "Yeah."

Yeah. That's what I get. I lost control after I got home. After she cooked me fucking breakfast. I fucked her on the floor like some sort of savage—or a teenager eager to get his dick wet. She tasted sweet. I can practically feel her on my tongue again. If I'm not careful, I'll get a hard-on.

My face pulses. I really could've used the bag of ice she suggested, but it's too late for that. I can only see a sliver of the world out of my right eye. My ribs hurt, too. They weren't immediately bruised, just red, but it'll probably show up tomorrow. I'm glad I killed those jackasses, but it was also a decision based solely on rage.

Father would expect me to be more calculating than that.

More like Aiden on a job, planning out his steps one at a time.

I chuckle.

"What?" Amelie whispers.

My smile fades. "I was just thinking about the mess I've made. Dad will probably throw in my face that it's not how Aiden would handle it."

"And that made you laugh?"

We arrive at the harbor, and I slowly set her on her feet.

"No. What made me laugh was the fact that this is *exactly* how Aiden would react if Gemma—" *Oops*.

Amelie narrows her eyes. "Gemma? Aiden's in love?"

"Nope," I lie.

She's not convinced. *Fuck*, he's going to kill me if she figures it out.

And in the next breath, she guesses, "Gemma West?"

"You've heard of her?" I mutter hoarsely.

"Oh, man. You said it was a West behind the attack that

killed Wilder. The Wests and DeSantises don't get along... aren't they mortal enemies?" She steps away, her brain's wheels spinning. "And he'd go all crazy, mass-murderer style, over her? Why?"

I tip my head back. "Amelie. Please stop."

She presses her lips together. I'm sure there are a lot more questions bouncing around her mind, but she wisely stays silent.

Besides, how do I explain that my father wanted to put pressure on the Wests a few years ago and had Aiden pick up their only daughter from school? Drove her around, did God knows what, and then returned her as if nothing had happened. Gemma was none the wiser, but it was a big *fuck you* from Dad to her father, Lawrence. He'd kidnapped her.

And that triggered a bit of an obsession.

He's still like that, pulling her strings from a distance. I don't know if she realizes she has a stalker, but with Wilder's death looming over our heads, I'm going to bet she'll find out soon enough.

"Is he going to hurt her?" she asks, stopping just in front of me.

"I don't know." I offer her my hand. "Want to come with me?"

She slips her hand into mine.

I tug her along, until we get to the marina. I feel the slight hesitation in her steps but keep going. Onto the rough wooden boards of the weathered dock, down to Paloma's catamaran. Antonio bought it for her on their twenty-fifth wedding anniversary.

La Bellezo waits for us around the corner, halfway down the dock. True to her name, she's a beauty. Amelie's eyes almost pop out of her skull. *La Bellezo* has a deck and a half, then of course the inside portion. But it's the half-deck that was built up that's the impressive spot. It houses the controls, and it's sleek enough that it doesn't get in the way of the sails. It's covered, too, for days when the weather is less than ideal.

I focus on Amelie, who gapes up at it.

"Sorry, I was expecting something... smaller. You own this?"

"No." I chuckle. "It's Paloma's."

"Who is that?"

I pause, then say, "My aunt. We're having dinner with her and my uncle later."

I help her step onto the stern and guide her up to the top deck. It gives us a good view of the ocean and the town. She waits until I sit, then takes the seat across from me.

"Tell me about your family?" she asks.

I shake my head and glance out over the water. "Nothing much to tell, really. I'd come out here in the summers and spend them with Mom's side of the family. Dad didn't love the idea, and everything felt controlled. Rationed, you know? I was looking forward to turning eighteen and being able to make my own choices, but she died before that could happen."

Amelie makes a noise in the back of her throat.

"I came out for her funeral. It was on my birthday." I've hardened myself to the idea of that particular tragedy, but it does sneak up on me sometimes. Like when I'm around Paloma, or in that restaurant.

"I'm so sorry."

I shrug. "It was a long time ago."

She covers her eyes. "I don't even know how old you are."

"Twenty-three."

"Oh." She glances at me. "That's not bad."

I tilt my head. "Why didn't you ask me how I got my injuries?"

"Because..." She sucks in a breath. "Wilder always told me he wouldn't tolerate questions."

I ball my fists. "That fucker." Damn, my anger is a force inside me. I lean forward and hook my hands around her calves, tugging her to the edge of her seat.

She squeaks and grabs my biceps. She blurts out, "I just... I thought that changing the subject was the right thing. And the breakfast was right there. And then we kissed, and..."

"I'm not my brother." I stare into her eyes. We're nose to nose, but she needs to know that I'm serious. "Are you hearing me? I'm not him. Whatever he told you, however he tried to groom you—"

She flinches. "He didn't."

I choke on my laugh. The poor girl is only nineteen. She was dealing with a twenty-five-year-old asshole who was going to take over every aspect of the DeSantis company in just a few years' time. His whole *life* had been about learning how to manipulate people.

"I'm sorry, but I can almost guarantee he did. But I just want you to be *you*."

She blinks rapidly. "Okay," she whispers. "Who hurt you?"

I exhale. "When we were teenagers, Wilder had a summer fling. Her name was Mariella Costa. Things didn't end so well. As in, like a fucking dumbass, Wilder knocked her up —then helped her get an abortion." I ignore her cringe. "As you might imagine, the Costas are upstanding Italian Catholics. They didn't take too kindly to Wilder's treatment of Mariella. They sent her away to live with relatives as punishment, and they've spit on the DeSantis name ever since."

"Wow," she mutters. She rises, pacing to the bow of the boat.

The sun catches her blonde hair, and I have to shake myself. Amelie is beautiful. I knew that before I even married her. But seeing her now...

She sheds the jacket and shakes out her arms.

"I was going to marry him." She turns back. "And he was running around getting girls pregnant?"

"Just one girl," I say. "As far as I know."

She pauses. "Did he love her?"

I wish I knew. But it would explain the changes in him after that summer. He did what he thought was right, but it ended up jeopardizing everything.

Amelie returns to the covered section of the deck, but she sits next to me now. She's so close, the heat of her radiates through my clothes. We both sit back, and I wrap my arm around her shoulders.

"This doesn't mean we're on good terms," she whispers.

"I know."

"So, it was the Costas?"

I heave a sigh. "Yeah. Matteo is Mariella's elder brother. *Their* elder brother, Cristian, has been the head of the family for the last few years. Their father died from cancer or something."

She shudders. "Matteo. That name isn't a coincidence to what happened in the alley."

"No, he's the one and only." I crack a smile. "Not *actually* the one and only, because the name is pretty popular. But he's the same one. He threatened to go to the house and find you. I guess he wasn't exaggerating."

"I'm sorry," she says softly. "I feel like an idiot."

I could say it's not her fault, but we're all allowed to feel like idiots every once in a while. And her actions directly impacted the lives of three men.

"Amelie or Ames?" I ask, a repeat of my earlier question. Maybe she'll give me a solid answer, this time.

She leans back slightly, meeting my gaze. Her pretty eyes narrow. "Everyone in high school called me Amelie. My sister calls me Ames."

And Wilder. She leaves that part out, though.

"And me?"

Her cheeks turn pink. "You can call me whatever you want."

"I quite like the sound of wife." I relish in her discomfort and the way she tries to put space between us.

Now that we're back on relatively neutral ground, I don't allow that space. She had her moment to freak out—and now we're back. Her and I, apparently on the same side. Even if it doesn't quite feel like it.

"Why did you decide to marry me?"

"It was an opportunity," I say honestly.

Her eyebrow tics. "An opportunity for what?"

I look out at the boats surrounding us and think of the best way to say it.

"To have someone of my own," I finally reply.

A claim, a prayer, a wish.

CHAPTER 12
Amelie

Ricardo meets us at the entrance to the harbor with a car. His expression is impassive, but he doesn't so much as glance at me. The coldness is a remarkable difference from an hour ago—and it's my fault. He opens the back door for me, and I slide in.

I almost apologize, but he closes the door in my face and crosses to the driver's side.

Luca doesn't say anything about his behavior and sits in front of me. In fact, he seems suddenly lost in his cell phone. Mine has been forgotten in the bedroom, set on a charger. I wonder if anyone cares enough to check up on me.

My sister, maybe, but definitely not my parents. Not unless there was a new development...

"I'm booking our flight back to New York," Luca tells me. "We're going to meet Paloma and Antonio for dinner, then get the hell out of here."

"A fast honeymoon," I murmur. The city flashes by through the window. "Are we leaving because of the Costas?"

He grunts his affirmative.

The sky darkens, and clouds roll in from the water. It

happens quickly—one minute sunny, and the next we're doused in gloom. I shiver at the temperature drop and pull on my jacket again.

Truth be told, I'm happy go home. If we stayed here, Luca might succeed in trapping me under his thumb. I might actually give in. But I must remain resolute. Strong.

A good wife satisfies all aspects of her husband's needs, Mom's memory whispers at me.

His *needs* can go straight to hell. He killed someone, after all. Two someones. I'd already decided that kissing was out, but there's an ache in my chest. It seems to breathe along with my heartbeat.

Too soon, Ricardo slows the car to a stop. Luca hops out and opens my door, offering his hand. I take it, peering around. The street is familiar.

"We're close to your house," I guess.

"Same street." He glances around.

"Okay. Well, we should..."

"Wait." He sidesteps, blocking me. "I need you to put this on."

I stare down at the ring in his hand. It's beautiful. It looks like a family heirloom. I balk at that. "I can't—"

"My aunt gave it to me this morning," he says in a low voice. "Before everything happened, I went to see her... She gave me this ring off her own finger. Just put it on."

I bite my lip and hold out my left hand. He smirks and slips the piece of jewelry on, and I glare at it. It's still warm from his pocket, but it's heavy, and just a bit too loose. If I flung my hand around, it would probably fly off. I make a fist and nod to Luca.

He takes my right hand and guides me into the restaurant. If I didn't know it was a restaurant, I'm not sure I would've guessed. Its dark-green door doesn't stand out against the white stucco building. The name is painted above it. Inside, we go down a narrow hallway and into the main dining area. It, too, is long and narrow. A swinging door in the back probably leads to a kitchen. There's a bar against one of the long walls, dotted with rows of barstools. Half of them are occupied. Opposite it are tables stacked next to each other. Patrons probably all know each other—or quickly become acquainted.

The tables are empty and bare except for one in the back. It's been made up with a white tablecloth and four place settings. A cluster of low candles in the center gives it some ambiance.

A man exits from the back, and as the door swings wildly behind him, I catch a glimpse of a dark-haired woman at a counter.

I don't know why I'm suddenly nervous.

Like... meet the parents nervous.

I've never met anyone's parents before, and I don't think Jameson counts. He was an imposing man before I knew I was going to marry one of his sons. But this is *formal*, even if it's Luca's aunt and uncle. They're the relatives who haven't been affected by the DeSantis storm.

Maybe I'm just some girl who Luca found and fell in love with.

That sounds nice. An escape from reality.

But then the man pops my fantasy. "This is your captive bride, hmm?"

He's medium height and bald as a cue ball, and Luca releases my hand to meet him halfway. The patrons glance behind them at the commotion but quickly return to their drinks. The two men hug and kiss each other's cheeks.

"It's been too long," the man says.

Luca beckons me forward.

My feet are stuck to the floor—and stuck on his first words. *Captive bride*. Is that me? Am I captive?

A hand tows me forward. Irritation flashes across Luca's

face, and he plants me in front of his uncle. I hope he doesn't plan on showing me that sort of greeting. My face is probably a mask of wariness, because he just chuckles and extends his hand.

"Antonio, this is my wife, Amelie. Amelie, my uncle, Antonio."

"Pleasure." I smile. Years of attending fancy dinners with my parents' dirtbag friends have schooled me in the art of little white lies. This is certainly *not* a pleasure, but what else can we expect from a captive bride?

Luca narrows his eyes at me, but I just turn my beam on him.

"Please sit." Antonio gestures to the table. "Paloma will be out shortly, and I will just top off my friends at the bar."

I slide into my seat, and Luca sits beside me. His hand immediately curls around my thigh, and butterflies wing around my stomach.

"What are you doing?" he growls under his breath.

I ignore the tone and flip my hair back. It's out of control today with the humidity, but I can't really be bothered to do anything about it. "I'm not doing anything," I inform him. "Let go. I want to make a good impression on your aunt."

Another lie.

They're stacking up.

He squeezes my leg, then slowly retracts it.

His aunt comes in from the kitchen, a wide smile on her face. "You must be Amelie," she says. She slips between the tables and takes my hands in both of hers.

I try to hide my surprise when she kisses both of my cheeks, and then my forehead. I don't get that affection from my family, let alone a perfect stranger.

"Welcome." Her accent is thick, and it adds to her charm. She takes the seat across from me. "Are you from New York, Amelie?"

I nod. "Born and raised."

"How was that?"

"Rose Hill is nice. It's outside the city, so nothing crazy really happened there."

"It's a rich town," Luca supplies.

"Right." Glancing around, I have to wonder if being rich is a bad thing.

"Antonio," Paloma barks, followed by rapid Italian.

He raises his hands in surrender and returns. "Excuse me," he says to us. "You know how they like to ramble on."

Paloma's eyes go to the ring on my finger, and I swear... her whole fucking face lights up. "He gave it to you! Oh, it looks beautiful. Let me see."

I extend my hand, and she grasps it. She turns it this way and that, only frowning a moment when it slips sideways.

"My fat fingers." She sighs. "I'm sure it can be resized. I appreciate the thought you took to wear it tonight."

I force a smile, although the fact that she's elated about this can only be a bad thing. It feels like a nasty trick. Luca and I aren't in love. We certainly aren't happy. We've just fallen into a weird circumstance.

Antonio asks Luca something in Italian, and he responds in kind. He grins at his uncle.

I try not to let the lost feeling show, but Paloma is still holding my hand.

She squeezes my fingers to catch my attention. "It's usually just me in the back. Would you like to see?"

I nod.

We get up and go into the kitchen. I can see the immediate appeal: it's cozy. More like a real family kitchen than the sterile environment I was expecting. There are sprigs of herbs hanging from the ceiling, and a vase of flowers on the corner of the large island.

"Luca visited me this morning," she says. "But he didn't walk like he was in pain, and his eye was not swelled shut."

I wince. "Right."

"So?" She opens the oven and retrieves a casserole dish.

I cross my arms. "Mrs..." *Shit*, I don't know her surname. "Paloma," I continue, "you should know better than anyone that the DeSantis name carries some weight. That weight isn't necessarily a good thing. I'm learning that faster than anyone."

She grunts. "Matteo and Luca used to be close friends, before the awful mess."

Before my dead husband-to-be knocked up a different girl—but she's a bit too classy to say that. Still, the fact that they were friends is... horrifying, if we're being honest. Luca shot him in the knee. Matteo...

I turn away. "That man is a monster," I say carefully. "He would've..."

"He would've what?" Paloma suddenly stands before me, her eyes wide. "You met Matteo?"

I swallow. "He threatened me, and Luca..."

"Enough," Luca booms from the doorway. He grabs my arm, drawing me to his side. He's angrier than I've ever seen him. "Do you know what happens when you drag innocent people into family business?"

"She's family," I sputter.

"I didn't think I would have to explain this to you like you're five." He's getting louder by the second. "You keep your mouth *shut*."

I open my mouth to retort, and he shakes me. Just once, back and forth, but my teeth clack together. The words get stuck in my throat.

"Go. Sit. Be *silent*." He pushes me toward the door.

I've never been more interested in fleeing—so I go.

Except I don't stop at the empty table. I fly outside and skid to a stop, gulping lungfuls of air. This whole freaking marriage was a mistake. Tears burn my eyes, and I swipe the back of my hand under my nose.

I've been silent about this situation for three years—and now he expects more of it.

"Are you okay?"

I sniffle and straighten my spine. *God*, Mom would smack me if she saw me like this.

A girl approaches slowly, her brow furrowed. "You seem upset."

"I'm okay." I exhale. "Just taking a break from..." I wave my hand back to the restaurant.

She laughs. "A boy? Or family?"

"Definitely a boy."

Her attention goes to the ring on my finger. "Ah."

I shove my hands into my jacket pockets. "Yeah, it's not a big deal. I should go back inside." Because standing out here is a little dramatic. Although Luca hasn't stormed out and dragged me inside by my hair, so I suppose that's a win.

They must be having quite the conversation.

"You want a smoke?" The girl holds out a pack.

If there was a bad habit I could secretly get into in high school, I did it. I drank and smoked and managed not to kill myself at summer parties. Because for a while, I just didn't give a shit.

And I'm starting to feel that way again.

I take one and lean in for her to light it. The pull of smoke into my lungs, the slight deprivation of oxygen, is an immediate rush. I let my breath out slowly and close my eyes. Nicotine bombards my system. Inch by inch, I release the anxiety.

"Thanks," I say, reopening my eyes.

But the girl is gone, and a face I never wanted to see again has replaced her.

Matteo.

A crutch supports some of his weight, tucked under his arm. His leg is in an air cast.

Honestly, I'm surprised he's standing.

I freeze. Now would be the perfect time to scream—and *definitely* a good time to run—but my muscles lock. The memory of him going to unbuckle his pants has fear paralyzing me.

He takes the cigarette from my lips and puffs on it. He blows the smoke in my face. "Quiet, little DeSantis bride. You're a curious creature. I don't think you're quite what you seem."

I ignore the fear and square my shoulders. "How's that?"

He shrugs. "You could've dashed back into the restaurant and been safe."

My gaze goes to the door, which is now blocked by the girl. She leans on it, staring down at her nails. She's got the same wildly curly hair as Matteo.

"Oh, shit." Recognition dawns—and then dread.

She's not a random girl offering a cigarette. She's Wilder's ex-girlfriend, almost-baby-mama, and the Costa princess. Mariella.

CHAPTER 13
Amelie

Matteo chuckles. "DeSantis told you?"

I grimace. "Yes."

"As I said," he murmurs, staring at me. "Curious."

"I don't..."

"Come," he says to his sister. He stubs out the cigarette beneath his shoe and motions for me to turn around. "Let's see dear Luca's reaction to *this*."

He wraps his arm around my shoulders and shows me his gun. Mariella takes the crutch, and Matteo leans on me. He puts pressure on me, indicating that he wants to go inside. The gun pokes into my ribs.

This is not going to end well.

"Are you going to kill him?" I ask.

He grunts. "Haven't decided, honestly. Might be easier to kill you."

Great.

We enter the restaurant. Luca and Paloma must still be in the kitchen. Antonio stands at the bar with his friends. It takes too long for him to realize we're here, and when he does...

He pales.

"Everyone out," Matteo orders.

There is *zero* hesitation. It's actually impressive. Mariella hugs the wall behind us as the patrons filter out, and it's just Antonio left.

"You, too, old man," Matteo adds.

"If you put bullet holes in my restaurant, your brother will be the one paying for repairs."

I close my eyes. He's going to get himself shot at this rate —but Matteo just laughs. He's unbothered by Antonio's vinegar. He replies to Luca's uncle in Italian, then shoves me forward.

"Mariella," he calls. "Go."

The door closes behind her.

Murmuring comes from the kitchen, loud enough to pick up the tone, but I have no idea what Paloma could be saying to Luca, or vice versa.

Matteo shakes his head. "What do you think, Amelie? Did his uncle go around and warn them? Is that what you were hoping for?"

I shake my head. "I wasn't hoping for anything."

"I was." He leans on me more. "I was hoping for any excuse to gut him."

The door opens, and Luca and Paloma come out. Paloma has that hot dish in her hands, pinched between two oven mitts. She gasps, lurching backward.

It's interesting to see Luca in action. He takes a second to process it—his gaze going from my face to Matteo, then the gun pointed at my side. He seems to check over the rest of me, too, but his expression stays completely blank.

Cold, even.

I strive to be more like him in these situations... but wasn't I just saying how I was frozen? Maybe this is the same. He's liquid nitrogen and I'm simply ice. Both frigid, but we're just... different forms.

Way to nerd out, Ames.

"How's the leg?" Luca asks.

Matteo grunts. "I'm not here for payback."

"Oh?"

"Paloma, dear, go outside. This way." He gestures behind us.

She sets down the dish and moves slowly past us, and I grit my teeth. She meets my eyes and nods once. The door closes behind her, and then only the three of us remain.

"What do you want?" Luca asks.

Matteo laughs. "What I *want* are my friends back." He's suddenly quivering with rage. A switch thrown in an instant. "But that's not what my brother wants."

Ah. A family matter, then?

"He wants to see you," he continues.

Luca barely suppresses his irritation. "He could've called."

Matteo grins, baring his teeth. "Why? He's here."

That gets a rise out of him. Luca takes a step toward us, scowling. "Matteo—"

"If you're about to appeal to my good *graces*, DeSantis, just remember how that went for you this morning." He jams the barrel of the gun into my temple. "I made a promise to this pretty little one. I think we should see it through."

My heart seems to want to burst out of my throat. The promise to test out my mouth and break my jaw? Luca wouldn't let that happen. He couldn't.

But I can't control my fear. I wasn't born into this life. I'm not hardened to it yet. In two days I've seen more death and blood than I could've ever imagined. My parents didn't prepare me to be courageous. They taught me how to swallow my thoughts, how to set a dining table, how to talk to politicians.

These men are as far from politicians as we can get.

Luca's eyes narrow, and he glances once at me before returning his attention to Matteo. If he thinks I can silently communicate what the *fuck* Matteo means, he's sorely mistaken. If he's going to break my face in, the least I can do before I go is bite his damn dick off.

That's a promise.

And the promise of pain, too, whispers at me.

The kitchen door opens behind Luca, startling him—and me. He puts his back to the bar—the only decent wall, really—to try and keep Matteo, me, and this newcomer in his sights. We're desperately outnumbered, him and I.

"Cristian," Luca greets him.

As if this night—screw that, the whole week—couldn't get any worse.

Cristian Costa smiles, and it's downright sinister. I shiver. Today was a bad day to try and test karma. The kickass black clothes and boots I pulled on earlier, feeling invincible? I should've gone with something sweet. Something less tempting.

"Bring him in," he calls. His attention comes back to his brother and me. "Put that fucking gun away, Matteo, and take a seat before one takes you."

Matteo doesn't respond, instead shuffling us sideways to the first table. He shoves me into a chair and slides into the one next to me, extending his injured leg.

"What do you want?" Luca finally asks.

Cristian raises his hand for silence. In the kitchen, something crashes to the floor. The door swings forward, knocked open by body weight. A man slumps to the floor. He hits it face-first.

Luca lurches, like he wants to go help but doing so would be detrimental.

I wince, turning away.

"Don't like blood?" Matteo asks me. "And you married a Mafia man. That's quite the problem you've got."

"It hasn't been an issue until now." I cross my arms to keep from revealing my trembling. I've got to be going into shock or something. "Did the Costas have something to do with Wilder?"

He snorts. "What has Wilder done now?"

Oh god. They don't know.

I press my lips together. What do I do? Do I tell them? Use it as a bargaining chip to get away? Somehow get us out of this mess?

Mariella steps over the man, wiping her hands on her jeans. The kitchen door can't even close because his legs block the way.

"Did you kill him?" Cristian asks her mildly.

"He got handsy." She glares down at him, stepping on his splayed fingers.

The fallen man emits a loud groan, and it sort of whistles.

"That's what you'll sound like," Matteo whispers. His lips brush my ear.

I stay perfectly still. Fear and loathing take up equal parts, and they've turned me to ice.

"That whistle? It could be a number of things, but I'd be willing to bet they broke your guard the same way I'm going to break you."

Horror fills me—not for his words, but because it's *Ricardo* on the floor. They found Luca's friend and hurt him just for this display of power?

For the fear, my father says. *For* your *fear*.

I squash it down. All of it. I can't afford to be horrified or scared. Wilder probably wouldn't have put me in this sort of situation, but I didn't marry a blossoming politician. I married his brother. The ruthless one. The dark one.

If anyone can survive this, it's him.

My gaze burns into Luca, searching for a sign that he knows how to get out of here.

Matteo's hand creeps up my thigh. He, too, stares at Luca, until the force of it catches Luca's attention. Matteo touches me through my jeans, and I close my eyes. I thought I had escaped this, but here we are.

My stomach is in my throat. Bile burns the back of my mouth. I'm not an ice queen. I can't control my revulsion.

"Don't you fucking lay a hand on her," Luca growls.

He lunges, and Cristian catches him mid-stride. We're so outnumbered.

Mariella's gaze is glued to the floor.

Help me, I want to scream.

"Now, now," Cristian says. "We're all friends here. Maybe this is the price you have to pay for us to leave you alive, hmm, Luca?"

A tear slips down my cheek.

I'm the price.

Funny—I haven't seemed to stop being the price people pay for what they want. Money, our lives. I'm worth everything and nothing at the same time.

Matteo's hand slips into my jeans, and there's nothing I can do to stop him—what can I do, if Luca can't? I can't face reality on this, even as it becomes crystal clear. We're probably going to die. This is payback for every fucking mistake I've made in my life.

I push at him, but he just slams my hands to the table.

"Don't fucking move," he whispers. He licks my ear. "Or I'll take out my anger on you. And maybe once I'm done with you, I'll go pay a visit to your mother? Perhaps a sister?"

The tears won't stop, even though I try to rein it in. I shudder when he reaches between my legs, prying me apart. His fingers are rough on my skin, little blades slicing me open. He curls his finger inside me, and nausea rises in my throat.

Luca's gaze burns into me.

Make it stop, make it stop.

"Stop," I beg. "Just stop."

"Say please," Matteo says, jerking his finger.

I ball my hands into fists. "Please."

His free hand comes up and grabs my hair. He yanks, and I suddenly have a view of his lap. His erection straining at his pants. I nearly fall out of my chair at the force of it.

"Louder."

Bargain with them. It isn't Matteo calling the shots—it's his brother. And his brother is letting this happen to torture us.

"I can give you Wilder," I choke out.

Matteo stills, but it's Cristian who answers me.

"Why'd you do that?" he asks.

Lie, Amelie. Seems to be something I'm good at. "Because he's the one who started this, isn't he?"

"Matteo," Cristian grunts.

His younger brother releases me and withdraws his hand. I almost fall over in my attempt to get away from him. I practically climb over the table, falling to my knees on the other side. It's Mariella who helps me stand, clutching my arms. She's a beautiful woman—I can see how Wilder would've been attracted to her as a teenager.

"I'm sorry," I whisper.

Her eyes harden. "He was nearly the death of me."

I dip my head. "Me, too."

She squints, puzzled.

"Amelie," Cristian prods. "I'll confess that I'm not the most patient man. *How* will you give us Wilder?"

Forgive me for what I'm about to do, I think in Luca's direction.

"He's vulnerable," I say. "Jameson wanted to get him out

of New York because weakness isn't allowed." I meet Cristian's gaze. "You should know that best of all."

His face betrays nothing. "So he's leaving New York."

"If I tell you where he's going, you have to let Luca and I go. And Ricardo," I add. I don't even know if he's alive or not, but I can't imagine abandoning him with the Costas. "We're leaving Sanremo. We won't return."

Cristian's eyes light up. "You won't return?"

I straighten and narrow my eyes. "Only when Wilder is dead."

"And what about my baby?" Mariella asks. "Wilder took me to a private doctor and forced me to get an abortion. He ruined *me*, too. I can't..."

I shake my head as understanding hits me. He didn't just ask her to go against her religion—he forced it on her. And why? Because he'd rather hurt an entire family than become a father. Than have a bastard floating around like Jameson. It hurts, and maybe she sees that, because she exhales.

She turns to her brother. "We take this up with Wilder, and him alone."

Cristian nods. "If that's what you want." He stands and goes to Luca, extending his hand. "A temporary truce until Wilder is dead. You don't step foot in Sanremo, and we don't kill you on the spot."

Matteo lurches to his feet. His face is beet red. "Brother. Luca *killed*—"

"Enough," Cristian snaps. "You want to settle this with Luca, dear brother? I think he might be just as inclined." He motions to Mariella, and she releases me to take his hand. They pause at the mouth of the hallway, and he looks back at me. "Where is Wilder going, Amelie?"

I swallow. My palms are sweating. It has to be somewhere believable. Somewhere...

"My parents have a house in France," I say slowly. "They

offered it to him after Luca and I got married." I rattle off the address. It's not far from here at all—they could take us with them to confirm it.

Cristian sneers. "How kind. I hope they won't mind a little blood in the place..."

"They have cleaners," I snap.

Mariella analyzes me. "Why are you doing this? You're a DeSantis."

I put my hand on a table, steadying myself. "Because what he did was wrong, and he deserves to go to Hell for what he did to you. I'd say the same about any man, family or not."

Luca's glaring holes in my head, but he can suck it.

Cristian nods. "I'll hold you to that. Just don't fucking kill him."

I can't tell if he's talking to Luca or Matteo. I press myself flat against the wall, hoping to stay far out of this—plus, I don't want Matteo to use me as a pawn again.

The door slams shut, and then it's just the three of us. Except this time, Matteo doesn't have a gun to my head—and Luca is *furious*. The facade he had managed to keep together shatters. If I was on the receiving end of that expression, I'd probably piss my pants.

Matteo doesn't, though. He just mimics his brother's sneer and grabs his crutch. I want to punch his face in.

Luca strides toward him and shoves him backward. Matteo pinwheels his free arm, trying to stay upright, but he tumbles back into a table. The gun he threatened me with is in the front of his pants, and Luca wraps his fingers around the handle.

They both freeze, and Luca grins. "I wish you had put up a semblance of a fight."

I instinctively turn away and cover my eyes with my hand. I'm *not* strong enough to handle this, if Matteo would somehow get the upper hand. Except, I keep waiting for a gunshot and none comes. Just a *snap* and grunt, then something hits the floor—a chair, maybe.

"Amelie," Luca calls.

I peek at them.

Matteo is on his knees in the center of the room, breathing hard. His legs are at an odd angle. Luca has Matteo's jaw in his grip, the gun now tucked into the back of his pants. Well away from Matteo.

"Come here," he says to me.

I unlock my legs and circle around, stopping behind Luca.

"He touched you," he confirms.

"Yes," I whisper.

"What else did he threaten?"

Matteo tries to jerk out of his grasp. Luca goes with the motion, shoving him back, and steps on his leg. A whine escapes from Matteo. Blood seeps up through his jeans. He's caught under Luca's shoe, and the pain flashes across his expression like a strobe light.

"What else, wife?"

Matteo stares at me. Now he wants mercy?

"He was going to break my jaw after I sucked his dick." I'm emboldened by Luca's presence and step forward, directly in front of Matteo. "But here's a secret, asshole. I would've bit it off if it came anywhere near my mouth."

"Go see to Ricardo," Luca says to me. "And don't look back."

I don't know why the idea of him avenging me is hot, but it is. Matteo seems well in hand, so I face Luca and cup his jaw, kissing his cheek. That isn't against the rules.

He turns quickly, catching my lips. He deepens the kiss, his tongue tasting my mouth before he breaks away. "Check on Ricardo."

I blink, shocked. *We said no kissing.*

Still, rather than stand there, no better than a lovesick

teen, I hurry to Ricardo. There's a pool of blood around his torso, but I can't see much. He's facedown, eyes closed. I check for a pulse carefully, waiting painful moments until I feel it.

Relief floods through me. He's alive.

I roll him over, bracing myself against the doorframe. He flops onto his back and groans.

"Holy shit," I murmur. A knife—one of Paloma's fancy ones, from the look of the handle—protrudes from his stomach. It's still in there, which I've heard is a good thing? But the front of his shirt is soaked with blood.

He reaches up, grasping at it, and I cover his hands with mine. They're covered in sticky, half-dried blood, like he wanted to staunch the bleeding before it became too much.

"You have to leave it," I say. "Until the ambulance arrives."

"Did you call them?" He's still whistling with every breath. His sides are moving weird with his breathing. Broken rib? Punctured lung?

Ambulance, Amelie.

Shit.

"Not yet." I release him and rise.

A scream cuts me off. I cover my ears, dropping back to my knees.

Silence.

Strong hands pull me up, and suddenly I'm in Luca's arms. My eyes are wide open—I couldn't close them if I tried. But the rest of the world seems to be moving disjointedly.

He sets me on the kitchen counter and grabs a phone off the hook. He leaves me there to see to Ricardo, and I don't know how long it is before paramedics rush into the restaurant. Luca lifts me, urging me to wrap my legs around his waist, and carries me out the back. He sets me in the passenger seat of a car and closes me in, then jogs around to the driver's side.

We zoom off down the street in the opposite direction of the rescue.

I have too many emotions, and I fear all of them. Relief, horror, terror. I'm worried for Ricardo, curious—and sick—over what Luca did to Matteo. We don't speak, don't stop back at his house, we just go.

I understand the mad dash.

If the Costas find out I lied...

I shiver. My jacket isn't cutting it anymore. Shock and the cool night air conspire against me, and soon enough I'm trembling like a wind-torn leaf. Luca cranks the heat.

"You saved us," he says softly. "Don't doubt that."

I wipe away an errant tear. Pesky things started falling a while back, rolling down my cheeks and neck, collecting in my shirt collar. "I condemned a man to death."

He grunts, then offers, "I didn't kill Matteo."

I bury my face in my hands.

"I wanted to. I did. But I don't think killing a Costa would solve our problems. It'd complicate them. But..." He tugs at my wrist, lowering it.

I meet his gaze before he has to look at the road again.

"I broke his jaw," he says. "He'll be eating out of a straw for a while."

I laugh. I can't help it. I tip my head back and let the giggles consume me, to run the last bit of my energy from my muscles. And once I'm depleted, I let my head fall to the side.

Luca doesn't seem stressed. He's relaxed behind the wheel, watching the narrow, curving road ahead of us. He switches hands on the wheel, resting one palm-up on my leg. I glance down and lace my fingers with his.

"How can you bear it?" he asks.

I sigh. "Which part? A lot of shit seems to keep happening."

We turn onto the airport road, and he pulls around to my

family's hangar. The jet is already outside, gleaming in the floodlights.

We park and climb out, and I don't wait for Luca. I trudge toward the plane. It's cold now, and goosebumps break out along my arms.

The pilot waits at the foot of the stairs and nods to me. "Welcome back, Ms. Page."

I smile. He's been my family's pilot for over a decade. We don't fly a lot, so he has other clients, but I secretly think we're his favorite. "Thanks for being flexible."

He nods. "Mr. DeSantis was persuasive."

Great. I hope he doesn't mean with threats, because we could end up crashing into the Atlantic Ocean. I wouldn't even blame our pilot, either.

I step past him and into the cabin, grabbing one of the thick blankets we keep near the front. I curl on a couch in the back, buckling myself in and making a little nest for myself. My eyes still refuse to close, though, because every time I do, I feel Matteo's hand on me. Forcing his finger inside me.

I shudder.

"Ready, miss?"

I sit up slowly. "Where is Luca?"

He shakes his head. "He said to leave without him."

I scoff. "Yeah, right."

The pilot regards me carefully. He isn't joking. My stomach does a weird swooping movement, and I throw the blankets off me. I bolt up the aisle and down the stairs, only taking a second to spot Luca's car. It drives away—but it has to loop around to get back on the main road.

I sprint for it and leap into the road, throwing my hands up. He's speeding toward me and might not be able to stop in time. I shut my eyes and hope for the best—but if he wants to leave, he'll have to run me over.

The car skids to a stop inches from me. The heat from the

engine and the glaring lights on my legs seep through my clothes.

Luca jumps out. "What the fuck, Amelie?" he yells. He comes closer, stopping inches away.

"You bastard," I scream, shoving him. It doesn't do much good. "You were going to make me leave without you?" I hit his chest, slapping at him with my open hand. "After what we just went through, you were going to put me on a plane and just—"

He catches my flailing wrists and yanks.

Our bodies collide.

"I can't leave," he says. "Ricardo, my aunt and uncle—"

"You promised me." My voice is barely above a whisper. "You promised that you'd protect me."

"And I fucking *failed*," he says.

"I told them we'd leave."

He lets out a short laugh. "Yeah, well, Wilder is dead, so I'd say you kept up your end of the bargain."

I cringe. "We have to go back to New York, Luca. They're going to kill me when they find out."

His eyes darken.

I stand firm. I have nothing left to bargain with. I'm pretty sure my worth has been ground into dust. He holds my wrists out to the sides, and I have to tip my head back to meet his gaze.

My vulnerability with Luca has shifted. I'm not afraid of it. I drop my guard and let him see the pieces I've been hiding —the fear and anger and relief.

His gaze lifts, going over my head, and I wish I could hear the thoughts running through his mind. How fierce is the debate to leave me?

"Stay on the plane," he says. "Get some sleep. I'll be back in an hour."

I try not to let his decision hurt, but it stings more than I anticipated.

"What are you going to do?" I ask.

He steps back and points to the plane.

I wasn't expecting an answer… but this is almost worse.

CHAPTER 14

Luca

Amelie trudges back to the plane slowly, almost daring me to call her out. I have half a mind to help speed her along, but this is the tiniest resistance she can manage. She didn't ask to come with me, and she doesn't argue.

She's hurting.

Once the pilot, Smith, seals her inside the plane, I climb back into the car. My first stop will be Paloma and Antonio's home. They live not far from their restaurant, and hopefully they made it back without complications.

This whole night was a fucking complication.

I should've known Matteo wouldn't wait to retaliate. I didn't think he'd be bold enough to touch Amelie in front of me. He was just asking for pain and suffering. I followed Cristian's wishes. I didn't kill him. But if Matteo comes out the other side of tonight without scars, I'd be impressed.

I hit the call button on my phone. It's early afternoon in New York, which could mean a number of things. But it's been just over twenty-four hours since Wilder was shot. Aiden either has a lead or he doesn't.

"Hello?" Aiden answers.

"How goes it?"

He's silent for a moment, then spits, "No one's talking."

I grunt. "Did you expect anything less? Everyone's afraid."

Of us, of the Wests. The whole town has caught wind of our feud, and our brother's death… well, it just depends on who can exert more force. Those trying to reveal the secrets or those trying to keep them hidden.

Lucky for us, Aiden is extremely good at pressure.

"Why are you calling?" he finally asks. "It's night one of your trip, technically speaking. Unless you got started on the plane."

"We're returning to New York tonight." I pass the road to the DeSantis estate. I won't be back there for a while, I would bet. Every minute takes me closer to family I dread to lose. But because of Amelie's bargain, I fear I'm going to lose them anyway.

"Why?"

"The Costas," I say.

This gets his attention. He demands, "Explain."

So I do. The whole grueling story, including what I did to Matteo's face. And his friends. I don't feel a lick of remorse, even when I remember how close we used to be. He lived right down the street, after all.

"You've really made a mess," he says. "But Amelie pulled one out of the bag."

"Is that even an expression?"

He chuckles. "You know what I mean. They couldn't have heard about Wilder—it was smart of her to trick them. Send them to France and broker a deal. I like her."

I grimace. "Don't fucking like her. Don't even think about her."

"Easy, brother." He pauses. "You okay?"

I turn onto my aunt's road and kill the engine. If someone's watching the house, I don't want to broadcast my arrival. It took long enough for the paramedics to show up, and if Cristian went straight to France, they could be minutes away from uncovering our deception.

We don't have a lot of time, in other words.

"I'm fine," I grunt. "I'll be better once I'm on the plane."

"Wait, wait, where are you?"

I hesitate. "I just have some unfinished business. I'll text you when we're headed back."

He makes a noise of affirmation, and I end the call. I didn't tell him it's fucking killing me to leave Sanremo like this. As if *I'm* a fugitive sneaking out of the city—or worse, driven out by a mob with pitchforks. That's sort of how it feels, although it just so happens my wife orchestrated everything.

I slip out of the car and hurry between homes, scaling a fence and dropping into a neighbor's backyard. I am nearly invisible in the shadows, and I have to hop over two more fences before I land in Paloma's patio. Light spills out from the kitchen.

I knock on the sliding glass door. It's covered by a gauzy curtain, but her shadow quickly falls over it. She peeks, then whips it aside and opens the door.

Wordlessly, she hugs me.

I return it, holding tight. This is probably what Amelie wanted—or needed—but instead she got me. A lump forms in my throat. How do I comfort a girl who just walked through hell beside me? Dump her on a plane and run away.

"What are you doing here?" Paloma demands.

I sigh. "I just came to say goodbye. I might not be back for a while. Until things settle, you know."

She pats my cheek. "I know. The Costas were watching my house, but Antonio and I know how to deal with them. We grew up on more violent streets than these. You go take care of your wife, and we'll be just fine."

I nod along to her words. "Okay. Can you check in on Ricardo for me?"

"Of course. His mother and I are close. Now go. I love you, dear boy."

I hug her again, and then I'm pushed back out into the night. Even if this is all I could accomplish, a deep part of me settles. I'm glad I was able to say goodbye to her, to set her on a path to look after Ricardo. Hopefully my old friend will be all right.

Instead of going to the car, I go in the opposite direction. Most of this city is built into a hillside, and Paloma's property butts up against a stretch of undeveloped land. It's rocky, but it beats climbing over more fences. I navigate by moonlight and step into a narrow gulley. It takes me between houses, past one street, then two, and finally dumps me out at a modest cemetery.

I know. I *should* get on a plane with Amelie and take her back to New York. But giving up feels a bit like leaving the Costas to run Sanremo. A bit like cutting off connection to my mother, too.

"I knew you'd come here." A body peels away from the shadows and follows me down a well-worn path.

Almost everyone's families are buried here. It's getting to the point where the next generation will be shoved into the mausoleum the town built last year. Space has been running out for years, but it only became dire in the last two. They refuse to create another one on the hillside I just cut through, because some are convinced it'll be needed for housing. And what's more valuable? It helps that cremation has gained popularity. I don't know why—who would want their grandmother sitting on a shelf, judging you for eternity?

Mariella keeps pace with me, maybe waiting for an answer.

I grunt.

"Talkative," she says. "What did you do with Amelie?"

"She's safe. Your brother—"

She grabs my arm. "He shouldn't have touched her. Even Cristian admitted that was crossing a line."

I raise my eyebrow. "But he allowed it."

"And then he allowed *you*."

I nod curtly and pull free, continuing on. "Shouldn't you be in France by now?"

She scoffs. "As if Cris would let me within three miles of Wilder DeSantis."

She shivers, and I glance over at her. It isn't cold—not for her. Her expression is peculiar.

"What?" she snaps.

"Do you still—?" I shake my head, unable to finish the thought.

I don't understand women. After spending time with Amelie, I'm even more certain of it. Especially since Mariella seems... hopeful. In her dream world, maybe her brothers find Wilder, beat him, and then she nurses him back to health.

I snort.

"Do not judge me," she says stiffly. "You don't know me."

I roll my eyes. "Right."

"Did my brother do that to your face?"

"One of your relatives," I reply. "Matteo said I shouldn't arrive in your city without calling ahead. Can't imagine he'll be saying much for a while."

"Hm." She grimaces. "He's in surgery, in case you were wondering. Since you used to be friends."

"I wasn't wondering."

She stops walking, and I keep going another few feet before curiosity gets the better of me. I turn around, only to find she's staring at a headstone.

Loathing sweeps through me. How is it that *I* couldn't

remember where Mom is, but she can? She's spent time here. She grew up in this town, except for her brief exile while she recovered from her parents' anger.

I stay back, and Mariella scowls at the headstone. My mother was a fierce woman, but she didn't put up much fight against Jameson. I wonder how well the girl knew my mother. Better than me?

That side of my heritage is slipping through my fingers. I wanted to heed its call. To stay here, build a life, learn my family. Not just Paloma, but the extended family. Travel Italy. Meet cousins I'd never heard of before.

The longing hits me square in the chest.

Amelie has steered my future off course.

"Did you know your mother was arranged to marry a Costa?"

I flinch.

Mariella glances and me and frowns. "No, then. Interesting. Everyone always leaves that part out. She was beautiful when she was younger. She showed me pictures, and my parents mentioned it a few times. They went to school with her. She was dragged away by Jameson and came back pregnant with you, so that... that ended things. But then he only came back for you, and not her." The hurt is evident in her voice.

Her empathy for my mom is surprisingly strong.

"Why hasn't anyone said?" I ask. "Why keep secrets?"

Shock colors my voice, but it takes a moment for the deeper ramifications to trickle down. I'm sure Amelie would put the pieces together quickly, if she were here. She's got a knack for such things.

It's the fact that Wilder and Mariella aren't the first instance of a DeSantis ruining something good. Jameson ruined my mother's prospects for happiness. And look what happened: she died alone.

"It's like water," she says. She hops up and winds away, through the headstones.

I gnash my teeth. "What does that mean?"

"You'll figure it out," she calls. Then laughs. "You better leave, Luca, lest my brothers have the same thought I did. And I believe your wife promised us you would leave the city." Softer, she adds, "You can talk to your mother anywhere."

Fucking hell. My anger for the Costas loops in Amelie, and I take a moment to rage at them all. She did what she had to do—but leaving here seems final.

It's like water. I'm going to have a hell of a time figuring that one out. But she's right—I've dallied long enough.

"Sorry, Mom," I murmur, touching my fingers to my lips, then the cool stone. "I'll be back someday."

CHAPTER 15
Amelie

The lights flicker on, and Smith ducks out of the cockpit to open the stairs. I didn't manage to get any sleep, but I think I dozed in the dark while Luca was gone. Hushed voices drift toward me, and finally Luca appears.

He glances around the cabin, at the front chairs where we originally sat, then farther back to the two couches.

I sit up slowly, keeping the blanket tucked around me.

"Let's get going," Luca says to Smith. "And can we get the temperature up in here?"

The pilot nods and closes his cockpit door.

Luca crosses the space and sinks to his knees in front of me. He brushes my hair off my face. "Are you okay?"

"Besides battling the feeling of total abandonment?" I try to be funny, but it falls flat. Neither of us smile. "I'm... okay."

He sighs. "You have blood on your face."

My eyes widen, and I throw the blanket off. He blocks my escape to the bathroom, gently catching my hands.

"I've got it," he says.

I sit with my hands in my lap, and Luca goes to the bathroom in the back. He returns with a stack of paper towels and resumes his position in front of me. He dabs at my face, then puts a damp one in my hand.

"I cleaned off your hands," he says quietly. "Do you remember?"

I close my eyes and lean into his touch. "I… don't. Everything is a blur."

"You had blood on your hands from saving Ricardo's life."

Grabbing the hilt of the knife before he ripped it out, holding my hands over his. And the awful scream that tore out of Matteo… I'd covered my ears. I must look crazy with two bloody partial handprints on my face.

My eyes fill with tears. "Is he okay?"

He nods. "He just got out of surgery. It only nicked his stomach, and keeping the blade in saved his life. Please don't cry."

I scrub my fingers, then wipe my face.

"Where did you go?" The question has been burning through me, but I don't know if he's going to answer me. I don't know if I can take another rejection.

"I went to see Paloma… and my mother." He lifts his shoulder. "Just thought I should say goodbye."

The intercom crackles, and then our pilot says, "We're next up on the runway. Please take your seats."

Luca offers his hand, and we go to the seats in the front. I pull the blanket along with me, although the cabin is already heating up. My jacket stays forgotten behind me.

Have you ever tried to sleep in a leather jacket? Not the most comfortable thing.

I tip my head back and exhale. "What's it going to be like in New York? You don't live on the estate with your father."

"I don't." He hasn't released my hand, and his thumb rubs circles over my knuckles. "I have an apartment in Brooklyn. I could've lived in downtown Manhattan, but I like the separation. Aiden lives in the tower, but he's not there much. It wouldn't be as suffocating."

I close my eyes. "I got ready in his apartment, I think. With Mom and Lucy. It was nice." And lifeless. It was very clear that Aiden spent little time there. "What's your place like?"

He contemplates that. "Quiet. Warm."

I shiver. "Warm sounds good."

"Are you still cold?"

We're in the air now, the plane leveling off above the clouds.

I nod.

He reaches over and unbuckles me, lifting me easily into his lap. He wraps my blanket around both of us, tucking my limbs in and shifting our weight. I loop my arm around his neck.

Don't kiss him, Amelie.

He has other ideas. His lips touch my temple, and my heart skips. It's a traitor.

"Close your eyes," he says.

I grip the front of his shirt. "I can't."

"Close your eyes and I'll tell you what I did to Matteo."

I shudder, but... a dark part of me needs to know. I didn't see him after that scream—all I know is that he's alive. So I meet his gaze, then slowly let my eyes shut. I rest my cheek on his shoulder, my nose brushing his throat.

He smells sweet, like honey and sweat. I want to bury my nose in his collar.

"Twice he threatened you, and once he touched you without permission." He speaks softly, a tone more suited for telling a child a bedtime story than this. "We grew up together. He has a fear of being forgotten—it's a middle-child symptom, I think. Of half a dozen kids, he was smack in the middle, and that meant he went to extremes to stay relevant. As a bastard son, myself, I empathized with him.

"Our friendship fractured once we got into more and more trouble, and then it shattered completely after Wilder's actions against Mariella." He goes quiet.

He acknowledges that what happened wasn't Mariella's fault, I suppose? And the blame rests on Wilder's shoulders.

"He most likely had a cracked rib from our encounter earlier this afternoon. A bullet in his leg. He obviously got medical attention earlier that day, and they must've dosed him up on painkillers. They can cause brain fog, slower reaction time..."

"I remember. I had my wisdom teeth taken out a few years ago."

He hums and tightens his grip on me. I have a feeling his story will take a turn for the worse, and my anticipation soars. He traces my arm under the blanket, ending at my fingers.

"I broke his fingers," he said. "They still held the smell of you. I crushed his hand under my heel, and then I broke his jaw. It wasn't even hard. He was on the floor, and I kicked his face. The crunch of bone... That's when he screamed.

"I didn't want to stop. I wanted to keep going until his whole face was a bloody mess."

"But you did," I whisper. My eyes are heavy now. Instead of Matteo forcing his hand into my pants, it's Luca's touch on my arm that I can focus on.

"I did. You needed me." He kisses the top of my head. "Sleep, if you can. We have a long flight ahead of us."

To my surprise, I do sleep.

Later, I wake up to him setting me on the couch.

"Do you feel better?"

I nod, suddenly shy. He just let me sleep *on* him. I probably drooled.

Oh god.

I try to wipe at my mouth discretely, but I catch his smirk. I scan his shirt for wet spots, my mortification growing. I don't like people watching me sleep, and he's seen me unconscious twice now. Three times if we include my hazy memory of directly after the shooting.

"Tell me," he says.

I tip my head to the side. "Tell you what?"

He puts his hands on my knees. "That you're okay. That I can do what I've wanted to do since we left the restaurant."

A thrill shoots up my back. I want more than anything for the memories of what happened tonight—and yesterday—to be erased. By Luca. Because what happened between us has shifted my heart. He saved me. Proved he'd protect me. And... well, the darkness in him calls to me.

I didn't know I could be dark, but I think we're all capable of it to some degree. For the briefest of moments, I picture Matteo's pleading eyes as I laid down his sentencing. *I* decided his fate.

"I'm not okay," I admit. "I don't know what to do with my guilt. And, with the exception of the sleep I just got, I haven't been able to stop reliving—" What's wrong with me that I can't even say it? I swallow. "I need you to erase that. So I remember *you*."

He doesn't move.

I glance away. "I'm not telling you this so you think I'm broken. I'm not—"

"You're not. I know." He holds out his hands.

I take them, and he helps me to my feet.

He stands so close, our chests almost touch. But we don't cross that distance. He just unbuttons my pants and drags them off my hips. I hold on to his shoulder and step out of the jeans, flinging them away.

He leans forward and presses a kiss over the top of my panties.

I suck in a breath and tighten my grip on him.

"This is mine," he says, sliding the fabric down.

I kick that away, too.

He walks me backward, and I hit the edge of the couch. I fall onto it, releasing a little yelp.

Luca grins. "Scared?"

I narrow my eyes. "No."

He parts my legs and runs his finger down my center. Hot sparks travel through me, and I gasp. I let my head tip back and close my eyes. When he pushes one finger into me, I'm right back at the restaurant. I tense.

"Amelie, look at me," he orders.

I crack my eyes just as Luca descends. His mouth lands on my clit, sucking hard.

I jolt at the suddenness of it, but *oh my god*. I can't tear my gaze away from him. He crooks his finger, teasing a spot inside me.

A second finger joins his first, and his pace quickens. He's playing with my body as if he owns me, and I can't tell whether I love or hate it.

Either way, this is going to be the fastest orgasm of my life.

"Luca, oh my god—"

It crests and breaks through me, over and over.

He doesn't pull out of me, but he sits back on his heels and watches his fingers. The sensation is light, but my thighs tremble.

"Stop," I moan. "Luca."

"Remember what I promised you?"

What? No.

"Lies, Amelie." He kisses the inside of my thigh. "How many did we stack up today?"

Oh god. And the fact that I only get wetter is proof that I'm into his games. I'm about to tell him screw it, I need to kiss him, but the words clog.

I don't *want* to get attached to him.

He doesn't slow—the pace he keeps is relentless, even as the waves of my orgasm ease. I shift, pushing at his hand, and he slaps my pussy. The pain of it, holy hell. I almost come on the spot.

"You like that, wife?"

"I don't—"

Smack.

He thrusts his fingers into me, and it doesn't just push me over the ledge—I fly off it. Stars burst behind my eyelids, and I clench around his fingers. Damn it. I moan, unable to stop the sound from escaping.

I reach for him—to push him away—but he just catches my wrists. He lifts my tank top, over the front over my head. He slides it down behind me, to my elbows, and ties off the material. I try not to think about how close he is. His face right next to mine, his arms looped around me.

My pulse quickens.

But all too fast—*or maybe not fast enough*—he sits back and admires his handiwork. My arms are slightly behind me, my tank top knotted at my elbows. It isn't uncomfortable. It thrusts my chest into his face, though, and that's exactly where his gaze goes next. My forearms and hands are free, but I can't really go anywhere. Can't stop him.

And my god, I think I *do* like it.

He just gave me two orgasms, but lust rushes straight to my core. I'm more turned on than I've ever been in my life.

"What do you want?" he asks.

I tilt my head. "I want to see what you're going to do next."

Surprise flits across his face.

"Okay," he answers. He stands and backs away. "Kneel."

I slip from the couch to my knees.

"Can you reach your clit?"

"Yes," I say.

He takes his shirt off, then his pants. "I'm going to fuck your mouth while you touch yourself. Don't hold back, Amelie."

I shudder, but I widen my knees and lean back slightly, pressing my finger to my clit. I'm already sensitive from what he did to me earlier. I let out a shaky exhale.

He raises my chin. "Open."

I do, gaze on his cock. I get the same thrill I did earlier. *Was it only this morning we had sex for the first time?* It feels like a week ago, at least.

I never expected things to move so quickly. Not physically. Not emotionally.

He grasps my hair and tugs my head back farther. The tip of his cock slides against my lips, my tongue. "You don't have control. Do you understand?"

I try to nod, but his grip in my hair tightens. "Yes," I manage.

"Tap my thigh if it's unbearable."

It's my only out before he slides into my mouth.

And he's right: I don't have control. He fucks my mouth hard. He hits the back of my throat, and I choke around him. I don't tell him to stop, though. I just take deep inhales through my nose when I'm able.

I push my finger into myself.

There's something dirty about it, but impossibly hot. I'm used, bound, but whether Luca likes it or not, *I am* in control. Of this moment. Of my orgasm.

He grunts and pistons into me faster. Tears stream down my face.

Ah, fuck.

I rub myself harder, matching his tempo. He sets a brutal speed, and I cry out when I come again. He pulls out of my mouth, his dick wet with my saliva. It bobs in front of me.

He drags me to my feet. I can barely stand—not after that. He supports most of my weight and wipes my face, then ducks down to kiss me.

I can't.

I turn my head away at the last moment, and his lips land on my cheek.

He doesn't say anything about it. Maybe he thinks I'm weird about kissing after oral. He sits and tugs me down. My knees go on either side of his thighs.

I stare into his dark eyes and try to see my future.

"Luca," I say hoarsely. "What's going to happen to us?"

He lifts me slightly, aligning with my entrance. He's *right there*, but now it's my decision to lower myself. I wait for his answer. My muscles tremble. I don't know how I'm still upright.

He cups my face. "We'll find a normal."

It's not the answer I want. I *want* to go back to school. To see my friends and my sister. To hunt down my demons and shoot them in the face. What I don't want is his idea of *normal*, which could be anything from keeping me locked at home, raising eight babies, to harboring me as a wife in name only.

That's a vicious fear.

But isn't it true?

The boys I dated in high school moved on to find their true loves, leaving me behind. The man I had thought I was going to marry was shot. Luca... he probably hates my guts. We're married, but that doesn't mean loyalty. It doesn't mean love.

It's just a license provided by the fucking state of New York.

"You're scowling, wife." His thumb presses into the space between my brows.

I jerk my head away. "Untie me, Luca."

He does so wordlessly, and I shake out my arms. I place them on his shoulders, lightly gripping him, and finally lower myself onto him.

We both groan. He stretches me out, fills me to the brim. Just when I think I can't take any more, he shifts his hips and slides the rest of the way in.

"What's wrong with normal?" he asks.

"You want to talk about this now?" I glare at him.

He presses his hand to my back and flips us. My back hits the couch. He traces the edge of my face with his finger. We're not moving, just... existing together.

And I want to hate it.

Kissing always felt more intimate than sex. And I don't know *what* this is, but I'm going to burst into flames. Or worse: catch feelings for Luca.

Both situations aren't ideal. I think we can agree.

"Fuck me, Luca," I say.

He sighs. "So many walls up in this pretty little head of yours. I didn't realize it this morning."

I shift, and he pulls out of me. My eyes roll back when he pushes back in. Each stroke is a different form of punishment. A different way to lose control.

"It's okay, Amelie. I'll break you down."

I shudder. "And me to you," I whisper.

He nods once. He tries to kiss me again, and I turn away. *Again*. He lets out a huff, and his hot breath touches my earlobe. His teeth follow.

I groan.

He moves lower, sucking on a sensitive spot on my throat just under the corner of my jaw. God.

I dig my nails into his back and rotate my hips. Finally, *finally*, he obliges. Maybe he's angry at me, because the force of his thrusts jolts my body. He bites my neck, moving down lower, and I can't even think. My mind scatters.

I lock my legs around his hips and grip his biceps.

A tremor runs through the plane, hitting a patch of turbulence. It doesn't stop Luca, though. I just hold on until he's had his fill. And suddenly his fingers are on my breast, pinching my nipple.

I moan, tensing, and he growls into my throat. He wraps his hand in my hair again, maneuvering my head to the side. More access. Another bite, his tongue. Sensation overload.

"Fuck." His pace becomes frantic, and then he stops.

Everything stops.

He comes inside me and lets out a hissing breath.

I hold him tight, although I couldn't say why. I'm worse than an octopus. It's like I've been flayed open, and only his skin will help me.

He pulls out, rolling onto his side, and meets my gaze.

Immediately, his finger is there.

"No," I say, trying to push him away.

He raises on an elbow and stares down at me. "I came inside you. *I* did. Not some monster who touched you without permission. Your husband." He pauses, maybe to judge my reaction.

I have none.

"Say it," he orders softly.

"That you came inside me?"

He narrows his eyes.

I have admitted to myself that Luca was my husband exactly *once*.

He's rubbing his cum into my clit, smearing it across my folds. I'm so damn tired, I can barely keep my eyes open.

"Stop."

"No."

I shove at his hand, but it makes no difference. I don't even have the energy for it. Too many orgasms. Too much emotion.

God, what I would give to hit the power button and end this nightmare.

"Luca."

"Wife."

I grimace. I can't help it.

"You would've called Wilder your husband."

He flicks my clit, and I cry out. I close my legs around his hand, because really? Enough. I shove against his chest hard, the force of it surprising even me. Shock flits across his face.

He must've been too close to the edge, because he topples off it.

I shoot upright, scrambling to my knees. Anything to get rid of the vulnerable feeling. He stares up at me, and we're both still.

I get the distinct impression that I'm the prey in this situation.

Run, Amelie.

I leap over him and bolt for the bathroom at the back of the plane. His grunt close behind me is the only warning I get before he fucking *tackles* me. We hit the floor hard, his arm protecting my head, and he maneuvers us so I'm in the cage of his arms.

"Stop. Fighting. Me," he snaps in my face.

"You're the one making things difficult!" I yell, throwing myself to the side.

He drops his weight on top of me.

I go perfectly still.

"We've been married for less than forty-eight hours," he says in my ear. "I don't expect love. But I do expect you to fucking *try*."

If I thought I might burst into tears—because it sure feels that way, with the lump burning in my throat—I'd be wrong. My eyes are dry.

"What's the worst that could happen?" he asks.

The thought of one of the Costas killing *him* pops into my head.

And I'm instantly mad at myself for even thinking it. The worst thing I could think of is him dying? Something deep inside me cracks open. It's worse than lust, because it creeps through me until I'm infected with it.

I'm not ready to call Luca my husband. To even test out the word on my tongue.

But he's asking for *something*.

After the past two days, I can do that.

"Kiss me," I whisper.

I give in for once. I put myself out there, even if it's just two words. Because I've always related kissing to vulnerability. My parents never kiss each other in front of me. I doubt they kiss at all. My examples of love come from a place of coldness, so this offering feels... right. I shed my mask for a moment, and the bright sensitivity of it hurts.

He searches my gaze for something, then abruptly releases me. He hops to his feet. "Not tonight."

All at once, those gates come crashing back down. How could I have been so stupid?

I climb up slower, watching him warily. When he doesn't do anything, I back up and feel for the door to the bathroom. I slip inside and close the door. My chest heaves, and I cover it with my hand to try to regulate my breathing. In the back of my mind, I know I'm hyperventilating.

The light automatically flickers on, and I grimace at my naked form in the mirror. My hair is a wild mess. The plane rumbles again, and it drops. I'm nearly weightless for a moment, and then the plane jolts sideways. I lose my balance.

I fall forward, and my forehead hits the glass. Pain lances through me.

I sink to the floor and close my eyes.

CHAPTER 16
Luca

I angrily tug on my clothes. I don't know why I've been thinking about Amelie with any sort of fondness—it's clear she views this as her duty. Something her parents raised her to do.

And that's what *I* need to start doing.

I'll get her pregnant and set her up in an apartment in the DeSantis tower. She can have a perfectly *fine* life there, and our child will be raised properly. Surrounded by our customs, our norms. He'll be brought into the family as the heir... unless Aiden suddenly gets his emotions in check and finds a wife.

Heirs are important. Family is important.

Wives... maybe not.

I thought we might have a connection. The way her eyes lit up when I touched her. She slept in my fucking arms, and I felt something I hadn't felt in a long time—*contentment*. It just goes to show how wrong you can be about someone.

But no. Then she had to open her eyes and decide to fight.

You like the fight, a deep part of me whispers.

I was furious on the drive back to the airport. Ready to strip her bare and fuck her until we were both exhausted. And then I could sleep. But instead, she got under my skin, and I was reminded about the trauma today has held for her.

I was raised on violence. Blood on my hands doesn't bother me. Yet walking onto the plane and seeing Amelie's face...

The plane lurches under me, and I grab the seat. It continues to move violently, and I stagger to the intercom. "What the fuck, Smith?"

"A storm, sir," the pilot answers. "I'm going to climb altitude to try and get out of this. You two okay?"

"Fine," I say and then turn guiltily back to the bathroom door. Amelie hasn't come out yet.

The nose of the plane tips up, and I hold on as we ascend. My gaze stays on the bathroom door, even as we level off.

Something's wrong.

I stand and scoop her clothes off the floor. A prick of guilt goes through me that she only has the clothes on her back. I should've asked Paloma for something else. A shirt, or...

"Amelie?" I knock on the door. "I brought your clothes."

She doesn't answer, and my gut instinct tells me that's not just her being petty.

"Amelie," I repeat.

I push the door open, but it only goes halfway before getting stuck. Still, it reveals the broken mirror. There's a dent in it, and spiderweb cracks have spun out from it. Chunks of glass are in the sink. Blood runs down it from the point of impact.

My heart stops.

I shove my shoulder and head through the door. Amelie is slumped over, braced up by the wall and the toilet. Her legs block the door. Her head hangs forward, face covered by hair. I'm overcome with a desperate urge to get to her.

I slide down and touch her ankle. Her skin is cold.

"Amelie. Wake up." I shake her leg and ignore the helplessness tightening my chest.

She groans, raising her hands to her head.

"It's okay, baby," I say. "I just need you to move your legs."

She complies, drawing her knees up to her chest. I nudge the door open farther and slip inside, immediately tipping her chin up.

There's a good gash across her forehead, and it's a bloody mess.

"Dizzy." Her eyes close again.

"It's okay, I've got you." I scoop her up and carry her out. She lets me maneuver the tank top over her head and arms, then her panties. I don't bother trying to get her jeans on.

Instead, I buckle her into one of the seats and tuck the blanket around her.

I hit the intercom. "Smith, do we have a first-aid kit?"

The cockpit door opens, and Smith emerges with a plastic container with an orange plus on it. He stares hard at Amelie for a moment, then turns back to me.

He's a peculiar man. I didn't much like his history, but he was all we had at our disposal.

"We should be landing in an hour," he says. "Do you want an ambulance standing by?"

"No." No, our family doctor should be able to patch her up. The idea of paramedics carting her off—after what just happened to Ricardo—turns my stomach.

"Very well. We're starting our descent in about a half hour." He returns to his cockpit.

He's not paid to worry. That's what I tell myself.

"What happened?" Amelie whispers.

I find a water bottle and twist off the cap. It takes her a moment to curl her fingers around it.

"Turbulence. You hit your head."

She winces. "That's why it hurts so much." She huffs. "We both look like we were in a fight."

"We were." I crack a smile.

The alcohol wipe is pungent. She doesn't fight me as I clean her skin. The glass didn't just cut her forehead, it left a series of scratches down the side of her face. It must sting like hell, although she barely flinches. Her gaze is glued to the water bottle in her lap.

"What are you going to do with me?"

I sigh. "I don't know."

"You never seemed like the settling down type." She's analyzing my expression.

"I'm not." I pause. "I mean that across my whole life—not just romantically."

Her eyes flutter when I get to her forehead.

"I'm afraid of a cage," she finally admits. "Of being shut away. You punish me for lies, but when I'm trapped, it makes me want to..." Her gaze snaps to mine.

I finally see some of the anger she's been hiding.

Wasn't I just thinking about shutting her away? For her safety, I suppose. Guilt filters through my thoughts.

"I know it's not a lot," she continues. "What I can offer. I feel like a failure most of the time. What good am I to you? But if you're going to be off chasing adventures, I need my own life, too."

God, she's ripping me apart.

I can't give her platitudes or promises. I just keep cleaning her face, and I press a bandage to the wound. She could hold it, but... damn it, I feel useful like this.

"We're starting our descent," Smith says over the intercom.

Amelie covers my hand with hers, and I jump.

She frowns. "I've got it. You should sit."

"That might need stitches," I warn.

She closes her eyes again. "That's fine."

I stuff the bloodied wipes into one of the wrappers and pack up the kit. Quickly, I shove it in one of the compartments at the front and return to her. I buckle myself in beside her, and we lapse into silence. The landing gear descends with a whine.

It won't be long now.

I text one of our drivers. My body aches, reminding me exactly how our day has gone. My eye is a bit better—the swelling receded, but I'm going to have one hell of a black ring around it.

"What time is it in New York?" Amelie asks.

"Just approaching midnight."

"I don't even know what day it is anymore." She chuckles, but it's laced with exhaustion. "I think I can sleep for a week."

I slip my phone back into my pocket. "The family doctor will be waiting at my apartment."

She groans. "Can't it wait?"

"Do you want a scar on your forehead the size of Texas?"

"No," she grumbles.

The plane touches down, and she squeezes my fingers tightly until we've slowed to a crawl. She releases me quickly, rubbing her hands.

I frown.

"The landing is the worst part." She cranes her neck to look out the window. "Maybe the turbulence beat it this time."

I grunt. I'm going to have to agree with her on that one. But with any luck, we won't be getting on another plane for a while.

"Um, Luca?"

I glance at her.

"Where are my pants?"

My cheeks get hot, and I scramble to grab them before our

pilot sees her. That's the last thing we need, because I'm pretty sure I wouldn't be able to control my reaction. I hand them over, and she slides them on under the blanket.

The plane stops next to the private hangar, and she follows me to the front. Smith opens the door, and the staircase unfolds. He steps back to watch us leave, his expression blank.

Halfway down, I turn and watch her. She's got both hands on the railings, and her legs tremble. I consider helping her, but she lifts her chin and glares at me like *I'm* at fault. And I guess I am—I'm blocking her way.

She keeps pace with me on the pavement, and we cross quickly to the car. There wasn't time to retrieve anything from the house, but Antonio might be able to manage to ship some things back to us.

I make a mental note to ask Amelie later if there's anything important. And then make *another* note when I remember the lingerie that was packed in her bag. I wouldn't mind getting that back.

We both sit in the back seat. The driver nods to me and clarifies which address I want to go to. I considered the tower in Manhattan for a brief moment, but all I want is to be home. To sleep in my own bed.

Sleep. There's a concept. It's been a while. I think I might've caught an hour or two on the flight out of New York, but that seems like ages ago.

It *was* ages ago.

We turn onto my street, and I glance at Amelie. Her eyes are closed again, but she's not asleep. She's too rigid. I doubt she's unaware of anything.

"We're here," I tell her.

Distance. That's what we both need.

The driver pulls to the curb, and we climb out. She stares up at the duplex, maybe marveling at its size. It isn't big by any means, but the house is surrounded by an iron fence. I own the house, and one of my cousins lives upstairs. She keeps to herself when she can, which is most of the time.

Her husband was killed a few years ago, and she's slowly withdrawn since then. It was the least I could do to offer her a place to live... and deliver groceries every week.

When I'm not in town, I make sure someone else does it.

Her lights are all off, unsurprisingly. The downstairs is dark, as well.

We head up the walkway, and someone steps out of the shadows on the porch. In the time it takes me to recognize the family doctor, I've tucked Amelie behind me.

"Luca," he calls.

"Dr. Matthews." I stride forward to shake his hand. "Thanks for coming."

He nods. He's a quiet man, bald, shorter than me by a few inches. He still manages to loom over Amelie, though, who has crept up to join us on the porch.

I unlock the door and flip the lights on, bathing both the living room and the porch in warm light. Amelie squints, raising her hand to block her eyes.

"Come in." I motion to the doctor to move past me.

Amelie steps through much more cautiously, like I'm going to slam the door and lock her in.

You bastard, a voice in my head admonishes, *that's exactly what she's afraid of.*

She trails the doctor toward the kitchen off to the left. I empty my pockets on the table that serves as a massive catch-all. My cousin must've been bringing my mail in, because there's a giant pile next to the little bowl for my keys.

When I reach the kitchen, I find Amelie at my small kitchen table, Dr. Matthews sitting beside her. He draws a needle through her skin and ties it off with sure, quick movements. Before our eyes, the gash closes.

He puts a long, narrow piece of gauze over it and tapes it

down. "Keep it covered tonight, then it can breathe. Keep it clean, rinsing it with an antibacterial spray if you need. I'll see you in a week to remove those."

She nods, and he quickly repacks his bag.

I follow him to the door, and he pauses.

"What are your injuries?" he asks.

I shrug. "Ribs, face. Ego."

He shakes his head. "Lift your shirt."

"It barely hurts."

He levels me with a look, and I roll my eyes. I'm pretty sure he considers Aiden's and my health his personal responsibility. As if Dad would shoot him in the head if one of us got hurt.

Well, more hurt than usual.

Come to think of it, he probably threatened something along those lines when Dr. Matthews was hired.

I raise my shirt and ignore the ache in my muscles. It does hurt, now more than ever. The adrenaline has officially left my system. Could be why I can barely keep my eyes open.

"Blurry vision?" he asks, shining a light into my eye. "Decreased or double vision?"

"No," I say.

He feels my ribs carefully, palpating my stomach with his hand. He must be satisfied, because he nods and sidesteps closer to the door. "Bruising, I suspect."

I smile. "That's what I thought."

He grimaces. "I don't know what you've been up to, but I suggest a few days off. Let your body heal. And your mind, too."

My smile drops fast, and he takes a step back.

"Goodnight, Doc." I close the door behind him and lean my shoulder into it. I give myself to the count of five to wrangle my emotions. Just another fucking reminder that

Wilder is gone. Somehow, it was a lot easier to handle in a different country.

Here, it'll slap me in the face.

Amelie, too.

I spin around, but she's gone.

A new emotion emerges, this one stronger than my anger. *Worry*.

Still, the apartment isn't big. Two bedrooms at the back of the house and one just off the living room. One and a half bathrooms. I find her in my bedroom, sitting on the bed. She has an apple in her hand.

I analyze her. Her tank top sits weirdly on her skin. The jacket was abandoned on the plane, I think, but neither of us thought to grab it. Her jeans are skewed. She's kicked off her boots already. They sit a few feet in front of her, knocked over as if she flung them off.

"I have clothes you can sleep in."

She dips her chin and takes another bite of the apple. Its scent hits me, and my mouth waters. We never got dinner. I escape into my closet and find a pair of basketball shorts and a t-shirt from one of the drawers in the back.

I hand them to her, and she in turn offers me the apple.

It feels like a trap, but I take it. She stands and puts her back to me. Curiosity nags at me, tangling in my stomach. She carefully removes her tank top and trades it for my t-shirt. It's giant on her, covering her ass completely. And then her jeans follow—and her panties, too.

I take a huge bite of the apple to keep from choking on my own tongue. There's no doubt about it: Amelie is gorgeous. She's taller than the girls I've dated in the past, with legs that seem to go on for days. Her skin is smooth and tanned to perfection—although that could've been wedding preparation.

She shimmies the shorts up, then glances back at me. "Are you sleeping here, or am I?"

I raise my eyebrows. "Didn't explore the other rooms, did you?"

"No." She frowns. "Why?"

"I don't have another bed."

She scowls. "Great. I'll take the couch."

I block the door before she can escape. "No. Take the bed, Amelie."

The fight leaves her, although her expression doesn't lighten.

"I have an extra toothbrush in the drawer." I point to the connected bathroom, then return to the closet to find my own sleepwear. The sound of the bathroom door closing reaches me.

I need a moment alone, bracing my hand on the wall and taking a few deep breaths. My ribs don't hurt that bad—it's manageable. I was able to carry Amelie around no problem... but I think that had more to do with the need of the situation.

Keep telling yourself that, buddy.

The problem is the sex. I haven't ever felt the need to explore any darker side of it before. Most of the girls I've slept with were fine with being bent over the back of a couch or shoved against a wall. Rough, yes. But if I think of Amelie trussed up, on her knees, my dick gets thick.

I tear my mind away from the image floating in my head and change, then slip back into the bedroom. I trade places with Amelie in the bathroom. Finally, I reenter the bedroom and cross to the bed. She's curled up on one side, and she rolls halfway over to stare at me.

"I thought..."

"I won't touch you," I promise. It could be a lie—I'm not sure, yet. Depends on how we feel in the morning, I suppose.

To my shock, she doesn't put up an argument. She just nods slowly and resumes her position with her back to me.

I climb in and stretch out, groaning slightly. Nothing beats the feeling of your bed after being away from it. I click the light off, and we're plunged into darkness. All I can hear is her light breathing.

"I've never slept with anyone," I say. "If I crowd you, just..."

She doesn't answer. Not that I expect her to. I flip onto my side and shut my eyes, matching my inhales and exhales to hers.

Sleep, I try to tell myself. The problem is, I don't want to dream of my brother. There's a reason I've been hesitant to close my eyes. Nightmares plagued me as a child, and I fear they will come back now.

"I can hear you thinking from over here," Amelie says.

She rolls to face me. I can barely see her in the darkness, just the faintest reflection of the street light outside coming through the cracks in the shade. Her eyes are open, on my face.

She extends her hand into the no-man's-land in the center of the bed.

"It's okay," she says.

I don't expect comfort from her, but I slide my hand into hers. She squeezes once, then relaxes. Her eyes close again.

And I do the best to mirror her calm.

CHAPTER 17
Amelie

I sleep like the dead. Something wakes me, though. A loss.

I crack my eyes open and catch sight of Luca climbing out of bed. My hand is still extended into the center. I'm still on my side. I don't think I shifted the whole night... and I wonder if he didn't, either. If his hand leaving mine was what woke me.

The thought is uncomfortable, so I draw my arm back to my chest.

He cracks the shades, and more light fills the room.

He's a graceful mover. It's weird, since he's a lot taller than me—and strong. He was able to carry me around the city yesterday. But his footsteps barely make a noise, and he retrieves clothes from the closet. He closes himself in the bathroom, and the shower starts.

Taking his hand last night was a risk. I wasn't lying when I told him I could hear him thinking—it was like he was projecting worry into the air. The fact that we fell asleep quickly after that is probably just coincidence.

And now *I'm* the worried one, because I sit up and immediately groan. The room whirls around me, and I fall back onto the pillows. I cover my eyes and concentrate on my breathing. It could be a concussion, I suppose. I'd felt a bit like a ragdoll being flung around the bathroom.

I'd never experienced turbulence like that.

"It's okay, Ames," I say to myself. I need to calm down.

The panic lives just under my skin, and as much as I try to control it, I can't. My breathing is short and fast, wild even in my own ears. I've been having more and more panic attacks. My heart races.

I used to get them in middle school, and then again when I was sixteen. It was the idea of being tied down, I think. And now I'm here. Brooklyn isn't so far from Rose Hill. But I can't leave if I can't stand—and that's my issue.

Mom knew how to bring me back.

She'd put her hand on my chest and push, trying to control my breathing. To match the pressure, the rise and fall.

She's not here now.

I push on my own chest, counting to three in my head for each inhale and exhale. I raise the number until I get to eight, and my chest unlocks.

"What happened?" Luca asks.

"Just dizzy," I manage. I drop the hand from my eyes and blink up at him. "I tried to sit up, and it did me no favors."

"Your head." He touches my cheek. "It's just as well that you stay here. I'll grab you Tylenol."

"Stay here?" I sit up slower. I can manage it if I stay focused on one thing—namely, Luca.

He ducks into the bathroom and reappears with two tiny pills and a cup of water. "When's the last time you ate? Besides the apple."

I grimace and swig back the pills and water. "I had a few granola bars on the plane while I was waiting for you."

I set the cup aside, and we both go silent. I don't know how to do this—it's clear he doesn't, either. His eye looks worse today. Less swollen, but the inner corner is an angry purple. He was used as a punching bag. I wonder if he only owns dark colors. The shirt I wear is navy. The one he picked is black.

His gaze sweeps down, from the bandage on my head to my eyes, nose, lips. Lower, over my throat and the collar of his shirt.

I tug at it, suddenly hot.

He spins away. "I'm going out. I need to see my father and Aiden. I wasn't planning on being away from my job, either. You just stay here."

I stare at him. He's going out, and he wants me to *what*? "Stay here?"

Apparently I'm a fucking parrot.

"Yes, Amelie. Stay."

I scoff and slide out of bed. "I'm not your servant. You can't order me around."

He doesn't even glance back at me.

The room tilts, but I persevere. You can't just walk away from someone in the middle of a discussion. Okay, an argument. But still. He doesn't wait for me, and I have to put my hands on both walls to manage the hallway without feeling like I'm a pinball.

I glance around for something to throw at him.

I'm just so *mad*. I've never been angrier, I'm sure. Not at my parents or sister or Wilder. He's going to leave me here to rot, just like I predicted.

"When will you be back?" I ask through my teeth.

"Later today. I'm sure you'd like to rest, right?"

"Fuck you."

I stop at the top of the hall, where it breaks out into the large living room. Kitchen to the right, dining area in front of it. It's all pretty open, which is unusual for these types of houses. The arched doorways feel like remnants of the original home.

He yanks his shoes on, glaring at the floor. "I'm trying to be nice," he says. "You're dizzy. You want to have a full day touring the DeSantis properties? Answering questions about Wilder? Smiling and accepting condolences for his murder? It's been two days. What do you think my family is going through?"

Something must've switched in his brain last night. Like a reset. Being back in New York has brought back out the ruthless version of Luca I'd always heard rumors about. For a minute, in Italy, I thought it'd be different.

But now his eyes are cold.

I'm separating from reality a bit, because it seems as if he forgot *everything* I told him. About being stuck. Trapped. And now he's watching me like he doesn't know who I am. He woke up to a stranger in his house, in his bed.

I regret every touch. Every nice word.

"Go, then," I say, unable to hide the defeat from my voice.

He does.

And I stay in my cage like a good little bird.

CHAPTER 18
Amelie

How many ways can a girl exhaust herself before she goes completely mental?

Asking for a friend.

Ha.

In direct opposition to Luca's sneering comment before he left, I do *not* want to rest. So I don't. I pace the house. I clean the kitchen, even though it doesn't really need it. I dust the bookshelves and pull out a few that catch my eye, but immediately return them when opening them cracks the spines.

I won't find anything useful in the books Luca keeps here if they're just for show.

And I continue on, even as my headache grows worse. If I let myself think about Italy—any part of it, or the plane ride home—my stomach flips. Nausea curls my toes, and I do end up puking twice.

The sky grows dark, and Luca doesn't return. I consider food. I've been iffy on hunger lately, not quite ready to commit to a full meal, but I finally peek in the fridge and freezer. The tub of mint chocolate chip ice cream brings a smile to my face.

If anything, I can handle that.

It's eight o'clock when I finally flop onto the bed. I was unsuccessful in driving myself crazy, but everything aches. The entire house is clean. *I'm* clean, and unfortunately smelling a bit like Luca. I've been in his clothes, using his soaps. Eating his food.

And yet, he is not here.

I close the blinds and crawl into bed, facing the wall. I promise myself I won't react when he comes back.

And I'm right. I wake to light streaming into the room, and I am triumphant... until I realize he never returned.

The ache that bangs around my chest surprises me.

My head doesn't hurt as much, and I inspect the stitches in my forehead in the bathroom. I tie my hair up, letting the wound breathe. He's not back, but I refuse to stick around for another moment.

For one, I have no clothes of my own. No possessions, even. I'd set out with Ricardo and hadn't even thought to bring my phone. Yesterday, it occurred to me that it's with all my suitcases at the house. What's shocking is that I didn't miss it until the early afternoon.

But in my hunt, I did find a wad of cash in one of the kitchen drawers. I couldn't say if it was emergency money or what, but I *do* know it's my ticket home.

Literally.

I tug my boots on, taking a deep breath after I rise. My head pulses, then the throb slowly fades. Armed in a sweatshirt that engulfs me, and my jeans and boots, I feel a bit better. I stuff just enough cash for a cab in my pocket and the rest in my boot.

It's a bit weird to be cut off from technology. I open his front door and take a deep breath. It's June. People will be leaving the city soon. College students and the like. I should be part of that, going home for the summer, running around with the kids I went to high school with. We're still young enough that it's a throwback to the *good* times. Before responsibilities.

I let myself out of the gate, then pause on the sidewalk.

Immediately, I'm weirdly overwhelmed. Not because of the clothes, or the neighborhood. Skyscrapers are visible in the distance, reminding me that Manhattan isn't far. No, it's deeper than that.

It could be me.

I'm the one different, irrevocably changed after... what, seventy-two hours?

But the air sits differently on my skin, and an intense loathing sweeps through me. I wanted to go home—but now I'm thinking anywhere but there would be better. A friend's house, maybe, if I hadn't isolated myself from everyone after graduating high school. It was too painful. I wasn't allowed to go to college. I was barely allowed to dream.

I brush away those intrusive thoughts. I cut off my best friend because she was allowed to have a future I never had a chance of. And it hurt. Yet... I couldn't tell her why.

My chest tightens, a pressure I can't will away. The first step to freedom is reconciliation... I think.

The real question is: which way to the closest metro station?

"You look lost," a woman calls.

I spin and immediately regret it. My vision lags, and I'm left clutching the gate.

On the second-floor porch, an older woman leans over the railing. "Amelie Page?"

I wince. "Yes."

She just smiles. "Rosalie DeSantis. Luca's cousin. I didn't attend the wedding, but I heard what happened. I'm—"

"Please don't," I blurt out. My skin crawls at the idea of an apology. "I'm sorry, I just..."

"Death is an oddity." She nods to herself. "You'll deal with it in your own way, I suppose."

She straightens and backs up a step, clearly done with the conversation.

"Wait," I call. "Can you point me to the closest train station?"

She considers me for a moment, then spits out directions and estimates it to be a ten-minute walk. And maybe that's a bit too much people-ing for her, because she backs away from the railing and disappears into her apartment.

Who am I to judge?

I'm almost at the station when I see someone I recognize coming down the sidewalk.

And it isn't a good someone.

"Amelie Page," an old classmate calls.

"Kaiden West." I cross my arms.

His friend nudges him.

"It's Kai now, actually."

"Ah."

The extent of our relationship was... well, actually, I think I might've made out with him at a party one time. It's a bit blurry. He was a soccer star, a year or two older than me. He used to deal drugs, I think. He's handsome, though. Everyone at school had a crush on him.

He had a way of making girls feel special.

And he's a West.

My stomach swoops. I'm an idiot.

By the time I was arranged to marry Wilder, Kai had graduated. And it wasn't until later that I learned about the feud between the Wests and DeSantises. Kaiden West was barely a blip on my radar.

"I'm Colin," the other one says, extending his hand. "Amelie is an unusual name."

I warily step forward and take it. "It's French."

He chuckles. "At least you didn't say Italian, right?" His grip is firm, moving my hand up and down.

I slip it away as soon as I can.

"Stop messing with her," a soft voice says from behind them.

They part for her, and a girl steps forward. "Gemma," she introduces. "Ignore my idiot brother. He likes to put his foot in his mouth."

"Right."

And then it clicks. *Gemma West*. The one Aiden would get all stabby over, apparently. Wasn't that what Luca said on the boat? Uh-oh.

Honestly, I want to be nowhere near this right now, but I'm very curious over my new brother-in-law's obsession.

"You went to Emery-Rose with Kai?" she asks.

I glance at him, then focus on her. She reminds me of Mariella Costa. Not in looks—they couldn't be more different in that regard. But she's swept along by her brothers, although maybe with a bit more spine in her. After all, she's taking charge of this conversation.

Ice drips down my spine.

Do they know I married Luca?

How could they not? I'm sure Wilder's death was in the papers—if I'm not actually staring at one of his killers. I'm glad I left the ring off today. It needs to be resized, I suppose, but there's also a freedom in not wearing it.

Just as I think that, Colin's attention goes to my left hand.

"I was two years younger," I say. "And you?"

Gemma grins. She really is beautiful. Her light-blonde hair is pulled back in a loose French braid, flipped over her shoulder. Her dress and the sweater over it give her a doll-like appearance.

I don't know where they're going, but she doesn't seem like the type to go knock down someone's door for money.

"Homeschooled," Gemma says lightly.

"Where's the ring?" Kai asks.

I jerk back. "What?"

"You married one of them, didn't you?" He rolls his eyes. "The least he could've done was give you a freaking ring."

"He did," I manage. "It didn't fit."

Colin narrows his eyes. "Are you staying around here?"

The warning sirens sound in my mind, and I have enough frame of mind to *not* look back the way I came. I'm glad I made it a few streets over—and that I'm not currently headed back. I press my lips together and narrow my eyes.

Gemma stares at me. "Which one did you marry? After Wilder—"

Colin makes a noise in the back of his throat. "Enough, Gemma."

Oh shit. I know that gleam in her eye. Recognize it as one I wore through most of high school. Like she feels something she shouldn't and is desperately trying to keep a lid on it. I don't know if her brother sees it. If anyone would know what to look for if they didn't experience it.

"Luca," I answer her. "I married Luca."

Relief crosses her expression—it's weird, but there's a little bit of fear in her gaze, too. Like the fact that Aiden didn't get pawned off on me is a good and bad thing. She nods and steps past me. "We're going to be late," she says over her shoulder. "It was lovely to meet you, Amelie."

"Maybe we'll meet again one day." I step aside and let the boys pass, and I stay immobile against the fence until they're halfway down the block.

Then I book it in the opposite direction.

My head threatens to revolt, but I push myself into a quick jog to get away from the Wests. As soon as I see the train station, I slow. My body aches, but I can't let that stop me.

I pause beside the row of taxis. I'm sure I'd have enough money to get to Rose Hill, but I hesitate. Going into Manhattan seems more unpredictable, and on the off chance Luca returns to his apartment to discover me gone... I don't want him to find me.

He's not going to bother going home—why should I?

I decide I can afford a moment of predictability and flag down a taxi. I want clothes of my own, and I think I have an old phone in my bedroom that I can reactivate. The urge to go back to my parents' house is too strong to ignore.

The driver agrees, naming his price, and I slide into the back seat. Once we hit the highway, I allow myself to zone out. The past few days have been insane, and now Luca's pulled a disappearing act.

The fact that it *hurts* is the worst.

We take an exit ramp off the highway, and I straighten. Anticipation chases my nerves away, and finally, we turn onto my street.

"Here's fine," I say.

He coasts to a stop in front of my neighbor's house, and I hand him the cash. Once he's gone, I cross the lawn and slip around back. It's a weekday—both my parents should be at work. I run my hand along the top of the door to the mud room, quickly finding the key. Lucy and I were latchkey kids before they sent her to live with our grandparents.

I pause, remembering the day they told me she was moving away.

We fought all the time, but what siblings didn't? That didn't mean I wanted her out of my life. I'd never cried so much. I had puffy eyes for a week. My parents acted like they didn't care—really, the relief on my mom's face that Lucy was going to be out of her hair made me furious.

After she left, the house was too empty. They didn't trust me to get home by myself, so Mom picked me up from school every day. And the loneliness increased.

I unlock the door and let myself in, embracing the quiet.

Lucy taught me a valuable lesson: I had to be perfect, or I wasn't any use to my parents.

And I *was* perfect until...

Nope. We're not going there.

The house is different. Subtle changes of empty-nesters, maybe? The kitchen table where we used to eat dinner is now against the wall, perfect for two instead of three. The mudroom was practically bare. No cups by the sink, or extra silverware in the drying rack. The extra fat has been trimmed, and that seems to include all traces of me.

If today was a normal day, pre-wedding, I would've waltzed in through the garage and dropped my keys on the hook. I'd kick my shoes off and maybe head to my room, or flop on the couch. I can almost taste the normalcy, except for the weird way my stomach keeps twisting.

It screams at me to get out of here.

I shove the emotions down and jog up the stairs to my room. I halt in the doorway, almost choking. A tornado must've gone through it—then haphazardly cleaned. My bed is made, kind of. The closet doors hang askew. I'm pretty sure I didn't leave any clothes on the floor, but even my hamper is empty.

It wasn't like this wedding took me by surprise.

I did my best to prepare. I put away the baubles and books I'd collected over the years, made sure everything was neat. Perfect, remember? Up until I said "I do," anything could happen.

And it did. The worst happened.

I drop to my knees in front of my nightstand and yank it open. I'm hit with a big dose of relief—the very top item in the drawer is my old phone.

A new SIM card and I'll be good to go.

I plug it in and hunt down a bag. Mom packed none of my favorites, which I should've foreseen. Why would she want her daughter on a honeymoon in a faded black *Three Days Grace* t-shirt? I locate it and grin, pressing the soft fabric to my face. Under my shiny, perfect exterior was... *is* an angry girl who just wanted a bit of angry rock in her life.

I smile, remembering the time Savannah and I snuck into the city to see them live. It was the single best night of my life. Until I got home.

The smile fades, and I shove the t-shirt into the bag. I pile in more clothes, and the pain in my chest deepens the more I find. It's like Mom didn't know me *at all* when she went through my room.

In the bathroom, I tug the hair tie out and shake my hair loose. My straightener is one of the things that *did* make it to Italy, but I'm sort of digging the wild hair. It's much more wavy than I realized. Every shower at home was followed by an hour of blow drying with a round brush, until it was gleaming and lying against my shoulders in large, sweeping flips. Otherwise straight except for those manufactured by heat.

"Gross," I tell my reflection.

Too many memories of standing in this exact spot, trying not to burn my scalp. Applying makeup. Smoothing my cheerleading outfit before games, curling ribbons. Waxing every inch of my body.

I'd be thrilled if I could never wear makeup again.

I put my spare hairbrush—the flat paddle brush that Mom always insisted did me no favors—in the bag and slip my shampoo and conditioner into a plastic bag, then shove that in, too. No more smelling like Luca.

My phone beeps in the other room, apparently on and getting some messages as it connects to the WiFi. It keeps beeping.

I raise my eyebrows and abandon the bathroom. There's nothing else I need, anyway. I'm becoming the definition of *low maintenance*. It gives me some sort of sick satisfaction that my parents would be horrified at my behavior.

Not to mention the stitches in my face.

There are smaller cuts, too, raining down my temple and cheek in a crisscross pattern. Those are minor. An annoyance.

Back in the bedroom, I toss my bag onto the floor next to the door and kneel next to my bed. Have I been paranoid since sixteen? Yes. And it's paid off.

I have to crawl half under the bed to find the canvas bag. It's taped to the support beams of my bed frame, invisible unless you know where to look for it. I figured, if anything, my parents would clean out my room and convert it into a guest room. No moving the bed required. New sheets, new duvet, and good to go.

I carefully peel back one of the strips of tape to check its contents. I've collected every pre-loaded money card from birthdays, holidays. Spare cash, when it wasn't suspicious for it to disappear, too. The result is almost five thousand dollars in untraceable money, and it all appears to still be here.

But I can't take it back to Luca's. I doubt he would respect my privacy... and it'll be safe in its hiding spot. The urge to take it and run fills me, but I have no doubt Luca would hunt me down.

It might take a while, at this rate, but...

No, I need a better plan. Where to go. A budget.

I nod to myself as I tape it back in place and slide out. I can do that. Figure out what the hell I'm going to do. He clearly doesn't give a shit about me. Italy was a fluke.

"No," I tell myself. "He just thinks of you as a possession."

I hate talking out loud. It's one of my worst habits. But it's not like I'm lying—he even said it himself on the boat: he married me because he wanted something for himself.

AKA: a toy his daddy couldn't rip from his hands.

Enough is enough. I'm *not* a toy, or someone to order around. I am Amelie freakin' Page, and I will show Luca exactly who he married.

CHAPTER 19
Luca

Aiden kicks my leg, and I groan. I've been away for less than a week, and the place has gone to absolute shit. Whoever decided to leave the construction permits in the hands of Reggie seriously fucked up. For one, he's dyslexic. Which would be fine on its own, but paired with an intense hatred of following deadlines...

Yeah.

"What?" I grunt at my brother.

"It's almost noon. Have you eaten?"

I sigh. I'm pretty sure I was just snoozing. I didn't sleep at all last night, surrounded by paperwork. I've got to pay a visit to a few people. Namely, the shipyard master who's been squawking a little too loud, and the woman on the city council who approves our permits. It should be pretty seamless, but *apparently* no one can do their fucking jobs.

"No," I finally say. "And I need some air."

He nods and leads the way to the elevator. When we step out onto the street, I tip my head back and sigh.

"You look like hell," he says. "Was he mad?"

He being our father. That meeting lasted longer than it

should've, too. I had to explain everything to both Dad and Aiden. Almost every detail.

I kept some things to myself, except a curt nod when Dad asked if our marriage was *official*. Consummated, in other words.

Aiden left after my story was done, so I fill him in.

"He's pissed that the Costas got the upper hand on us, and seemed extraordinarily angry that Amelie bartered by giving up Wilder." I recall his expression and shake my head. "She told them he was at her parents' summer home in France, which was honestly brilliant. It gave us time to get out of the country."

He scoffs. "Because they'll be even more furious when they realize they've been duped by a girl who only married into the family the day prior."

"What would you have done?" I ask suddenly. He and I align on some things, some actions, but in other ways we couldn't be more different. "If Matteo had been touching—"

"I'd slit his throat," Aiden says without hesitation. "Put a blade in Cristian, too, for all I care. *No one* touches what's mine."

I nod along to his words, and guilt hits me that my reaction wasn't *his* reaction.

"Of course," he continues, "if you kill someone, you have to deal with the consequences. If you killed Cristian and Matteo, who would take their place in the family? Someone in the room? Mariella, maybe, or a cousin who only saw the aftermath and not the circumstance it was born out of?"

I grind my teeth. "So, what are you saying?"

He claps me on the shoulder. "You were in an impossible situation."

So was she.

We step into a deli and grab sandwiches, eating on our walk back to the tower.

"Pretty sure Mariella harbors long-lost love for Wilder," I mutter. "I felt bad we didn't tell her he was dead."

He shrugs and takes a huge bite of his sub. He doesn't seem particularly bothered one way or another, and I suppose he's right. The Costas are an ocean away. It doesn't really matter to him whether she's upset or not. He probably doesn't plan on returning to Sanremo. Not when he's suddenly the heir.

"Has Dad been treating you with kid gloves?"

He shoots me a glare. "No. I've been avoiding him—and I don't plan to stop just because you're back."

I grunt. "Fine. Want to come with me to see the councilwoman?"

She's a *little* promiscuous, which would usually get Wilder's attention. I should've known that wouldn't appeal to Aiden, because his expression asks, *Are you fucking dumb?* A hard no, then.

"Fine," I repeat. "Are you going to be any help?"

He shoots me a baleful look. "I reminded you it was lunchtime." He flicks something off my shoulder. "Speaking of, did you sleep there?"

"I pulled an all-nighter," I say. Which fucking sucked. "Everything is a mess. How did it go sideways so fast?"

"You're asking me? Who put Reggie in charge?" He laughs, then sobers quickly. "I've got to go, anyway. Sam's been talking to an arms dealer who's seen an uptick in West purchasing."

I narrow my eyes. "Like they're preparing for something?"

"Possibly."

For once, I'd like some real answers.

"When are you going home?" he asks. "You know, to the wife? You said you consummated the marriage, but understandably you didn't want to say how it was in front of Dad. Did you fuck her just to get it over with?"

This coming from the man who's barely noticed any woman in years. Of course he would feel that way. *To get it over with.*

That's the last thing I wanted.

"Sometimes I like her, and other times I'm wondering what the hell we're doing."

He snorts. "It's been less than a week, brother."

"And in that time, her fiancé was killed on the altar, I got blindsided by the Costas, she ran away and nearly got assaulted, I killed two people—"

"Okay, okay." He holds up his hands in surrender. "Why are you here, then? Go home and figure it out."

We stop in front of the tower's doors, and I contemplate what he's saying.

But then I remember that New York City is all I have left, now that Italy is barred to us, and the anger flushes through me all over again.

"I've got work to do," I mumble. More things to organize, permits to straighten out, people to see—and one person to avoid.

Besides, Dr. Matthews was pretty sure Amelie had a mild concussion. She won't make it out of bed, let alone out of the house.

Aiden's laugh follows me back to my office.

I fall back into my chair and lift a piece of paper. It's a note from our construction company, Woodrow Builders, that we've been shorted three pallets of concrete mix from one our suppliers in upstate New York.

I rub my eyes and grab my coat. I guess I'll start there.

CHAPTER 20
Amelie

I pull into the parking garage below the DeSantis tower. I have no doubt my parents will call me *now*. The guard nods to me, and the little blockade rises. I tap my steering wheel and park close to the elevator—just in case I need a quick getaway.

This car has been mine for three years. It was my sixteenth birthday present once we got back home from France. I'm pretty sure the extravagance of it was supposed to mask the horrified expression I was walking around with. All I could think was that in three years, I'd be married to Wilder DeSantis.

And here I am, *not* married to Wilder but still very much trapped in the family.

Okay. Deep breath, Amelie.

I slip from the car and hit the button for the elevator. Once I'm in, I swipe the keycard over the sensor. It changes to green and allows any of the upper floor buttons to be pressed. I found this keycard on the table in the front foyer at my parents' house, and I'm sure glad I recognized it. Otherwise I would be stuck waiting for permission...

And that doesn't fit with Operation Luca Can Suck A Dick.

It's a working title.

Jameson's office is on the twenty-fifth floor, and I could've sworn I remembered passing an office with Luca's name on it, and another with Aiden's. I'm not sure why Aiden needs an office, but whatever. Wilder's office was giant, in the corner across from his father's. We visited there the morning of our rehearsal dinner to sign the marriage license.

My nerves rise. I *had* signed a marriage license, and Wilder, too. Our parents stood around us. And then Dad took it and said he'd file it.

The next thing I knew, Wilder was dead and I was signing another piece of paper.

Oh god.

I cover my mouth, holding back nausea. What if I'm not actually married to Luca? If it was a ruse, and I'm really a *widow*?

Operation Luca Can Suck A Dick just transformed into recon.

The elevator chimes, announcing my arrival on the twenty-fifth floor, and I step out carefully. It's quiet, and it occurs to me that it shouldn't be. It's Wednesday, the middle of the day. My eyes immediately ache under the bright lights.

And yet, it's a ghost town. No one stops me from striding down the large open space. This could be a bullpen-style work atmosphere, but instead there are couches in the center. The only offices appear to be for immediate family.

Which means if I get caught, I'll have no excuse.

The light is off in Luca's office, and he left it unlocked. I close the door quietly behind me but don't bother with the light switch. He's got a decent view from this angle, and there's enough natural light for it to be sufficient.

But since he's clearly not here, where did he go?

Frustration sweeps through me. I could've forgiven the nature of a workaholic. But what if he went out with someone else? A woman he actually liked instead of... me.

There are papers in neat piles on the floor. They're arranged in a semi-circle, like he spent time sitting on the floor to organize them around him. I kneel where I imagine he sat and frown.

I don't make sense of most of it, although it doesn't stop me from riffling through the pages. I rise and go to his desk, then slowly perch in the leather chair. More papers, but these seem to be correspondence. Printed emails.

My gaze catches on a familiar company: Page Printing, Inc.

My father's budding empire, made of paper and ink.

Luca's words from our rushed little wedding come back to me. He had told Dad, *Our protection is a security system. The promise of force if you meet resistance*. But I never asked myself why Dad would need so much protection. That's where my fault lies.

I assumed the printing referred only to the newspaper—which is officially my dumbest assumption. That the protection is for when the journalists move to attack everyone except the DeSantis family. A full takedown via media... and public mob.

Funny, isn't it? How a company that has its fingers in the journalist side and the printing side would turn to the DeSantis family for help. They're the very people who *should* be making headlines for their crimes.

But this paper in front of me is an invoice for services rendered: cleaning and distribution.

And listen, I may be dumb in my younger assumptions, but my eyes are wide open now. I would bet anything that Dad's been slowly adding specialty ink and paper to his inventory. Just enough to not cause suspicion.

A private company, however low profile, printing *money*?

Whether with a government contract or not, it's bound to draw attention from all sorts of people. And if he's able to scrub it clean through his other businesses, or through the DeSantis businesses...

God. No wonder he was so willing to sell me off. The DeSantis family is giant. Their name alongside ours is enough of a security to keep Dad's company out of trouble.

But it didn't save you.

I set the paper down and replace the email from the builder on top of it.

My next stop needs to be Dad's office. Surely he would've had to file the marriage license *after* my wedding to Wilder. We signed on a Saturday morning. The wedding was Sunday. Everything would've been closed.

I breathe deeply, resisting the urge to go check Jameson's office.

My hand is on the door when voices drift toward me.

"Aiden, go check for the report in Luca's drawer," someone says.

I'd bet money that was Jameson.

Shit. I jump away from the door, thankful that the walls aren't made of glass. I consider hiding under Luca's desk, but if the drawer is his *desk* drawer...

I swing behind the door just as it opens, stopping a hair's breadth from my nose. Aiden saunters in, shuffling some things around. He doesn't make any other noises, and when he leaves, the door remains open.

Carefully, I peek through the narrow gap near the hinges.

Jameson's office door closes with a *snick*, and footsteps return.

Suddenly, the door flies shut.

I squeak. Caught.

Aiden raises his eyebrows, looking me up and down. "Well, well."

"I—"

"Save it," he interrupts. "This is the most interesting thing to happen today."

I'm at a loss for words. My mouth opens and closes, before I finally settle on shut. Better to just stay silent, anyway.

He leans against the closed door, contemplating me. "Well?"

"Well what?" I snap.

He grins. He really is quite different from Luca. Besides their height—*tall*—and dark hair, Aiden seems fairer. More heritage from his white mother's side, I would guess. They're only half brothers, in any case. Luca's skin is a darker complexion, his eyes closer to black than gold. Aiden's skin is honey-kissed. Green eyes. Tattoos peek out from his shirt collar.

They're both lean, though. I'd guess that comes in handy for being an assassin—and whatever it is Luca does. Actually, he never really mentioned what his role is in the family. I understood on an innate level what Wilder did. He was in the public eye—maybe not as much as he wanted, not yet, but he was getting there. He would've been one of the politicians pulling the strings of the city.

New York is just a big puppet, moving to whatever beat her dictators want.

And can't I relate?

He keeps staring, so I sigh. "I came to see Luca. He's not here."

"How'd you get here?"

I frown. "Why?"

Aiden narrows his eyes. "I'm not the one caught in someone else's office, am I?"

I glance around. "I didn't see your name on the door."

That... that gets him. He cracks a smile. "Okay, touché. What were you going to do when you found Luca? Kiss him? Kill him?"

"I don't know." *Lie*. I was going to give him a piece of my mind. But that bluster seems far removed from my current state. Now I just want to go home and take a nap.

"You look like you're dressed for war," he offers. "And I think you might be right. Luca needs some war."

I stare at him.

I mean, he isn't wrong. After careful consideration of a plan at my parents' house, I changed out of my black jeans and Luca's oversized sweatshirt. I picked a shirt I love, a dark-green satin peplum with a plunging neckline. It goes all the way to just above my bellybutton, held closed over my breasts with fine ribbon.

I found a gold necklace that wraps around my throat like a collar, then added shiny leather leggings and heeled boots.

My hair is pulled back in a French braid, some curls left loose to accent my face.

The only makeup I chose was mascara and lip balm.

"Okay, come on."

I squint. "What?"

"You really knocked your head hard, huh? Come with me, and I'll take you to Luca."

Oh. I move out of the way, then follow him down the hall. It's still quiet, but the most important thing is that Jameson doesn't come out of his office.

We don't speak until we get to the parking garage, and Aiden double takes at my car.

"A bribe for agreeing to marry Wilder," I say sweetly, patting the hood. It's a Porsche Spyder. Dark blue. A few years old, of course, but still in good condition. Even at sixteen, I knew a nice car when I saw one.

"I'm driving," Aiden says, holding out his hand for the keys.

I laugh. "No."

For a moment, I think he might pout—but then he grabs

me, patting me down until he hears the clink of my keychain. I... well, I panic.

Is this not similar to what Matteo did to me?

I shriek, batting at him, and he flies away from me.

"Jesus, Amelie," he swears.

"What the fuck is wrong with you?" I scream. "You had to know what Matteo did."

I shudder, turning away from him. I actually felt myself softening. Like, hey, maybe Luca's scary brother isn't *that* scary. The rumors about him might be true, but I might be able to get along with Luca's family.

Wrong.

He's not only scary—he's an asshole.

The keys dangle from his fingertips over my shoulder. A silent apology, maybe, but not good enough. My skin crawls, and I can't get the panic to loosen its grip on my lungs. I'm breathing too fast again.

"Hey, hey, I'm sorry," he says. "I thought you wouldn't..."

I spin to face him, snatching the keys back. "You thought I wouldn't *what*? Be affected by trauma? By Matteo violating me? By anything that has happened this week?" I shove him, ignoring the surprise on his face. "Don't touch me. Ever."

He opens his mouth, but I don't want his apology. The same way I didn't want Luca's tenant's sympathy. Some things just make everything worse, and this qualifies. I unlock my car and slide into the driver's seat.

Aiden climbs in a moment later.

"Where are we going?" I ask once we're past the guard booth.

He points to the left. "He went to see a city council-woman," he says. "Something about permits, I don't know. I block him out when he gets going."

I scowl at the road, automatically annoyed that I have no idea what he's talking about. Luca has meetings with someone in government? Regularly? And permits... I guess he's talking in relation to that construction company they own. Woodrow Builders.

It would appear that he's more in the public eye than Aiden.

The thought of telling him about seeing Gemma, her brother, and Kai crosses my mind, but then I shuffle it back. I'm still pissed that he grabbed at me.

"Take your next left," Aiden says.

I glance at him, then flip my blinker on. Manhattan traffic sucks—maybe I should've let him drive. *If he had asked nicely, I would've*. He stares out the window, his face impassive.

Brother-in-law.

I try it in my mind, and it just feels... weird. We coast to a stop at a red light, and I peek at him. Then away.

"Why do you keep looking at me?" He catches my gaze before it snaps back to the road.

"Just trying to..." I shrug. The light turns green.

"Trying to what?"

"Picture you as a brother." Ugh. I shake my head. "Weird, right?"

He faces me. "You're trying to picture me as a brother."

Ugh, men. "No."

"You literally just said that, Amelie."

"I know I did, but I didn't mean it like *that*. I meant it like..." Like I wish I could backpedal out of this conversation. "I've only had my younger sister. So it's different."

"Huh."

I roll my eyes. "Forget I said anything."

"No, no, I see where you're coming from. You've had to fend for yourself against shitty parents. Hell, they totally sold you off like cattle. Eh, maybe a painting? They're more valuable, and what Dad got for your marriage... But yeah, I get it. It's why you came back to the tower with your armor."

"It's not armor," I mutter.

"You can pull over here," he says, gesturing to his right.

I swerve across the lanes and to the curb, and only a few cars honk. Mild for New Yorkers. He shakes his head and points to the building we're parked in front of.

"He's probably in there."

I glare at him. "Okay, so get out."

"Why?"

"Because you're not sitting in my car while I go *march into battle*, as you say."

He grins and hops out, barely waiting for me on the sidewalk. He leads the way inside, three steps ahead of me. The lobby is all white marble and glass, and a woman frowns at us from behind the receptionist desk.

"Can I help you?" she calls.

"Just looking for my brother," Aiden replies. "He had a meeting with..."

I think back to the names signed to the permits.

"Councilwoman White," I supply.

The woman checks her computer. "They should be done soon."

I narrow my eyes, and she pales. Maybe she recognizes the last name, or maybe it's my perfected bitch stare. Either way, she doesn't say anything when I lean over and scan her computer screen.

Sandra White. The name rings a bell from Mom's many lectures. If I wanted to make it, she reasoned, I had to know who everyone was. The strings they pulled. She even wanted to get in a room with the councilwoman. Hell, she might still want a quote from her for the magazine. Dad's one business concession for his wife was to allow her the freedom of a monthly magazine.

While not what Mom might've seen herself doing, she relishes the power and prestige of it now.

"Thirty-fourth floor," I tell Aiden, striding to the elevators.

He doesn't follow.

I ignore it. It doesn't matter, anyway. This fight is between Luca and me. The fact that I'm bringing it to a business meeting with a councilwoman... I sigh. I've got more tricks up my sleeve, at least.

Sandra White and her fellow council members recently helped pass a law restricting government oversight into privately funded construction zones. I don't know the specifics, but as long as the permits are filed, then those zones now have free rein. It's the sort of thing Mom would jump on —an exclusive interview.

Wait.

Of course the DeSantis building company would benefit from that.

Fuck a duck, how deep does this family's influence go?

"Miss?"

I jerk toward another receptionist.

"Are you here to see Councilwoman White?"

Either I say yes and she asks what my name is—thus figuring out I *don't* have an appointment—or I say no and she asks me what the hell I'm doing here.

And I'm not sure I have an answer for that anymore.

So I fall back on old talents.

"Hi! I'm so sorry, yes, I'm here to see the councilwoman. I'm Amelie Page. Councilwoman White promised my mother an exclusive for our magazine, and now that the construction bill passed, she was hoping to collect." I flip my hair over my shoulder. "I can come back, of course, but unfortunately the deadline for printing this month is tonight..."

"Oh, dear. Well, do you mind waiting? Her current appointment should be over soon."

Better than barging into her office, I suppose.

I nod and wander away, putting distance between us. My cell has automatically connected to the WiFi here, and I send a message to my mother.

Me: *About to be face-to-face with Sandra White.*

She replies almost immediately, and I'm surprised she doesn't have a million questions for me. I know I would.

Mom: *Congratulate her on the bill and ask where her focus is next.*

Mom: *Ask about her dog, Jacks.*

I hesitate to type out my next question. This would constitute a conversation with my mother, and I don't know if she's capable of that.

Me: *Dad never filed the marriage license Wilder and I signed, right?*

Silence.

The office door opens, and Luca steps out.

Oh shit. Okay. Get it together, Amelie.

The sad thing is, he doesn't notice me at first. He turns and shakes the woman's hand, and her name matches my memory of her face. Relatively young, ambitious. Newly divorced and, well... thriving.

It makes me think if my parents hadn't been hung up on the idea of protection from the DeSantis family, where might they have pushed me? Politics? Law? Somewhere to benefit the Page name, of that I'm sure.

Luca's made it almost all the way to the elevator when I step forward, out of the shadows.

"Amelie Page, Councilwoman," I introduce, sticking my hand out.

Sandra White's eyes light up, no doubt landing on my last name.

Wilder's death has been kept under wraps and out of the media, as far as I could tell. No one was in the chapel except my small family and Luca's large one. Of course, it's only been three days since he died in front of me. Plenty of time for a fancy write-up in the *Times* and a funeral announcement.

"Amelie," she repeats. "We met before."

"At the charity dinner you hosted," I say. "I was in the area and hoping to help my mother out and get your quote? Since it was so impressive how you carried it through the council."

She laughs, waving her hand. "Oh, Elise taught you well. Aren't you a beauty?" Her gaze strays to her assistant, then back to me. "I do have time for a quote. Would you like to join me?"

I glance over my shoulder. Luca stands next to the elevator. I wasn't sure how he would take it—I'd go for anything, really—but he's pissed.

Good. So am I.

I flash him a brittle smile and slip into Sandra's office.

She's got a wall of windows, and a bookcase completely takes up another wall. It seems to be the way of things for politicians. Law books all stacked to display at eye level, whatever award or accolades framed beside them.

I analyze them while she goes to her desk.

I asked myself if my parents would've wanted me in law or politics? If I asked Sandra, she would probably say both. Her law degree comes from Harvard. Undergrad at Brown. She's barely thirty and already had a healthy amount of bills pass with her convincing.

"Amelie?"

I straighten and step away from her Bachelor of Science. "Sorry, just admiring. You've made a lot of headway in your time on the council."

"It's been an uphill battle," she says.

I catch a glimpse of a dog photo on her desk. "Jacks, right?"

"Good memory," she murmurs. "Your mother is quite

persuasive. I don't think I've met privately with a journalist in years. Not since before I was elected."

"I'm—" I pause. I guess, in a way, I *am* a journalist. Investigative.

Investigating the DeSantis family.

I *will* figure them out. Uncover all their secrets. It's suddenly a need pulsing under my skin, this sick sort of curiosity. I want Luca to suffer for it, too.

To recover, I dip my head. "Still new to being referred to as a journalist. My mother wanted something different for me."

To be a housewife.

Her attention goes to my left hand. "Wilder DeSantis was that something different?"

Fuck. "It was," I say carefully. "I'm not sure that's the direction I'm headed in."

I mean, come on. Talk about being in bed with the enemy. All I have to do is remember how I felt waking up this morning completely alone. Or the way Luca and I spoke to each other before we left.

"Do you know Luca, then?"

I press my lips together.

She narrows her eyes. "I just couldn't help but notice you have some bruising on your face. And the stitches, of course. He had a black eye."

I shrug. "Coincidence. We're not well acquainted."

She hums.

I take out my phone and hit the 'record' button.

"So, what would you like to say about the success of the bill passing? And where is your next focus?" An idea sparks inside me. This next focus could be what her and Luca were discussing. If she's in his back pocket, how much work does she do to make their lives easier?

I've driven by construction sites that have been run into the ground—almost literally—by bureaucratic red tape, politics, schemes. And ones that have had to practically sell their souls to get built. Page Printing went through something similar.

Even just getting a loan to finance—*ugh*, there were many nights I sat at the top of the stairs and listened to my parents lament the system. But this... they managed real change. Whether it pans out or not is anyone's guess.

She smiles. "I'm thrilled that my colleagues and I were able to pass the bill. A lot of effort went into protecting the smaller contractors who will benefit from less oversight. Of course, permits will still need to be filed appropriately, but the burden is now on government officials instead of another corporation with something to lose."

I tilt my head. "And you're the one who signs off on the permits? Or rejects them?"

"I do."

"I imagine this is where it comes in handy to be your friend," I joke.

Her smile is tight. "I imagine so, Ms. Page—or, is it DeSantis now?"

I almost grimace but hold back at the last second. It shouldn't be a surprise that she knows. Or, at the very least, suspects. Wilder's death has been kept under wraps, except for some gossip that may not have reached her ears. That announcement will probably come to light soon.

No, it's the way she wields my brand-new last name. Not so much like a weapon against me, but a shield for herself. Protection. A plea for me to stop this line of questioning? For the first time, I wonder what they have over her to get what they want. If Luca or Wilder or whoever usually visits her office brings bribes or threats.

I try to see through her exterior, to the heart of the matter.

"And next on your plate?" I ask.

"Cracking down on gun trafficking," she answers. "Safety

in this city should be a top priority, and I fear this has slipped off the priority list in recent years."

I nod and click off the recording, stowing it back in my purse.

"You married a DeSantis," she says, "and you're asking *me* about immoral conduct?"

"I was sold into the family," I say, my voice soft. "And you... well, I don't know how they got you. But I'll figure it out."

I don't wait for her response.

I incline my chin and say, "Thanks for the quote, Councilwoman." And then I get the hell out of there.

CHAPTER 21

Amelie

It's funny how my parents operate. Page Printing, Inc. owns a newspaper that pretty much operates freely on its own. It doesn't need my father's oversight. He just collects his share of the royalties each month. The paper was acquired from the last CEO who, if memory serves correctly, had a gambling problem *and* a women problem. As in, he liked women who weren't his wife a bit too much.

Anyway, that was how the *New York Star* came to us. We were already printing the newspapers for a few of the other weekly papers, those too small to have their own press like the *New York Times*. It seemed like a natural acquisition.

The magazine is my mother's pet project. A glossy, thick thing full of too-thin models and those folded-page perfume adverts. The monthly run usually has a spotlight feature on a few people. Headliners that sell it.

And the councilwoman, with an impressive résumé and fresh off a win, seemed like a natural choice.

But now I'm thinking the only reason Mom picked her was because of her agreement with the DeSantises. If every single decision from the last three years can be traced back to them.

I hate it.

I hate their influence.

Wilder's death peeled my eyes wide open to what goes on in this family. They want absolute control—of course. They've got their fingers in everything.

I need to go back to Luca's office.

Maybe Jameson's, if I can manage it...

They're hiding something.

No—they're hiding *everything*. I'm no better off than an outsider, but my hunger to know them drives me on. The glance into Luca's work has piqued my curiosity.

The councilwoman closes the door behind me, and I pass the receptionist's desk. It's empty, and I don't spot Luca at the elevators. Maybe this move wasn't enough to rattle him, and he's home. Or downstairs, having a laugh with Aiden.

For all I know, his brother warned him we were coming.

A hand wraps around my mouth, yanking me backward.

If I wasn't two steps outside the councilwoman's office, I would be alarmed. But my spine hits a chest that seems way more familiar than it should, and I don't put up a fight.

Luca drags me into a small room, dark except for the light seeping in under the door. A supply closet, if I had to guess. He flips me around, and his hand slips from my mouth to my throat. His fingers curl around, digging into my skin.

It might be a warning, but I've never been more turned on.

"What are you doing here?" He leans in and touches my hair.

I smile. "You're the one who wants to play games, Luca."

He squeezes suddenly, cutting off my air supply. My mouth pops open, and I grab his wrist with both hands. My lungs sear.

Fuck our vows. I'm going to kill him for this.

I bring my knee up between his legs as hard as I can manage, and his grip loosens. He lets out a pained wheeze, and I shove him away from me. He hits the metal shelves and stares at me like he's never seen me before.

I shake my head. I can't be in here anymore. I can't be around him.

When I came here, I was looking for... a way to validate myself, I think.

I twist the doorknob, and Luca's hand slams into the wood next to my head, forcing it shut.

"Lock it," he says. "Keep your hands on the door."

Something must be wrong with me, because I obey. A dark thrill goes through me, a pulsing that only danger seems to awaken. Danger and Luca.

He yanks my hips back against him. His erection digs into my ass.

And then he pushes my leggings down, all the way to my ankles. The last time he knelt behind me...

I automatically shudder when his hot breath hits my bare skin. His teeth graze my butt cheek, biting before he rises.

"If you make a sound, I'll stop," he promises. "Nod."

I do. How did I go from wearing armor, ready for battle, to this? In a dark closet, naked from the waist down, and I'm panting in anticipation.

He slams into me in one go, and I lurch. No sound escapes my lips. This feels dirty and secret, and the twisted part of me loves it.

"You're soaked," he murmurs, pulling back out. "You like this? The threat of being caught?"

I don't answer. I shift, bracing my forearms on the door. He slides against me, and I almost moan. It's right behind my teeth, threatening to break free.

He moves, then. Enough talking. Enough waiting. I take

each of his thrusts and shove back, the delicious fullness of him creating waves of dizziness. They crash through me, so much so that I can't quite tell if I'm still standing. Just his fingers on my waist, his length ramming into me, my damp palms on the door.

Everything else has ceased to exist.

He reaches around me and flicks my clit.

I'm too stimulated. By the situation, by him. By our mutual anger. This sex isn't made from love, that's for sure. I feel his annoyance and I hope he can sense mine.

He flicks it again, faster, and my orgasm shatters me.

I press my mouth into my arm, suppressing the noise that comes with my shaky exhale. He comes only a minute later, stilling inside me.

And then he's gone, sliding free from me. I stay against the door as he tugs my leggings back up. They snap into place, covering our wicked deeds.

"I'm going to remember this," he says in my ear. "And when I get home tonight, my cum better still be on your skin. Between your thighs. I own you, Amelie."

I shiver.

He unlocks the door and gestures for me to step back.

And then the fucker leaves me.

I touch the edge of my head wound, probing one of the stitches. My head kills. Dr. Matthews said something about no strenuous activity, probably. If I had been listening.

I push my shoulders back and ignore the wetness that seeps between my legs. It's like he's still here, still against my back. I'm immobile for a long moment, just trying to breathe.

And then the claustrophobia takes over, and ice creeps over my skin.

I can't stay in here.

Snatching my purse from the floor, I crack the door and make sure the coast is clear before booking it to the elevator.

No one waits for me in the lobby—I can only imagine Aiden intercepted Luca and left with him.

The work of Mafia men is never done.

My car is thankfully in the same place, and I lock the doors as soon as I'm in. There are a million places I could go to leave this place, but it's like I'm tethered to Luca. I have no doubt he'd find a way to track me down and drag me back, kicking and screaming.

I own you, he said.

It's repulsive. The idea of being owned, of being reduced to a possession. It's a running theme in his words, his actions. He *married* me, but I'm no better than a puppet for him to position in his house. He'll pull my strings, use me, fuck me.

The pain of that realization burns. My chest is on fire. I can't cry here, though, even as a lump forms in my throat. I can't lose my mind in front of a government building in downtown Manhattan.

I swallow it down and swipe under my eyes, checking my face in the rearview mirror. I came here and did what I wanted. I rattled Luca.

But I think he rattled me more.

I take the long way back to Luca's house and park down the block. I don't necessarily want my car to be tied to his house, so I hop out and walk the rest of the way. The upstairs porch where Luca's tenant leaned out to help me this morning is empty. She's a peculiar woman.

Once I'm inside, I kick off my shoes and immediately freeze.

My *parents* are here.

At Luca's dining table.

"Amelie," my mother gasps, shooting up. "What happened to your head?"

I squint. "What are you doing here?"

Dad seems equally concerned, which is a fucking first. He

doesn't rise, though, and instead waits for my mother to shepherd me to the table. She grips my chin and turns my face this way and that, inspecting the damage.

"Your hair," she murmurs. "You were out? Like this?"

"Is there something wrong with my hair, Mom?"

She grimaces. "We've discussed this. And you were with Sandra White? What were you thinking—"

"The opportunity presented itself." My voice is monotone, and I fall into one of the chairs. Them being here is suffocating.

A whole new form of claustrophobia.

"Is Luca here?" I ask.

Mom tsks, returning to her seat across from me. "Honey, we need to talk."

I narrow my eyes, and she reaches into her purse. She removes an envelope and slides it across the table to me. I don't touch it, even under their stares.

"You're not talking," I say softly. "What is this?"

I wish, for once in my life, I could be more like Lucy. She doesn't give a fuck about my parents. Not in the traditional sense. That's probably one of the reasons they sent her away—they couldn't control her anymore, and control means everything to my parents. Just look at me, and where I ended up.

They didn't care when I was, in their words, *sowing my wild oats*. An expression usually said in reference to eager, horny boys, but they slapped it on everything 'bad' I did. The parties, dating, drinking. "Oh, she's just getting it out of her system," they would say.

I wanted to scream every time they brushed me off. I feared it would build up in my chest until I exploded.

"This is your marriage certificate," she says. "It came to our house yesterday."

My throat tightens. "That was fast," I manage.

"Open it." Dad pushes it closer to me.

I retreat. I can't help it. I pull my hands back from the table, clenching them in my lap. There has to be a reason, right? That they're here, looking like the world is ending.

Mom makes a face. "Stop being so dramatic, Amelie. It's a piece of paper."

I straighten. I don't think I'm *dramatic*. I just... have an unhealthy amount of fear at seeing my fate sealed with the courts of New York State. Like the ring and the sex and being ordered around by Luca wasn't enough proof for me, I need a piece of paper to confirm it.

So I face my fear and pick up the envelope, carefully sliding my finger under the seal. It pops open, and I remove the marriage certificate.

Amelie Page and Wilder DeSantis...

"No."

"You're married to Wilder," Mom says.

I don't need it spelled out, but I can't form the words to tell her off. To question this. He's *dead*. Died in the ambulance. So this piece of paper is...

"We haven't received a death certificate yet," Dad says. "So as of right now, you're still officially married to Wilder."

"Because the one with Luca must not have been filed," Mom adds. "Or it was, and disregarded because they received this one first."

I drop the paper, and my heart drops like a stone, too.

Down, down, down.

I didn't escape Wilder.

I think of Mariella's fate, and how he wove it together with mine. With Luca's. And my mind snags on every interaction between us and our families. The way I'd never touched him except a few times, our hands brushing. A kiss to my knuckles.

The only time I felt his body against mine was after he had been shot.

And I'm married to *him*. Not the one who saved me. Who irritates me. Who has infiltrated my heart in a matter of days.

I know better. I know better and yet I'm still falling for the bad guys in my story.

"What now?" I barely recognize my own voice. Monotone, even. "I'm not married to Luca?"

Inside, I'm a disaster. The ring Luca gave me may as well be a sham. I should return it to Paloma, so she can save it for him to give to someone worthier than me.

Someone who didn't manage to marry his brother.

"Now, we're taking you home. Just temporarily, until we figure out what to do. This complicates things, as you can understand." Dad raises his hands. "We've already talked to Jameson, and he's allowed us—"

"Allowed," I scoff.

"He's *allowing* us to bring you home," Mom finishes Dad's sentence. "Isn't that better than the alternative?"

Is it? I don't even know what the alternative might be.

They expect a certain answer, though. An affirmation that they're doing the right thing. And I'm nothing if not well-trained.

I nod, pasting on a smile. "I've missed you both."

Mom returns my smile, relief apparent in her eyes. "We've missed you, too. Come on. Do you have your bags?"

I glance toward Luca's bedroom. I haven't been here long enough to even think of it as mine yet. "I have some things to pack. But, um, I got my car. So I can meet you at home."

They frown.

"Long story," I mumble. "I'll be right behind you."

They leave, and I lock the door. Knowing Luca, he won't be home for hours. It's plenty of time to pack up and make my escape, but my skin crawls at the idea of returning home. I was under their thumb there, and that's the life I'm returning to. I won't have an excuse to *sow my wild oats*.

I'm not married to Luca.

My heart squeezes, and I lean over the table. My cheek touches the cool wood.

They left the marriage certificate. It leers at me, inches from my nose. Wilder's printed name, his scrawled signature beneath it. Hadn't I hoped that Dad didn't send it in on time? Hadn't I wished, just today, that the right marriage license would make it to the courthouse?

I should know better than to *hope*. Hope is a dirty word designed to tear us down. Because where am I now, after all that time spent wishing and hoping and searching the sky for shooting stars to hang my dreams on?

I hoped for love and I got Wilder's cold charm.

I wished for a future and I got Luca's cage.

So, as of right now, I'm done. There's no ring on my finger. I might be a DeSantis in name, but my husband is dead.

My laugh bursts out of me. I'm a fucking widow. I smack my hand on the table, unable to contain the giggles. My stomach aches from it, muscles clenched. God, it's been forever since I've truly laughed, and *this* is what gets me.

Eventually, I pick myself up and go to the bedroom. I contemplate writing a note, but there's nothing to say. I've been here for two days and I have absolutely no possessions here. My purse on my shoulder, my WiFi-only phone in it. I didn't even bring in my bag of clothes from the car.

I leave the marriage certificate on the table and walk out the door.

I manage to get halfway to my car before someone calls out my name. I glance back, biting my lip. Luca storms toward me, his face a mask of fury.

"Where are you going?"

"Away," I snap.

He stops in front of me. "Why?"

"Because you're an asshole." I cross my arms. "Do you disagree?"

"That's not it."

He narrows his eyes, then grabs my arm and drags me back the way we came. I have no choice but to go along with it, unless I want to be *literally* dragged. He's furious—but not as mad as he's about to be.

Adrenaline kickstarts my heartbeat. It gallops in my chest, the anticipation of how he's going to react almost too much to bear. But he takes me into the house and releases me.

"I told you to stay, wife."

I laugh. "You should pay closer attention, Luca," I admonish. "Things change faster than you might think."

He tilts his head.

I raise my hand, pointing to the table.

He goes, staring down at the paper without touching it. It might burn him if he does. But his face goes from angry to... scary.

"Tell me where you were going," he grits out.

I lift my chin. There wouldn't be any point to caving to the fear now, would there? Not when I'm suddenly, remarkably expendable. Wilder managed to do what he agreed: he married me. And it happened in almost the exact same manner Luca married me, with no flourish. Our parents as witnesses.

I don't think there's a force on earth that could save me from Luca's wrath.

"Home," I say. "My parents were here to collect me. I told them I would drive myself."

He glances around. "You let them in?"

"No." I narrow my eyes. "That's your only take on this? You're asking if I let them into your house? Fuck you, Luca."

Some thought enters his mind, and unknown terror rips down my spine. I don't trust whatever he's thinking, and nothing protects me anymore. Wilder's death—and my lack of marriage to Luca—basically solidifies that.

Run, my fear whispers.

I turn and sprint for the kitchen. There's a door there that leads to a backyard, although I hadn't explored it more than drinking my coffee out there yesterday morning.

His arm wraps around my waist, and he swings me off my feet.

"Luca—"

"Be quiet, Amelie."

I struggle against him, but he holds me at an angle that prevents me from doing any lasting damage. He carries me outside and throws me in the backseat of a dark sedan, then climbs in beside me. A minute later, someone slides into the driver's seat. There's a wall of glass between him and us, so dark it's almost black.

Luca stares at me.

I press myself against the opposite door, reaching for the handle.

"Don't make me subdue you," he threatens.

I glare at him. "I was leaving," I seethe. "Going home. Isn't that what you wanted, anyway? For me to be out of your hair?"

He shakes his head and looks away. "You don't understand."

"I understand perfectly well that I have had *no say* in my life up until now." I spread my arms. "But Wilder isn't just my almost-husband who died. He's my *dead husband*."

I hate that this is a weapon against him, but he let me in. He let me in when we were in Italy, and now I'd like to think that I can read him. The slight flinch in his expression, the way each time I repeat the word *husband* and connect it to Wilder, it's a little stab.

But I'm so fucking angry.

We cross the bridge into Manhattan, and I sit up straighter.

"Where are we going?"

He glares holes in the side of my head, but I ignore him. My gaze is glued to the highway we're on, trying to anticipate which exit we'll take. Where Luca plans on taking me.

Maybe he just wants to go to dinner.

Ludicrous idea, but my stomach growls. I haven't eaten much today—actually, haven't eaten much in the past week, if we're being honest. I've been feeling the effects of it much worse recently, compounded by the headache that won't release me.

The silence between us is thick with tension.

"How does it feel?" I ask him finally, once I understand we're not going anywhere special. We're going to the DeSantis tower.

He takes my bait. "How does what feel?"

There's a bump, and we descend into the darkness of the parking garage.

I finally look over and meet his stare. It burns, but I force a nonchalant voice when I tell him, "To know that you lost to your brother. Again."

He sneers. "My brother is dead, Amelie. I have you now."

My expression drops. He opens the door and offers his hand.

Inexplicably, I flash back to right after the wedding. Him reaching in the car, offering his hand. Demanding I get out.

I ignore his hand and brush past him, stepping out myself. Part of me still clings to the hope that we're headed to Jameson's office. To right a wrong, I suppose. Produce Wilder's death certificate, file Luca's and my marriage license.

He follows me into the elevator and swipes his card, then hits a button for one of the higher floors. Above the offices, close to Aiden's apartment, if I didn't know any better.

A chill goes through me.

The *ding* of us arriving at the floor cracks our silence. My belly is a nest of snakes. I almost can't make myself get out of the elevator, because I know now what he's doing. My old fear is coming to bite me.

Like it's a living, breathing thing, it climbs up my throat and takes my voice hostage. Luca's hand finds the back of my neck. His fingers curl into my skin, pressing softly. He leads me that way down a short hall. There are other doors here, labeled with brass numbers.

I dig my heels in. "Stop."

But I'm helpless to stop this.

"Luca—"

His attention comes back to me, silencing any question I had. Sometimes he feels like a different person. Like a monster slips in behind his features and takes control.

He unlocks a door at the end of the hall and guides me inside. Sits me on the bed, then releases my neck. He straightens to his full height and backs away.

I bolt to my feet. "Why?"

He inclines his chin, opening the door and pausing in the threshold. "You said it yourself, Amelie. You wanted to go home, and here you are. Your new accommodation." His gaze goes to my belly. "The only thing that can save you now is if you're pregnant. Welcome home, Amelie."

I race toward him, and he slams the door in my face. I hit it with my shoulder and grab the knob, but it's already locked. It doesn't even rattle.

Wild fear overtakes me, and I pound on the door. *I can't do this.* This is a prison a thousand feet off the ground, designed to make me weak. But I'm *already* weak. My heart jackhammers, threatening to explode out of my body.

"Let me out, Luca. Please. Please let me out." I claw at the door handle like he might change his mind. Tears pour down my cheeks. My eyes are burning. "Please, Luca, I'll do anything. I'm sorry. I'm so sorry."

I slap my hands against the painted wood until I lose feeling in them, and I slide down the door to my knees.

"Luca. I'm sorry. I won't try to leave you or run away. But you can't leave me in here. I can't—" My throat closes, and I can't breathe for a moment. I suck in a sharp breath as stars burst behind my eyelids. "I won't do anything bad. I'll do—I'll be what you want. Okay?"

In the back of my mind, I register this as a panic attack. My chest has an elephant sitting on it, and the room tilts under me. I'm losing my mind, a little realization that terrifies me. My reaction is pure fear. I hit the door again. "Are you still there?"

Something thumps against the door on the other side. His hand? His head?

"I know you can hear me," I say in a low voice, hiccupping slightly. "Please, Luca, you can't keep me here. I promise I'll be good. I'll do exactly what you say. Anything. I just... you need to open the door. We can talk about this."

He doesn't respond.

I sag to the side, bowing my head. He's sitting there and letting me beg, and he's doing *nothing*.

"Let me out," I try again. "I'll go crazy in here, Luca, and I'll never forgive you for this. *Please* open the door. Please don't leave here."

I don't know how long I go on for. Hours or minutes. My voice is hoarse by the time I eventually stop talking. Stop begging.

He's gone. There's no way he could listen to me this whole time, drinking it up like some sadist.

Right?

I've got nothing left to give. He's reduced me to nothing but a pleading mess on the floor. I handed him my dignity and let... I let this happen. I told him my fears, laid out the best way to trap and destroy me. And he *has*.

Screw hope.

I run my hands under my eyes, wiping away the wetness. My eyelids are puffy. I scrub my face, and my fingers scrape at the stitches above my eyebrow. I'm filled with the intense desire to tear them out, to uglify my face. Mom liked to remind me I got here because of my face. My beauty. Cheer captain, a plethora of friends, and I knew how to behave in public. Those were my good graces, my lucky charms.

I've truly lost my mind, because I'm nauseous at the thought of relying on my face for anything. I don't want beauty if it leads me here.

Powerful men like to contain beauty. Trap it, kill it. My soul aches, a pain that radiates deeper than my bones. I'm tired of being the pretty thing in the cage.

If he's going to keep me under lock and key, the least I can do is become... *other*.

I do it before I can back out, yanking on a stitch. It rips through my skin, and I gasp at the sudden sharpness of pain. It dampens the ache in my chest, though. Just a little. Hot blood rolls down my temple. I pull out the second, third. I keep going, nearly gagging, until I can't feel anything except the riot on my skin.

I rise, tracing my bloody fingers along the wall to the bed. The room spins around me. It's like when Lucy and I would hold each other's wrists and spin around as fast as we could, until everything else was a blurry mess.

It's all I can do to lie down and close my eyes. I focus on my head, but the agony of Luca's betrayal is cold. I can't keep it out.

CHAPTER 22
Luca

I'm seething when I arrive home. Aiden waits for me at the front door, and he follows me inside. We have bigger things to worry about than Amelie and Wilder. Namely, finding Wilder's killer. But this is all I can think about. It nags at me.

Aiden advised that I not rush to accuse my father of anything, and instead told me he'd meet me here.

And here he is.

"Well?" I demand.

"Easy." He waves me in ahead of him, then goes straight to the dining table while I turn on the lights. He reads the license with a blank expression. "He died. This license isn't valid anymore."

"Except we don't have Wilder's death certificate yet. They're delayed, apparently, due to the cause of death." I rub my eyes. "She threw it in my face."

"And you...?"

"I'm keeping her safe," I snap. "She's still a DeSantis to the rest of the world, and that means she's in danger. Always.

Constantly. And she refuses to follow directions, so I'm keeping her away."

He watches me passively.

I blow out a breath. "She'll be fine. Plenty of food, on-demand movies..."

Only one person knows I brought her to the tower, and I only told her because she has to feed Amelie. Slipping food in the door and then relocking it shouldn't be terribly hard for Catrina to manage. She's a troublemaker, but a reliable one. Especially when it comes to family.

I have no doubt, if I hadn't left a camera outside Amelie's room—and told Cat as much—Cat would be more likely to do something. Like try to spring Amelie free. And I just can't let that happen. Not now.

Aiden shakes his head. "What do you want to do?"

I grimace. "I want to kill Michael Page."

It's not technically his fault, unless he filed it after...

"She will never be free of me," I say, more to myself than Aiden. I don't know why she makes me feel so damn crazy. I hate her. I'm possessive of her.

And she's married to *Wilder*...

God, it just spikes up every bad nerve in my body. If he wasn't already dead, I'd kill him myself.

"Don't do anything tonight," Aiden suggests. "Straighten this out with Dad once you're calm. Tomorrow, maybe, or next week." He pats my shoulder and goes to the door. "If you don't want to stew on it, you can help me with a little West project..."

I perk up. "Anything for a distraction."

He smirks. "I've been tracking their movements. It's only been a week—less than that, actually—but they're all acting odd. Tonight, we're watching Lawrence's family."

"Recon," I repeat. "You want me to sit in a car with you? For who knows how long?"

He shrugs. "Yeah."

I stifle my sigh. He dropped what he was doing to come here, and I can still feel the fury slipping under my skin. It's like gasoline in my bloodstream, just waiting to reignite.

"Fine. Let's go."

CHAPTER 23

Amelie

I wake up, and for an instant, I forget where I am.

And then, like it has for the past two weeks, everything comes rushing back: the marriage certificate, Luca dragging me here, being locked in this room. I've avoided my phone, because up until yesterday evening, I didn't have a charger.

My jailer hasn't been back. He pawned off the responsibility of keeping me alive on one of his cousins, a girl named Catrina. She said to call her Cat, but I haven't managed to find it in me to be that... nice.

She is, though. Nice.

She seemed sympathetic when I lost my mind every night. Something broke in me, and the urge to get out of here fills my throat. It hasn't left me, like anxiety crawling through my veins. My heart seems insistent on reminding me I'm the caged bird.

Trapped, trapped, trapped, it sings.

She passes the food through the door and closes it again, the lock in the handle, a deadbolt. Two clicks that burrow in my ears. I've cried until I couldn't breathe. I've screamed.

No one is coming to help me.

It's the worst to know you've been broken. Defeated. This is the fate I was terrified for, and now it's here. My mind exaggerates my fear. It shows me an eternity in this room, hidden away from everyone. What control do my parents have over me now?

It's Luca who holds me captive.

I focus on him. His face. The way it felt to fuck him.

And then I contort those memories. I twist them into something small and meaningless and angry. It's how I survived high school. It's how I survived every day of the three years before my marriage. Take what hurts you and make it small.

It took a while to convince Catrina to bring me a charger. I wrote my request on the napkin when she swung by to clear out my plate, and it was two whole days before she nodded to me through the crack in the door. I offered her a tentative smile, and she lit up.

So, she's nice, but I'm not.

I'm just so not in the mood to deal with it. Or her. Or anyone.

I've got a scream building in my throat. It sometimes grows strong enough to seal off my words, but I don't let it out. It's different from the screaming pleads, my begging.

Shame burns inside me.

I *begged* Luca. And Catrina. Any time there was a noise outside my door, I was reduced to a begging, crying mess.

I've never been that person, but Luca managed it. He's not even here to witness my destruction.

Oh, but what glee he must have. What a proud man he is now, holding his almost-wife captive. He can't even look at me. He hasn't stepped foot near my door since he put me here.

My eyes are open now, the reality creeping back in.

Along with the charger yesterday, Catrina gave me the

front page of the *New York Times*. I never thought I'd make the news, let alone the front page of a national paper, but here we are. One of my mother's favorites of the engagement photos Wilder and I posed for months ago is front and center, with *DeSantis Darling of New York Fatally Shot* as the headline.

I couldn't even read it, except to scan for the funeral information. I didn't want to hear about how *good* he was. I imagine it's lies, anyway. Glorified in death, aren't we?

The funeral is today.

Two weeks gave me plenty of time to contemplate my life —good, bad, ugly. Luca's words play in my head on repeat about pregnancy being the only thing to save me. Those words haunt me, too, because it seems the universe has a sick sense of humor.

I occasionally touch my arm, just to remind myself that the birth control is still there.

Everything hurts. I never let Cat see that side of my face. She would've immediately told Luca, and then Dr. Matthews... *no.* I'm hoping the gash scars. It's already closed, pink and puckered. Actually, some of it is an angry red, splotches of skin. It bled terribly. I woke up in the middle of the night with blood in my eye, my hair, the pillow.

I smiled when I turned on the light, swaying. They didn't question my desire for new sheets, and I refused to give the old ones back. I tucked them away in the bathroom, a memento of bravery.

Or stupidity.

It's going to be a good scar, though. My nails did the most damage as I pulled out the stitches, raking down the closing skin. The little scratches around it have all scabbed over and flaked away, leaving smooth skin in their place. My head doesn't even hurt, really, except for an occasional twinge.

Or when I cry too hard.

The door unlocks. The sound has become something like nails on a chalkboard, and I wince. It opens as far as the chain lets it.

"Amelie?" Cat calls. "You awake?"

I throw the covers off and swing my legs out of bed. "Yeah. One minute."

She waits. The chain over the door makes me feel better about the cage, if only slightly. That while I'm locked in here, I still have control over who can enter.

It's not an even trade—not even close. But I'm a desperate girl who will do desperate things. They shouldn't underestimate me.

I go to the door, and she hands me my breakfast one item at a time. An apple, a toasted bagel smothered in peanut butter and honey, carefully wrapped in a napkin. A coffee.

"What time is the funeral?" I whisper through the door.

"Eleven," she answers. "I don't know who's taking you, but L—"

"Don't," I snap. His name is off limits. His face is off-limits, because I'm pretty sure I want to bash it in if I ever see him again.

But you are going to see him again, I remind myself. *Today. At the funeral.*

As my brother-in-law.

She sighs. "They asked me to give you this. To wear."

She passes a dress bag through the crack, and I take it from her. She's done that a few times, handing me clothes. A toothbrush and toothpaste. Shampoo, conditioner, a razor. Things that Luca clearly didn't think about before he put me in here and tossed the key.

"Thanks." My jaw tightens. "So, they'll probably get me around... ten? Ten-thirty?"

I imagine her automatic nod before she realizes we can't see each other. "Yes," she verbalizes. "Probably."

"Could you hold on?"

She goes silent, but the door doesn't close. I set down the food and unzip the bag. Typical man, to provide a dress but nothing to go with it.

"If they want me presentable, I need a few more things." I step to the side so I can see her. Just a sliver. One eye, the curve of her lips. I list what I'd like, jewelry and shoes, makeup. Her eye gets wider. "Please," I finish. "It's a funeral, but it's also the only time I'll have been outside in two weeks. I want to feel..."

"Yeah, I can do that," she says softly.

"Okay. Thanks," I repeat.

I close the door and take my breakfast to the desk. It's set up like a hotel, minus the luxury of a television: desk, bed, nightstands, closet, and bathroom. As I said, not a lot of options for entertainment.

But I've had plenty of time to plan.

The bloody sheets are visible from here, folded on the edge of the tub. I don't know why, but it steels my resolve. I know the lengths I'm willing to go. Luca cracked me open, and now we both have to live with the demons that come out.

My plan. The flimsy thing I've been hanging my hat on.

I sent a fleeting text before I shut my phone off. It was exactly a week ago. The text led to a number, which led to another name. Another number. It felt like I was being guided along a path, only to confront a gunman at the end.

I rub my eyes. I'm tired.

The nightmares have gotten worse, showing me Wilder's death over and over.

In my dreams, I scream until I'm hoarse and my voice dies away. It's always just me, him, and the masked gunman standing in the choir section above us. He never shoots me, though. We stare at each other until he disappears, and I fall through the floor.

Without fail, I land in the alley in Sanremo, surrounded by

three men. They shove me through the wall, and Matteo catches me in the restaurant. There are more people with us, a whole audience who watches him unbuckle his pants.

Sometimes I jolt awake, my heart pounding out of my chest. Other times, it isn't until his hands are on me that I am yanked into consciousness. And more recently…

It worries me. Last night, I woke myself from a dead sleep with a scream on my lips. I clamped my hand over my mouth. I sat in silence for minutes, wondering if someone would come running.

They didn't. I didn't know if any sound had burst out of me before I was really awake or if it was all in the dream. The terror of it, though, took too long to subside.

I haven't slept well except the first night, and I think that was more like unconsciousness due to the blood loss.

"The plan," I mutter to myself. I glance at the dress on the bed. Whatever happens, this will be worth it. I open my recharged phone and take a deep breath. I have one shot at this. One option. I was warned the last number I received would only work once, that if I messed up, it was over. I press dial and close my eyes.

What if they don't answer? What if they refuse to help me?

"Hello?" a buttery-smooth voice answers.

"I need your help," I blurt out, my tact out the window. "Please don't hang up. I think they might've told you I was going to call, and I have no one else I can ask. No one who would be able to help me."

The voice on the other end of the line is quiet, then, "What did they do?"

"He… they're holding me hostage." *Dramatic as always*, I scold myself. But aren't I being honest? How many times have I begged to be released?

"Your marriage didn't protect you," they say, and of course

they know who I am. Of course this is probably the least surprising thing to happen to them today. "Not for long, anyway."

"Please," I whisper. "I need to get out."

"Where?"

"Doesn't matter. I have a plan beyond that, I just need your help to get away from them. The funeral is today. It might be my only chance." I'm desperate, trying to hold on to hope with both hands again. I should know by now that hope can kill me.

They sigh. "I have to remain anonymous in this."

"Yes. Of course."

"The funeral, then?" They seem to consider our options. "It's the only time you'll be in public, but heavily guarded."

"A distraction," I guess. "Something to draw their attention."

"I'll take care of it." Then, "You owe me a favor, Amelie Page. That's my price. A favor of equal measure."

"Deal," I breathe. I'd be willing to promise them my first-born. Anything to escape. This could backfire. This could go so, so wrong. But there's hope again, pulling me toward optimism.

But I can't stay here one minute longer.

CHAPTER 24

Luca

My father straightens my tie. "Are you ready?"

I try not to scoff. Over the past two weeks, family has poured in. Italians from New York City and beyond, those DeSantises who scattered and retired, who went beyond to try to spread our fortune, flock back. Some I know, some I've heard of. Others are strangers.

But the funeral is today, and everyone is somber. We ate together as a family, packing into the restaurant on the seventeenth floor. We'll save the stories and the drinking for later, after we've laid Wilder to rest.

Now, we're back in Dad's office that seems to overlook the rest of the city. Maybe it's just a matter of perception.

"How is Amelie?" he asks.

"Fine." Still breathing, I think.

Cat hasn't said anything, and I imagine she would let me know if my wife... my *not wife*... was dead in her room.

"Aiden will collect her," he says. "And you've had time to consider whether you're actually ready for marriage. It would be easy enough to shuffle her off, let her go back to her life in Rose Hill. That's what her parents are pushing for."

I stiffen. "Are they asking about her?"

His eyebrow tics, and that's the only tell he has before his hands tighten in my jacket. The man is the same height as me, and it's questionable who's stronger. But right now, with the darkness in his eye, I have no doubt he'd shove a knife in my eyeball if it served his purposes.

"I've let you live with this fuck-up," he growls, "wondering when you would come to your senses. But you keep her imprisoned here, and I've told her parents that she's happy living here. I'd like to think our fragile agreement with the Pages *does* go up in smoke because you can't see past your ego. At least then I would have an excuse to discipline you."

I shake him loose, taking a few quick steps back. "It's not my ego."

"It fucking is your ego, son. You've made such a mess of things in less than a month." Pity flashes across his face. "You compare yourself to your brother, over and over again. When will you stop?"

"When he stops taking what's *mine*!" I slam my fist into the wall, puncturing a hole clean through the drywall.

He watches me impassively. "And this is why you won't go near Amelie at the funeral. Do you understand me?"

I narrow my eyes and clench my jaw. I can only offer him a single nod, hating myself because of it.

He pats my shoulder, and that's the end of it. We go downstairs and climb into one of the waiting SUVs. This feels too similar to the wedding. The vehicles lined up, the suits. We weren't quite so stoic, then.

No, before? We celebrated.

Wilder, Aiden, and I had been out on the town the night before. We snuck out of the tower and went barhopping across Manhattan, and the three of us stumbled back to Wilder's apartment in a drunken haze. Wilder kept saying it wasn't the end for him, but we all knew it was. Amelie was captivating, even at sixteen. If she couldn't manage to hold Wilder's attention—or his dick's attention—then their marriage was doomed.

It rankled me how he spoke about her. A trophy wife. Someone to schmooze the politicians with, to have on his arm as he rose through government. "One election at a time," he said. It was practically his slogan.

And yet, when she'd walked down the aisle toward him, she hadn't radiated happiness.

There was a smile, and she kept her chin high, but deep sadness in her eyes, too.

I try to think of a time—any time—in the past month that I've made her laugh. And I come up empty.

"There," Dad murmurs.

The elevator doors slide open, and Aiden and Amelie walk out. She steals my breath away. Her golden hair is coiled up, leaving only a few curls down around her face and sweeping over her forehead. There's a black lace veil over her face, almost obscuring her stormy eyes and blood-red lips. It clings around her chin. Black stones in her earrings. The dress is black and flowing, the plunging neckline almost too revealing for a funeral. But she's paired it with long ropes of silver that hang around her neck.

It's similar to the one she wore to see the councilwoman.

I have to tear my gaze away from her.

I have to stop thinking she's mine.

"Let things settle," Dad orders. "Try and forget about Amelie Page—especially since we have more important work to do here."

I kill my protest that I can't forget her. That I *won't*. Maybe he recognizes the hungry look in my eye. For weeks, I've forced myself to stay away, thinking I could get over her. That while I've claimed her in every sense of the word, there's a darker undercurrent to my desire. Worry, maybe.

Fear.

Loving Amelie might just tie me to New York. It'll certainly chain me to this family.

But then she's stepping into the SUV ahead of us, her long, tan legs flashing, and she disappears completely from view.

Aiden gets in her vehicle, and that's it. Our caravan begins the drive to the small chapel outside the city. Amelie will recognize it from her wedding, but it's an important place to our family. Security has been doubled—an effort put into place by Sam, Cat's brother—and Dad is confident that it's safe.

Or maybe we're having the funeral here to draw out the killer again.

I swallow, suddenly wishing I had paid more attention to the plans. Asked questions. If we're waiting for a trap, I need to be vigilant. Wilder's death was a shock—I wasn't prepared for violence. My mistake.

Now I've come to expect it. My black eye healed, my ribs only twinge occasionally, but the remnants are a ghostly reminder of what happens when I don't pay attention.

The people I care about get hurt.

"Luca, are you listening to me?"

I wince. "No, sorry."

"I was just about to tell you that it's time you have more responsibility in the company. You've done good work, especially with Sandra White. She had a particular taste, but it seems you've been able to fill Wilder's shoes easily."

I've met with the councilwoman three times in the past two weeks, and she's nothing more than an annoyance. Wilder fucked her to keep her complacent, but that isn't my style.

She's another wedge to drive between Amelie and me. Like a distraction would help redirect my thoughts.

Amelie already owns it all.

"That, coupled with the fact that you can't return to Sanremo—"

"Can't?" I raise my eyebrow. "Amelie's deal with them was that we only had to stay away until Wilder was dead."

"Which, no doubt, they'll be furious about." He shrugs. "You can't risk it. I know your mother is buried there—"

"Don't." I pinch the bridge of my nose. "Seriously, don't."

Any hope of returning there is snuffed out.

Mom used to take me for walks in the afternoon, telling me stories of her own childhood. She'd grip my hand so tightly, as if to impart that I wasn't alone.

And here I am, drowning in loneliness. My brother is on the hunt. My father is psychotic. Amelie surely hates me.

A hopeless situation, it would seem.

And we have to bury Wilder today.

Well, not quite. He was cremated, and his ashes await us at the chapel. After, we'll make a procession to the mausoleum at the back of a local cemetery, and they'll polish and bless his name on a plaque, nailed to the marble.

I hop out of the car the minute we arrive, stalking across the grass to the chapel doors. Sam stands guard, waiting for us to arrive.

I shake his hand. "How does everything look?"

"Fine," he says. "Quiet."

We glance out across the lawn. Dad, Aiden, and Amelie climb the steps. Dad has Amelie's hand looped around his bicep, and they take position on the step above Aiden and me. Sam slips away.

The family comes in waves of black, filing past us into the chapel. They pause to shake my hand or pat my shoulder, greeting Aiden much the same way. Their eyes alight on Amelie, and understanding—and pity—fills their features. They clutch her hand or hug her, depending on their boldness.

I understand, suddenly, why she chose a veil. It's just another layer to the mask she has carefully slid back into place.

Her parents come up, pausing in front of Aiden and me. Her father shakes my hand, and her mother inclines her chin. They express their sympathy and move on to their daughter. Both hug her, one after another. Lucy isn't with them. And even with her mother's arms wrapped around her shoulders, Amelie's face is bland. She wears the proper expression: a slight frown, the corners of her lips dragged down by what someone might consider grief.

I once wanted to break through Amelie's mask. To see what was under the surface.

She glances at me, and the mask drops. Naked fury radiates from her, so quick and plain that I almost reel backward. And then it's gone, her face smooth. She smiles politely at the next person, reaching out for them with black-gloved hands.

Finally, everyone is inside.

Dad and Amelie lead the way down the aisle, pausing to pay their respects to Wilder's ashes. A portrait of him is set up on a stand next to the display, surrounded by flowers. If I didn't know her better, I'd think she was actually heartbroken by his death. And that's exactly what Dad wants people to believe. She trembles a bit as she reaches forward, pressing two fingers to the Wilder painting's lips.

They take their seat, and Aiden and I are next. The whole place is too silent. What a tragedy this should be. Two brothers confronting the eldest in his final stage. Past his final stage, I suppose. He's been dead for almost a month, cremated for just under that. Dad has dodged questions about his death certificate. The medical examiner told me he couldn't disclose his findings. I want to rip into them all, but we're supposed to be gutted by this sad, awful day.

But... I'm not. I've got a clusterfuck of emotions inside me, but I don't feel grief. I'm not upset. If anything, I'm *mad*, as mad as Amelie is at me. If I were alone, I'd smash his urn and kick a hole through the stupid painting.

Because he was an idiot.

He reached too high, too fast. Thought he was the most clever, the brilliant darling son Jameson DeSantis wanted him to be.

Maybe he was that, but he was also something else.

Difficult.

Self-possessed.

As charming as a snake, and just as deadly.

And if someone like him can be snuffed out in an instant, what does that say about the rest of us?

Aiden nudges me. "Come on."

We take our seats on the opposite side of the pew from Amelie and Dad. My nerves are shot, and I can't help but crane my head back to stare at the choir section. Two of our men are up there, and one catches my eye and nods. The steps of the altar where I knocked Amelie down is now masked by a cream rug, no doubt hiding the bullet hole that almost killed her. I can't help but feel on the edge of my seat, waiting for the next bad thing to happen.

I blow out a small breath and try to relax.

The ceremony starts, and the solemn music cuts through me. I rub at my chest. Wilder was... hard to get along with. But he *was* my brother. Now, more than any time in the last month, do I feel the connection to him. The tug of family, of loss. Sadness that I couldn't have thought possible opens up in my chest.

I glance at Aiden, but he's impassive. Heart of stone, that one. Sam's at the side entrance, staring holes into the priest who talks of Wilder like he knows him. He talks of his accomplishments, of the wedding. Gazes turn to Amelie's stiff form next to my father.

And then, abruptly, it's too much for her.

She stands and walks slowly out the side door, past Sam. I lurch to follow, but Aiden latches on to my arm. I lower myself back into the seat. Every muscle screams at me to chase after her.

"We have men outside," Aiden says under his breath. "If she needs air, give the girl a damn minute."

I stare at the door, and the minutes tick by. I can't even pretend to pay attention. Someone is doing a reading at the podium, a passage surely about death and God's welcoming arms. It turns my stomach.

She slips back into the chapel just as the priest welcomes Jameson up to the podium to speak about his son. They asked if I wanted to say anything, but I couldn't manage it. I don't think Aiden had it in him, either.

My attention snags on her for a second before Dad starts.

"Wilder was a complicated man," he says.

I force myself to focus on Dad. On his words. If anyone should be in mourning, it's him. He loved Wilder. Poured all of himself into his first son. Feels like a bit of a waste now, doesn't it?

That's the asshole part of me speaking.

"He loved," Dad's saying now. "He got to spend precious time with his family and new bride. And..." Something catches his eye in the back of the room.

Aiden and I follow his gaze.

Lawrence West walks down the center aisle.

My brother's hands clench, and I have to push down my own sudden flare of anger. *His* family is responsible for Wilder's death. How dare he come here. Our blood was spilt in this very chapel. Dad's glare bores into me and Aiden, and I glance at him. His subtle head shake is enough for me to lean back on the bench.

Lawrence slides into a pew on Jameson's side, ten rows or so back. He's like a magnet, our attention being sucked toward him. Aiden's anger is white-hot, but he keeps ahold of himself.

Dad is still going on about Wilder, barely having paused to acknowledge his rival. He finishes, and our family rustles.

"Let us pray," the priest calls, motioning for us to bow our heads.

I'm not exposing the back of my neck with a West in the room. Like he might whip out a machete and cut off my head here and now. But across the aisle, Amelie doesn't seem to have any trouble. Maybe she didn't pick up on the tension or doesn't know Lawrence West's face.

Oh, how I wish I were away from this.

I can't wrap my head around what I'm supposed to do. I'm Aiden's second—and now *only* brother. What was once an empty title of third son, often forgotten, now gets dragged into the light. There's no way I'll ever be free of this place.

The priest steps down the altar and gestures for Dad to come forward. We stand, too, and meet him in front of the table with the urn and flowers. The man motions for someone to take the urn, and we all pause when Amelie steps forward. She lifts it in her arms, cradling the ceramic to her chest. She doesn't look at any of us.

The priest's altar boys stream past us and stop, waiting to frame us in like white-robed guards. Aiden takes some flowers. Dad picks up the portrait. And I follow behind, empty-handed.

We pass Lawrence West, whose gaze leaps from Amelie to Dad to Aiden, then pauses on me. I keep my face blank, hopefully. Amelie's parents are teary-eyed across the aisle. More cousins. Cat and her brothers. Familiar faces. New faces.

We'll all get to know each other tonight.

The smell of incense sticks in my nose long after we exit the church. We don't wait, climbing into the cars that will take us to the mausoleum. Dark clouds blot out the sky, threatening rain. What began as a beautiful day seems to have taken a turn for the worse.

Aiden and I slide into one car. Dad and Amelie in the other.

"That was fucking bleak," Aiden says.

The driver grunts his agreement.

"Why was Lawrence there?" I shake my head. "It doesn't make sense."

"Why not? Any opportunity to throw something in our faces. And all he had to do was walk in a bit late." My brother grimaces. "The sooner this day is over, the better."

"Agreed," I murmur.

It takes a while to get to the mausoleum. We wait for people to get into their cars and line up behind us, and then, finally, we move.

The cemetery is big and sprawling—a marked difference from the one in Sanremo where my mother is buried. Sharp sadness cuts through me that I'll never see her grave again.

It's never because of my father, because of Amelie, because they'll kill us when they figure out how they were tricked. A slight against the Costas won't be forgiven. Not when she used a dead man as a bartering tool.

I'm ashamed. I shouldn't have let her do it. I should've been able to protect her more. What Matteo did… he deserved to die.

I just keep failing.

"Luca." Aiden drags me out of my spiral. "We're here."

I grimace. "Right."

We climb out of the car, and I follow Amelie and Dad. Aiden sticks behind, maybe waiting for someone. I don't linger.

Dad puts his hand on the small of Amelie's back, guiding her up the marble steps. This mausoleum is a giant stone structure, something straight from Europe. It has wide, carved marble pillars guarding the entrance. The dark oak doors are at least twelve feet tall, adorned with swirling decorations.

They're propped open now, admitting us inside.

It's much lighter than I expect, with a cool breeze running through from another open door. Skylights dot the ceiling, and lamps are mounted on the wall around the octagonal-shaped room.

Every side is taken up with marble slabs cut into rectangles of varying shapes. Some are occupied and marked. Others empty.

Amelie has set down the urn, and the priest unfolds the easel for my father to set down the portrait. Cat approaches with the flowers Aiden had carried out.

"I'm going to see my parents," Amelie whispers to Dad.

He doesn't even blink, lost in thought. Or, perhaps, distracted by Lawrence's arrival. He's here now, in the back of the room. His cold gaze travels around, creating a little bubble of free space around him. I pivot to warn Amelie not to get too close, but she's already gone.

"Luca," Dad snaps. "For the love of God, do not do anything stupid."

The priest coughs and tugs at his collar.

Dad, to his credit, turns red. "Sorry, Father."

"Quite all right," he murmurs. "Trying times for all of us. If you boys need anyone to talk to, my door is always open."

"Thanks." Aiden appears beside me. His voice is laced with sarcasm.

The priest misses it—or chooses to ignore it—and beams.

"Where is Amelie?" I ask, craning around. I catch sight of her in the back, speaking to one of my cousins. I have to blink a few times before I realize it's my tenant, Rosalie. The fact that she would leave the house is touching. But she must've recognized Amelie from before...

"Leave her," Dad says. "She'll be allowed to fade out of the spotlight."

Unlike you. I can hear his thought ricochet around my head.

The priest makes it short, just saying a few more words before blessing his burial spot. Their team will be by later to crack open his space, no bigger than a drawer, and seal him in. I shudder at the thought.

We file outside, and I glance around for Amelie again.

I can't help it.

Her back is to me, and this time she's with her parents. Her veil is off, dangling from her fingertips. I can only imagine what questions they have for her. The tales she might be telling.

But she's coming back with us. Back to the tower, to her room.

"Luca," someone calls.

I'm waylaid by Cat.

"I'm worried," she says.

"About?"

"You. Amelie."

My annoyance flares, and I brush her off. "Don't, Cat."

"You can't just keep her locked up forever, Luca. That isn't right."

I *know* it's not right. It's eating me up inside. But losing her would be worse, and nothing ties her to me anymore. She's free-floating, adrift, and I can only physically stop her from leaving me.

It's desperate.

Wild.

I can't control myself around her.

And now she won't even look at me—but that's about to change. "Leave me alone, Cat," I toss over my shoulder. "This is between us. I didn't tell you about her just so you could judge me."

"You told me so I would keep an eye out for her," she argues, following close behind me. "And I *am*. She cries every day. Bet your cameras don't pick that up, do they? Her sobs and pleading for me to release her?" She yanks me around. "The only reason I don't is some fucked-up loyalty to you, but I can't do it anymore."

I stare at her. "What are you talking about?"

She glares. "Which part, asshole?"

"The sobbing."

I shake my head. Her desperate attempt to get out almost killed me—but it was in her best interests to keep her there. In my best interests, too.

"You're an idiot." She slams her hand into my chest, and the unexpected force knocks me back a few steps. "Such a fucking dumbass. How about you go talk to her, huh? Instead of the shitty, controlling way you've been treating her for the past two weeks."

I shake my head. It doesn't dislodge her words, though. It makes them stick worse.

I ignore my newfound dread and spin around, trying to find Amelie again. There are so many fucking people crowding me, trying to get in a word. Is this how Wilder felt at family functions? Everyone wanting his ear? His promises?

I shoulder through them and come face-to-face with Amelie's parents.

"Where is Amelie?" I demand.

Michael raises his eyebrow. "You're asking *me*?"

"We should be trying to get answers from you," Elise adds, bolstered by her husband's anger. Her words are worried, though. "Honestly. We haven't heard from Amelie in two weeks. We might not be the best parents in the world, but she's always checked in—"

"I—" I narrow my eyes. "She was just talking to you."

They exchange a glance.

"What?" I demand.

Michael frowns. "We haven't spoken with her. We were talking to a lovely young woman, but not our daughter."

I glance around, rising on my tiptoes to try to see over the taller bodies. There are a few blondes, but none like Amelie.

"You didn't see her," I repeat.

"Well, we saw her at the chapel." Elise purses her lips. "You were right next to her."

I have to swallow a few times so I don't cuss. I mean, the f-word would be the least of our concerns if Amelie is missing. But I could've *sworn* it was her. She wore nearly the same thing...

"Fuck," I let loose. "She planned this."

Her mother rears back. "Planned *what*?"

"To escape." I leave them standing there and race back to one of the cars. I have no idea where she's going, but I need to make sure. I can only imagine she'll board her parents' jet. Her pilot wouldn't question it, not really.

So I have to beat her there.

CHAPTER 25

Amelie

TWO HOURS EARLIER

I shake out my arms, nervous as hell. There's a little voice in my head that's telling me this will all be for nothing—I don't have a chance. My contact will fail, and I'll go to the funeral and then be shuffled right back into this room.

No one has been in here in two weeks.

I haven't touched another person in *two weeks*.

My heart cracks at that. Cat's been a lovely jailer, but she had her orders. Did she ever try to release me? Fight for me with Luca? I'm not counting on it. Even if she had, it clearly fell on deaf ears.

I test out my voice in the bathroom, and it comes out scratchy. Figures, since most of my nights have been wrapped in nightmares. And the times I didn't wake up screaming, I usually wore my voice out trying to get someone to let me out.

It would be easier to just... go with it. To stay in this room until something happens. But that would be like allowing Luca to grind my face into the dirt. It's humiliating enough as it is, dealing with Cat. I've worn the same clothes for two weeks, washed them in the sink every other day, tried to preserve the fabric. I loved that outfit. I felt fierce in it.

Look, now. It's my prison uniform.

My heart beats faster at the idea of escape.

If I don't do this, I'll lose myself. I just know it.

"See how stupid you are, Amelie?" I ask my reflection, pinching my cheeks. "You think a bird with broken wings can still fly."

My phone goes off just before Aiden collects me from my room, and reality pushes in. This is my *one* chance. The image of Luca's foot pressing my cheek into the floor resurfaces, and I shudder.

My resolve comes in waves, but my anger toward him is constant.

The text tells me to find a reason to go outside during the service, all the way outside, even if it's only for a moment. I don't know why I trust the person on the other side, but I do. I can't afford not to. I need to be an actress for today. I need to convince the DeSantises that I'm sad but not broken.

I have to be glued to Jameson's side for the duration of the day. And if not him, Luca or Aiden. Possibly both.

I hold my palm to my chest in the elevator, trying to regulate my breathing. It's weird, I can almost feel the scrape of my soul against my heart. The pain of it.

"You okay?" Aiden asks me.

I don't respond. I need to pull the pieces Luca shattered back together, and I can't speak without my voice shaking. I can blame that on the day. On what I'm about to do.

Escape.

Leaving the room has kicked up some other emotions. Worse, still, because they don't fit into the narrative. My whole body thrums with the desire to run, and quieting my adrenaline is the hardest part. It's a drum beat that moves me, forces me forward.

"Amelie." Aiden touches my arm.

I jerk away from him. "Do not touch me." It's reminiscent

of when he tried to take my keys, and I freaked out on him. "I'm not okay. Why would you ask me that?"

He nods slowly, and he hits the emergency stop button. The elevator halts, and the regular lights flip over to dimmer ones. I squeak, moving as far away from him as possible.

"You're very clearly not okay," he says, leaning against the far wall. He crosses his arms. "Dad will want to talk to you. To ensure you know your role."

"My role," I repeat.

"Grieving widow. It's overwhelming, I'm sure, to be the center of attention. All of us will be watching you."

I *am* overwhelmed. And uncomfortable.

I lack sadness, or empathy, or pity.

Wilder died, and that's been the least of my concerns.

"The veil makes you look badass, though," he says, then hits the button to restart the elevator. "Don't tell anyone I said that."

I grit my teeth. "Don't worry, I don't plan on speaking more than I have to."

We ride in the SUV in silence, with no sign of his brother or father. We're in a caravan of black cars, though. They could be in any of them.

They plant me beside Jameson on the steps of the chapel. My skin crawls. Luca is *right there*, and I've never wanted to stab someone so badly. Does he see what his imprisonment did to me? It's driving me mad. But I refuse to look at him. Any of them.

The procession begins. It's in place of a wake, I realize. They don't want to draw out the mourning, and now it's time for my acting to begin. I paste on a small frown, befitting a widow. The veil helps hide the fakeness, although it seems like I'm a beacon for everyone. The one under the microscope.

Did she love him?

Poor girl, barely a bride before he died.

I heard they married in secret and consummated it before their ceremony.

People are not subtle.

The funeral passes in a blur. A few people read, they talk about death. I'm going to explode, so I stand and cover my mouth, hurrying for the side exit. The man at the door lets me pass, and I burst outside. I suck in large gulps of air and eye the parking lot.

Nothing stands out.

I spin in a slow circle, trying to regain control of myself.

My first day outside in two weeks, and I still feel shackled. I should be hopeful, right? Cautiously optimistic?

Hope is the thing Luca used to break me. To shut me away.

Hope and I aren't on speaking terms.

I return inside, sliding back into my seat just as Jameson goes to speak. The whole room's atmosphere changes slightly, and I wonder if this is part of the distraction. If someone will extract me now.

I don't turn around.

And then it's over, and I'm still here. I'm still beside Jameson as he puts me in the car and closes us in, and I can hardly breathe because of the space he takes up. If anyone will see through my plan, it's him. I'm almost positive he's going to question me, to blame me.

But we ride in silence, and, damn it, a nervous sort of light blooms in my chest. I wouldn't call it hope, but... this has to happen here. Here, or I go back to the DeSantis tower and maybe I'll never see the light of day again.

I try not to tremble when Jameson steers me into the mausoleum. I grip the smooth ceramic urn that contains Wilder's remains, my palms sweaty. This building is better suited for giants than the likes of us. Whoever built it intended to awe its visitors. The sky is already gloomy, threatening to rain—perfectly fitting for today—but it just adds to the structure's imposing nature.

We walk into the belly of the beast.

The priest appears, and I set down Wilder. Odd to think of him like that, reduced to *literal* ashes. It's how I pictured Luca breaking me down, but there's something comforting about Wilder like this. He can be filed away in the back of my mind. Not a loose end, not my husband, just... ash.

I press my lips together and imagine how I must seem now. Staring down at the man who would've been my husband. My future derailed rather quickly, and it's been downhill since then.

Except the boat.

Loathing fills me. My own mind is working against me now? I squash down everything that happened in Sanremo. The truth is, I could've lived with what happened in Italy. It's Luca's betrayal that came after that hurts the most.

For the briefest of moments, I'm jealous of Ricardo and the knife in his gut. He has a physical reason for that agony, while me... I'm rotting away with no visible signs. I could carry on like this for a while, until I'm just a dead girl walking. No one would miss me when I die.

The pain of it hits me.

I thought *Luca* would miss me. I thought he was on my side.

The fact that I trusted that, trusted *him*, and I turned out to be wrong? That might be the worst part.

I refuse to glance at Luca, even though he's very clearly eyeing me. His gaze burns my skin, and I can't imagine what he sees.

People file in, and my phone buzzes against my hip. I can't check it, so I guess what it says: get away from Jameson and Luca. I murmured an excuse about finding my parents, then dive headfirst into the crowd. It's thick with their relatives at this point, and they all seem to want to touch me. *Again*. They didn't get a good enough look at me at the wedding three weeks ago, apparently.

And they won't get a good look at me now.

Everyone loves a tragedy, and what's more tragic than young love struck down too soon?

I shake my head, acting to be more upset than I am, and make it to the far door. I successfully avoid my parents, who stand in the center of the room with some people I recognize from the tower. Concern is etched across their features, and I almost pause. Almost go to them.

I stop myself.

They didn't come to my rescue. They put me in this position to advance themselves. For protection. I was their sacrifice long before I was Luca's caged bird.

The only other exit is on the opposite side of the mausoleum, around a corner. I pass a small alcove, headed for that exit, and someone grabs me. I let out a sharp squeak before they release me, and I come face-to-face with my savior.

My double—Gemma West.

She grins at me. She got my dress nearly identical, somehow. Her feet are bare, toenails painted deep red. "You okay?"

I nod, exhaling, and that damn hope inflates me without warning. She's here. We're doing this. The swell in my chest is almost unbearable, like I inhaled too deeply. My chest hurts, but in a good way.

"Sorry." I realize I'm staring. "I just didn't think this would happen."

She nods, but she doesn't do anything drastic, like try to hug me. "I need your veil. And shoes."

I kick off the heels, and she helps me unclip the veil. She holds it for a moment, arranging her hair like mine. She quickly nails down the finer details—the rest, the broad strokes, she managed to get just right before she even saw me.

"How?"

"Luca's not original when it comes to dresses," she murmurs. "We've been keeping an eye on everything since Wilder..."

I nod once. "Say no more."

She turns me around and pulls my hair loose from its coil, shaking it out over my shoulders. Her fingers against my scalp are soothing, and I close my eyes for a moment. Human contact at its finest. A lump forms in my throat.

Why is it that my supposed enemy is the first one to show me a kindness?

Now is not the time to lower my guard. Not with Luca just around the corner.

"I hate pins, don't you?" She flips my hair over my shoulders.

I face her again, and her eyes go wide. She runs her thumb along the scar, cupping the side of my face. The gesture is, again, unexpectedly kind. I swallow, even though my throat feels closed, and will my eyes to stop burning.

"You have to survive this," she says firmly.

"I will."

She smiles and retreats, taking a denim jacket off the armchair beside her. She holds it out for me to put on, and it feels weirdly like another layer of protection. She gives me a pair of sandals and slides my heels on, then gives me a once-over.

"How do I look?" Gemma splays out her hands, doing a small twirl. With the veil, her hair, the dress, and shoes... We aren't identical, of course. She's an inch or two shorter than me. Her hair is a shade closer to wheat than honey. Under the veil, I can barely tell that her face is more angular. That her eyes are hazel instead of blue.

If anyone gets close enough to see her eye color, we're all screwed, anyway.

"Perfect." My chest is tight. Too tight, really. I struggle to inhale as the reality of the moment hits me. This is it—she's the distraction, and I've got to run. Now or never.

She grips my hand. "This is the fun part, Amelie."

I tilt my head, confused.

"You get to *fly*." She presses a piece of paper into my hand, then throws her shoulders back. She stares at me for a moment, her dark-green-brown eyes burning into me. And then it hits me that she's analyzing my expression, and she mimics it. The purse of my lips, the set of my brow. Small details that will trip up anyone who has an idea of me in their head. The veil helps, too.

"Go," she urges.

I always thought I'd pick fight, not flight. It was how I operated in high school. I seized opportunities, crushed girls who didn't have a backbone. I played my fellow students and turned vicious when I didn't get my way. I was a mean girl.

But this opportunity is flight, and I seize it.

I step outside and tip my head back. The air is cool, and I take a deep breath. It smells like rain. Looks like it, too, judging from the dark clouds. I quickly reel myself back in. Anyone could see me and shout an alarm.

There's someone leaning against a blue car, and I have to squint to make sure I'm seeing correctly.

Kai West.

Of course Gemma managed to rope in her cousin. I'm more surprised that her brother isn't here—but then again, I know Kai. I don't think I'd be as willing to get into a car with the other one. Colin.

I walk across the grass and pause in front of him.

"Hey," he greets me. "Welcome to your great escape."

I glance behind me at the silent mausoleum. We're well away from where the DeSantis clan parked, but nerves still race up and down my spine. "We're not gone yet."

He nods and opens the back door for me. I slide in, huddling deeper into the denim jacket, and then we're slowly pulling out. I count my heartbeats pounding against my ribs. We pass the row of DeSantis SUVs, the few guards out front. Kai lifts his hand and waves at them, and they respond in kind. I busy myself by staring in the opposite direction.

It's almost *easy* how quickly we get out.

Don't fall apart yet, Ames. I still need to enact the rest of my plan. I focus on all the times I *wanted* to fall apart growing up, and somehow muscled through. Fights with my parents. Grappling with my future. Lucy being torn away. That old strength is a muscle I haven't used in a while, and I call upon it now.

"Where do you want to go?"

"My parents' house," I say immediately.

He frowns. "You wasted our help on *this*? Going—"

"No," I say quietly. "I just can't leave without my passport."

It occurred to me while I was stuck in that room that we didn't go through customs—not when we arrived at the private airport outside of Sanremo and not back in New York. I'm not sure what kind of strings the DeSantises had to pull to make that happen, or why they would even want to.

But I'll definitely need my passport now, and I can guess exactly where it is.

He goes silent, and I stare out the window. I'm strung up tighter than a mouse trap, ready to explode at the slightest sign of danger. We arrive in Rose Hill quickly, and he coasts to a stop in front of my childhood home.

It's déjà vu. Like I might've fallen asleep in the car, and now I'm in the nightmare version of my life. Or maybe I'm still in the room in the tower, destined to beat my fists against the door.

"Stay here," I say. "I'll be back in two minutes."

He sighs but doesn't stop me. I rush in and straight to Dad's study, to the safe behind a painting. It's a bit cliche, but he takes his role in the Mafia life seriously. Apparently. The combination is a mash of their anniversary and my birthday, and it beeps at me before swinging open.

Memories choke me. Sitting in here while he checked over my schoolwork, having 'the talk' about Wilder, marriage, expectations. Something Mom should've been telling me, but instead Dad took the lead. Every conversation seemed clinical, guiding me to an expected outcome.

Marriage to Wilder, being able to survive as a Mafia wife, becoming a mother.

Our passports are on the top shelf. I flip through them and stuff mine into my purse, then pause. If I take anything else, I'm guaranteeing my parents will look for me. If I don't... they might just think I've been magicked away by Luca again. And that will buy me time, because no doubt Luca won't be forthcoming about my escape.

He can't admit failure, not when their deal hinges on our safety.

I'm just assuming that extends to me.

So I ignore the cash, the stacks of paper documents, anything else that could catch my interest, and slam the door shut. I replace the painting and go upstairs, then skid to a stop. The bag I had packed—the one that's supposed to still be in my car, parking on Luca's street—leans against the closet.

I kneel, hardly breathing as I go through it. Everything is still in here, like my parents couldn't decide what to do with it... so they did nothing.

My last stop is the cash. The gift cards. I rip it from under my bed and scramble out, shoving it into my bag.

Before I leave, I pivot and stare at the house. At everything it held for me. My parents. Lucy.

The house stands for *nothing* good.

I go back upstairs and duck into my parents' bathroom, which is above the front living room. I plug the tub and the little hole that's supposed to prevent overflow, then start the water. I do the same in the sink, turning the faucet to full blast. I repeat that in my bathroom and stand back, watching until the sink overflows. It doesn't take much time. Water pours over the edge, running in streams down the cabinet. It pools on the floor, soaking the bath mat.

It's the least this house deserves.

I lock the door behind me, wishing it the worst.

Kai shifts when I slide into the passenger seat. I keep my backpack between my legs and click the seat belt into place, then raise my eyebrows at him.

"Where are we going?" he asks.

My cheeks get hot. "Oh, right. Newark Airport."

He stares at me.

"What?" I snap.

"You? On a commercial flight? I can't picture you navigating a busy airport—have you done this before? Wait. Did your parents' jet have to land there?"

I roll my eyes. "I'm not an idiot, Kai. They'll expect me to stay in New York, at the very least. Newark is close, but it's New Jersey. Totally different jurisdiction. And my parents' pilot... he doesn't take orders from me. He'd probably rat me out. And at the very least, he'd need to file his flight plans. That's more trackable than disappearing on a commercial flight."

"That's true," he allows.

I don't doubt the DeSantis reach—but they'd need a federal agent on their payroll to get my name. And I have the added benefit of paying cash, forgoing the usual means of tracking someone. It seems like everything has lined itself up correctly.

I can't fail. I can't go back. But a large part of my system is still in shock. I can't really process my escape until I've reached my final destination. Until I'm safe.

Safe—that's a concept I don't think truly exists. No, I'm going to be as safe as I can be, and then I'll carve out another path for myself. A bolder Amelie.

I have about five thousand dollars to my name—enough, for now.

It has to be enough.

CHAPTER 26
Luca

I *have to find her.* The thought spurs me out of the mausoleum. I can get in one of the cars and be at the airport in thirty minutes. Twenty if I speed. The need to find her sinks its claws into my throat.

Dad catches my arm and shoves me against the pillar before I even make it to the stairs. I fight him for a second, until he slams me harder. My head cracks on the marble, and I force myself to stop resisting him. A bump on the back of my head is the least of my worries if he chased me out here.

"Just what the fuck do you think you're doing?" He leans in close, eyes narrow.

Yep, he's pissed.

"Amelie left," I say. "She can't—"

"Get it together, Luca. Your whole family is watching you. Seeing how you react to this. Looking for *weaknesses*. I don't really give a shit about what Amelie does, because from here on out, she's not a DeSantis."

I blink and try to make sense of that.

He shakes his head and sneers. "What, you think they're all sympathetic? They're vultures. They want what we have—

they think they *deserve* what we have because we share blood with them. They're wrong."

"Dad." I stare out at the cars. They're so close, but I've never felt more stuck. "I need to go find her."

"You need to put your family first," he says. "What about Aiden? When they come for him because they think he doesn't have his brother's support? There's blood in the water, son, and we're closing ranks to protect ourselves. They'll just as soon kill Aiden if they see any hint of weakness."

I blow out a breath. The glint in his eye is dangerous—it's a warning to back off. And how could I not? I've seen how he reacts to our enemies. To plausible threats. He's merciless—that's how he got here. And he must've had people who supported him.

His brothers and sister.

That's why he's standing here today, in control of this family. He fought for it. He wanted it. But he had help along the way. And Aiden... Aiden doesn't have anyone else left except for me.

The guilt takes the wind out of my sails.

I wince. "Sorry."

He releases me. "It's a tough day, which means it's even more important to stay vigilant. We get through the weekend, and we'll reassess. Got it?"

I nod. Reassessing sounds like a joke, but it's the only thing I have right now. So I grit my teeth and do the unbearable. I go back inside, knowing Amelie has just slipped through my fingers.

CHAPTER 27
Amelie

My phone vibrates, and I lift my eye mask to read the message.

I'll be in touch to collect my favor.

A massive one, I would think. I type back that I understand and slip the phone into my pocket. Now that I'm awake, I sit up straight and try to stretch the best I can in my seat. I slide my window shade up and take in the dark sky. Faint traces of pink and gold are creeping up from the horizon, heralding the sun.

We'll be landing soon, I suspect. Sleep still tugs at me, so I lean back and close my eyes again. I leave the mask up, though, because when the sun hits my face, I want to feel it.

It's been ten hours since I left New York. Ten hours passed in the blink of an eye, and I can't help the smile that creeps across my face.

I did it. Partially, anyway. I'm not there yet. I haven't gone through customs, I haven't secured a place to sleep tonight. I hate to admit it, but Kai was right: I hadn't flown on a commercial plane before. I never had to check a bag—I still didn't, but that's beside the point. Going through security and customs, waiting for my group number to be called to board, was a brand-new experience.

If I wasn't constantly looking over my shoulder, I might've enjoyed it more.

My money didn't stretch far. As it turns out, it's *expensive* to fly spur of the moment. It's now early morning, and it reminds me of landing in the private airport outside of Sanremo with Luca.

I was so fucking naive. About absolutely everything.

Somehow, I managed to grow up thinking bad men were above me. That they wouldn't stoop to mess with *me* when they had bigger fish to fry. But that's not right. They will because they can. Because I was beautiful.

But they won't now. I've taken my beauty and turned it into something fierce. It keeps me warm in the center of my chest. I've never felt lighter than I do right now.

Gemma told me to fly, and I've come untethered. The plan that was slow to come to me has clicked into place, driven by that wild fierceness in my heart. It leads me forward, as if the path is a string and I'm at the end of it, being reeled in.

"You okay?" the man beside me asks. "You're crying."

I open my eyes and touch my cheeks. "Oh."

"You all right?" he repeats.

He's got an accent I haven't heard in real life before. A brogue, maybe Scottish.

"Yes." I wipe away the liquid and rub it between my fingers. Tears of happiness, maybe? I left my old life, but it still drags behind me.

His gaze flicks to the scar above my eye, the hollows of my cheeks. There are dark circles under my eyes, too. I'm sure I look like a train wreck.

He nods once. "You seem like a survivor."

I am, I almost say, but my stomach flips at accepting that sort of honor. True survivors are so much braver than me.

Stronger. So I say, "I don't think of it that way. I barely made it out, and I'm..." *Broken*. Can't finish that thought, either. I've got jagged edges and scars aplenty.

Lucy and I used to joke about people who lost their marbles. We'd scatter our colorful marbles across the floor and wonder what it would be like to go crazy.

I fear I'm there.

He taps my arm. "But you're alive. Right? Breathing and kicking. And now you're on a plane, all by yourself, and I don't know a lot of young women who would do that. Perhaps that's daft of me, but I would disagree with your assessment. You seem like you've survived a whole lot, and you're better for it."

My eyes burn, and I look away. The sun is just now creeping up. It's this small ball of red-orange, blazing a path through the sky.

"Thank you," I say quietly.

"Any time. I will admit, I get a bit protective when I see a young lass traveling by herself. It's because you remind me of my daughter." He gestures to his forehead, where my scar is. "She was in a car wreck. Her scars don't define her, and I get the sense yours don't, either."

My smile wobbles. I need to pull myself together. "They don't. I'm hoping not, anyway. I'm Amelie, by the way."

He shakes my hand. "Gordain McRae. You ever find yourself in Scotland, come look us up."

"I appreciate that."

Soon after, the captain makes an announcement that we're starting our descent. I press my nose to the glass. I keep my eyes fixed on the scenery, relishing the view. I can't remember the last time I sat back and enjoyed it like this, and something loosens in my chest.

There's a bump and sudden rush as we land. I sit back, tearing the forgotten eye mask from my forehead and stuffing it in my bag. It has the airline's logo on it in the corner, a promotional item for those traveling overnight. Besides a long layover in Dublin, the flights have been smooth.

I wonder what sort of favor Gemma West will ask of me, and when. I didn't put any restrictions on it, mainly out of fear. She could've just said no to my request for help and hung up. I was desperate. But with time comes clarity, and I can't help but contemplate the gravity of owing a West anything at all.

I shiver.

The plane parks at the terminal. I stand along with everyone else, happy to stretch my legs. My row buddy hands me my bag from the compartment over our heads, and we slowly file out. From there, it's relatively quick through customs, our passports stamped, and then... I'm out.

The steady flow of French conversations around me is immediately soothing. We never flew into the Nice airport—there's a smaller one closer to our summer house—but it was the closest international arrival I could find. I follow the signs to the taxis, my backpack and purse my only possessions.

I'm weightless.

I find the taxi stand, and when it's my turn, I ask a driver if he'll take me into Italy. The first shakes his head. So does the second, inching forward until I'm out of view.

"Mademoiselle?"

I duck down to peer in the window of the third taxi.

"Where do you want to go?" he asks in French.

I tell him, and he pauses. Considers me. I don't break my stare, and he names a price. It's a little high, but I'm asking him to drive just over hour, and he'll be out the money if he doesn't catch a fare on the way back.

I exchanged half my money for euros at my layover in Dublin, and I discretely count it out in the backseat as we set off. Luckily, the driver doesn't try to make any small talk. We hit the highway headed for Sanremo. I've always enjoyed the ride—although it's about a half hour longer than it would be from my parents' house. The highway cuts through the mountains—both over tall bridges and into round-topped tunnels that engulf us in darkness—and then eventually spits us out near the ocean.

"Wait," I call. "Can you turn off here for a moment?"

He meets my gaze in the mirror. "Here?"

I sigh. "I'll pay you extra. Please."

He nods and follows the instructions I deliver in bad, broken French. We stop in front of my parents' house, and I climb out. I tell him I'll only be gone a moment.

I can't even say why I have a desire to come here. It doesn't look none the worse for wear, considering I sent the Costas here on a witch hunt. I pull my keys from my purse and find the one for the front door. The deadbolt slides back with a dull, satisfying *thud*, and then I'm in.

It seems… the same. Untouched.

The furniture is covered with white fabric to protect it from the dust. It's been thoroughly boarded up since the last time they were here. They came without me, I think, in the fall. I couldn't go because of dress fittings, a doctor's appointment, and Mom placed some of the engagement party decision-making on my shoulders.

"You're going to be a wife," she'd said back then, before they'd left. "It's time you learn how to put together a party. To follow through. And maybe think about taking a little responsibility for your life."

Her words hurt. I rub my chest now, walking through the downstairs. I didn't think the Costas would go through and destroy anything just for the sake of it, but I wasn't positive.

"I took responsibility," I mutter to myself. The engagement party was fine, not particularly exciting at the DeSantis estate, but a beautiful evening out. I pause in the kitchen, tilting my head. The people my parents pay to close up the house always used to put the chairs up on the dining table, but they're all down and tucked in.

There's a cup in the sink, tipped upside down.

I sit heavily in one of the chairs. Wilder and I sat here on my sixteenth birthday. He and his father filled the space. Aiden and Luca, too, but they had left us alone. We were uncomfortable. I was, anyway. Sixteen and destined to get married to a stranger. No matter how beautiful, I couldn't seem to justify it in my head.

My brain feels like it's playing a record and keeps skipping forward, missing blips of the conversation. I can't recall what we talked about. He smiled a few times, trying to be less intimidating, maybe? Turning on his charm.

I wonder how long he knew about this.

All of a sudden, I stand and grab my chair, throwing it across the kitchen. It skids and falls on its side, then hits the cabinets. The noise is impressive, but it doesn't satisfy me. The anger in my chest hurts, burns worse than flames. I scream into my hands.

Broken little thing. That's what they'll say about me.

I don't go upstairs. I would rather not see my old room. There's a picture of Wilder on my dresser, and I remember staring at it, trying to convince myself I could love him someday.

I hope my parents' house flooded while they were gone. That the bathroom floors upstairs gave way, crashing water down into the living room, the kitchen. That they always smell a bit of dampness.

"Had enough of a tantrum, Amelie?" I ask myself. The bitterness is full force at myself. "Jesus. Grow up."

I right the chair, slamming it back into place at the table. The cup can stay—maybe my parents will question *their* sanity. And then I sigh, trying to release some of my anger. It comes on too quickly, and I could point fingers... or I can close my eyes and breathe.

After a few moments, my heart rate slows. I don't feel guilty leaving this space. So with one last shudder, I leave. I lock the door behind me and don't look back. I can't.

Thankfully, the taxi is still waiting for me.

"Sorry," I apologize. "I'm ready."

He sighs, and off we go. I lean forward as we go through the final tunnel twenty minutes later, and the landscape opens up. A smile creeps across my face. It was a whirlwind trip with *him*, but I've got nothing but time now. The Costas will ensure Luca doesn't follow me, as long as I can remain off their radar.

Safely, with any luck.

"Here's good." The street is quiet, and I pay him before slipping out and into the garage. It's unlocked, thankfully, and quiet. I hurry upstairs, bypassing the first floor. I'm not ready to face it, with memories lurking just out of reach. In the bedroom, my bags are just where I left them.

No doubt someone would've sent them back eventually, but it couldn't have been a priority. Not with Ricardo's stab wound, and the restaurant, and whatever unrest we left with the Costas. I sit on the bed and grab my phone off the charger.

There are a million notifications that I quickly scroll through, then swipe them away. Most came to my other phone through WiFi, but there are a few messages that didn't. I go to those, first, and click on my sister's name.

Lucy: *WTF AMELIE? WHERE ARE YOU?*

I consider calling her, but I can't pull her into this. Not now.

A lot of the other texts are from old classmates from Emery-Rose Elite that saw my picture in the paper. My engagement photo with Wilder that was used to announce his death. Some are shocked. Others want to know why I didn't say anything. Of course I didn't tell anyone—I'm not sure why everyone is acting so surprised. Or sympathetic.

They're the ones who forgot about me after high school. They went on to their fancy colleges, moved into the city or away entirely. My so-called friends just... left me.

I set down my phone and stare around the bedroom. We didn't come up here together, except to pass each other for the shower, so it's relatively safe.

But unfortunately, I can't hide up here forever.

I go downstairs and pause on the last step. It's easy to remember how he looked walking in with fresh bruises, the immediate concern that coursed through me. The way his eyes bored into mine when I stood between his legs.

I hold on to the railing and squeeze my eyes shut so I don't catch the other details.

There is where he ate me out, and *there* on the floor is where he fucked me, and *there* is where I blew him, cooked him breakfast, worried over the word 'wife'.

I grit my teeth and open my eyes, forcing myself to see it all. Everything from the open living and dining area, to the kitchen, to the sliding doors that lead onto the patio. *Here* is where I find my courage, and *here* is where I will find myself. In this spot. In this house.

Piece by piece.

I am encroaching on Luca's space, and I hate that it's so very clearly his. But unlike my parents' house, or the summer home across the border, or Luca's Brooklyn apartment, I like this space. My stomach knots thinking about the what-ifs.

What-ifs, much like hope, can seriously bring a person down. Because if only we had stayed here, none of the ugly bad things would've happened. The Costas would still be pissed at Wilder, and Luca would've still killed two of their men, but we would've walked out of that together.

Now? Not a chance.

My only option is to make this house my own—and that means learning all its secrets.

Over the next three hours, I tear the place apart. Someone as cunning as Luca must have secret hiding places all over the house, and I intend to find them all. It's bright by the time I'm ready to stop. My muscles ache, knees sore from kneeling and crouching. I hike the stairs up from the garage and call my hunt complete.

When I made my first discovery, I laid out a blanket from the couch in the center of the room, and now a pile of weapons has accrued.

"Okay, you got this."

I can't say I'm an expert—that would be laughable—but Dad and I tried to bond over firearms once. How to check if a cartridge is loaded in the chamber, how to eject the magazine. We went over cleaning and assembly, but that's long since slipped from my memory.

I wonder what Luca would do in my place. If he'd go to the Costas or keep his head down.

Stop. My mind keeps tripping over itself to get back to him, and I hate that part of me. The part that let him in, even a little bit.

The first time I tried to truly open up, he dismissed me. And when he realized we weren't married, he locked me away. He listened to my screams. He reduced me to begging. And he did *nothing*.

I touch my scar. It's grounded me in the past, and it does so now. Just another layer of armor I've added. I seem to keep piling it on, even though Luca slipped through my defenses easily before.

I pour myself a cup of coffee and sit at the edge of the blanket, then take a deep breath. The best thing for me is to have a purpose.

Step one: go through everything. Figure out which guns

go with which ammunition, if any are loaded. Fill the magazine just in case.

Step two: I need something more than coffee. The dairy products in the fridge have expired, and a girl can only live so long on the frozen waffles I found.

Which leads me to step three: decide what the hell I'm doing here.

It isn't enough to just exist. I came here for a reason. Vague as it is, I felt a connection to this city. Two of the three people who ruined my exploring are dead. One is probably wandering around with his jaw wired shut. I don't know about Cristian or Mariella, but I hope they don't expect me back. That they won't be searching for me.

The only trouble is that, by now, word had to have reached them of Wilder's death. And I'll need to suss out their level of anger.

Hmm.

I examine my fingernails. I ripped them to shreds these last few weeks with nothing better to do. My hair has lost its shine. I need sunshine and fresh air. Exercise. My body was once fit enough to flip through the air and land one-footed in a cradle of hands. And now, two weeks of captivity, my muscles ache. My abs have disappeared into soft skin stretched across my belly.

Step four: self-care. As soon as I figure out all this shit in front of me.

I cast a longing glance at the patio and sigh. Then I get to work.

CHAPTER 28
Amelie

It's dark when I finally venture outside. My anxiety climbed steadily higher and higher, and now my stomach seems to be in my throat. I slip out of the garage and immediately into the shadows. I feel a bit like a fugitive, but I make it down to the other end of the street without incident.

I sorted everything I found earlier today, including some of those canisters that I *think* emit a flash-bang, and... seriously, only Luca would be crazy enough to keep a few grenades.

I put those back where I found them.

That left me time to microwave the frozen waffles and douse them in powdered sugar and syrup, then lie in the sun. I napped on a lounge chair, my first solid sleep in weeks. When I woke up, I showered and scrubbed myself down with the soaps left over in the bathroom.

I tried not to let the fact that these were *his* scents ruin my shower, but I couldn't help it. And I hated it. I let out a ragged sob under the water, and suddenly I couldn't stop the flood of tears. The grief of what I'd suffered flowed through me, and I cried until I couldn't breathe.

It wasn't just what I went through that gutted me. It was the raw loneliness that managed to worm inside my bones. I *missed* Luca, even as I hated him. I craved his touch as much as I wanted to hit him.

The water ran cold by the time I stepped out.

My hair is now loose, wildly wavy. Makeup covers the dark circles under my eyes, but not the scar on my forehead. Never that, not again.

Before I left, I filled a magazine and slid it into the tiny black pistol. I didn't realize there were holsters meant for *inside* the waistband of your pants, really finalizing a concealed carry. It now sits safely against the small of my back, burning a hole in my skin.

I don't know if this, or the knife strapped to my forearm, will protect me. But it sure does make me feel better.

The restaurant glows from within, the light spilling out onto the street when one of the patrons leaves. Their chatter drifts toward me. It's all melodic Italian, and I close my eyes for the briefest of moments. It's hard not to picture Luca and his uncle sitting at the table, conversing in the foreign language.

I wait for what feels like ages, hidden between two houses across the street. Last time, we were only there for what felt like moments before the Costas came. And now I can't afford to be trapped again. So I crouch in the darkness, trying to remain patient.

I wonder if Luca has any idea where I am. If he's half as tormented by my absence as I was by my cage. I hope he suffers for it. I rock back on my heels and contemplate what Luca would look like when he self-destructs. Wild? Out of control? Or perhaps he'll just shut down.

My mind spins through scenarios.

Finally, my patience runs out. The street is empty, showing no signs of anyone watching from obvious places. Some houses around me are lit up, and others seem empty. I go across the street and into the restaurant.

The tables are mostly full, save for two. I'm impressed at the noise level in the room—there's conversation, but it isn't overwhelming. The bar on the left side is equally busy, only a few stools free. Antonio is behind the bar with another man—one I recognize immediately.

Paloma, I would assume, is in the back.

A tugging sensation fills my chest, urging me forward. I slide onto a stool and wait, and it's only a moment before Ricardo stops in front of me. He doesn't see me. Not really. He asks me something in quiet, quick Italian. The staccato of it is pleasant, even if I don't understand much of it.

I stare at him.

He doesn't look awful, as I dreamed. My skin remembers the warmth of his blood, the protruding knife. How pale he was, lying on the floor. I blink away those images.

No, Ricardo's cheeks are full, his body straight. I'm cautiously relieved, but I have to wonder if he hates me for what happened. Maybe that's why he won't meet my gaze—he clocked me when I came in and has decided the best course of action is to ignore.

"Ricardo," Antonio calls.

Ricardo's gaze lifts, and he locks on to me. His eyes widen, like maybe he doesn't *really* believe I'm sitting here. Last time we were both in this space together was traumatic at best, and then we just... left.

My cheeks heat.

"Ricardo," Antonio repeats, stopping beside us. He glances at me, then double takes. "Amelie?"

"In the flesh," I say weakly. I eye Ricardo. "How are you?"

"Alive, thanks to you." His voice is soft. "Is Luca—"

"Not allowed back." I shrug to cover the bite of my words. "Probably."

Being here is strange. Dreamlike. I spent too much time in this room in my nightmares, and chills now skitter down my back. I shift on the stool, antsy. I came to see them. To begin to make amends, apologize, maybe just... let them know I'm here.

The guilt I hold is another sharp edge inside my chest.

"I'll get Paloma." Antonio moves past Ricardo and to the kitchen.

"Why are you here?" Ricardo leans on the bar.

I sigh, contemplating how to answer. To tell him the truth of what his best friend did? Who's to say he'd even believe me?

While I waffle, he pours me a glass of wine.

I take a sip, and the flavor is bittersweet on my tongue. I don't like wine—never have. Clear liquor sometimes, beer. I'm not sure I like this red liquid, but it suits the mood. I take another sip. "I need to finish some things."

"Really."

"Yes, Ricardo, we left pretty suddenly, and I have unfinished business here." My annoyance reaches a sudden flashpoint. "I am allowed to operate with my own agency. Is that a problem?"

He scowls. "No."

"You didn't put up a fight when we went exploring."

His eyes darken. "And how did that turn out?"

True.

"Do you happen to know where I can find Mariella?"

"Amelie," he warns.

Oh shit. How could I forget that *she's* the one who stabbed him? What was her excuse—that he got handsy? I shift, suddenly uncomfortable. "Never mind."

I stand, ready to rush away. I can talk to Paloma later. Tomorrow, maybe, or next week...

But Ricardo grabs my wrist, pressing it to the bar. "Don't judge me, Amelie. I tried to stop her from entering the dining area after she came in through the back door. I grabbed her shoulders, and she..."

"Stabbed you," I finish. That guilt digs a bit deeper. "You're sure you're okay?"

He grins. "I'm flattered that you're worried about me. But I'm healing. I'm fine."

"Amelie." Paloma stands in the swinging door of the kitchen. There's no trace of blood under her feet, or any sign at all of something bad happening here.

I shiver.

"She stays in an apartment on the water," Ricardo says under his breath, almost too soft to hear. He releases my wrist to scribble something on a piece of paper. He shoves it at me, then turns away.

I slide it into my pocket and cross the restaurant to Paloma. I stop in front of her, suddenly shy. Our single conversation a month ago was short-lived, and internally, I brace myself for her to react as my mother would. How would Mom feel if her home was stormed by men who wanted to harm us? If a man was left bleeding in her kitchen?

She wouldn't take it well, that's for sure. And the blame would rest on my shoulders.

But Paloma just pats my cheeks with both hands, then pulls me into a hug.

After my initial surprise fades, I sink into her and return the embrace. She's warm and solid and she grips my shoulders with sureness.

And wouldn't you know it?

That's my undoing.

My eyes burn a split second before I burst into tears. I can't seem to stop all the ugliness that comes out. Because when's the last time anyone hugged me like they cared?

Certainly not my parents. Luca didn't give a shit. My sister might be my only exception, but she's so far removed from my life.

Paloma shushes in my ear, quiet noises that penetrate over my distress.

This is the cry of a desperate, lonely girl, and I can't stop.

Why is Paloma the first person to hug me in over a month? And the last person before her... Lucy, I think, after Wilder died. And the further back my memory stretches, the more I realize how cold my life has been.

It's like my parents were trying to condition me for the Mafia life in the only way they knew how: by making me unaccustomed to affection. To not expect it, and certainly not need it.

But... doesn't everyone need affection?

"Oh my god, I'm so sorry." I hiccup on my words and try to step away. "I don't—"

She doesn't let me go. Her hand comes up and cradles the back of my head, stroking my hair, until I let out a shaky exhale. She doesn't stop her quiet murmurings that I don't quite understand, even if I get the gist. Nonsense babble you might tell a crying toddler.

"I'm okay," I murmur. My cheeks are hot, and when I straighten, I quickly wipe away the wetness on my face. "Sorry."

She frowns. "Do not apologize for your emotions, Amelie. Come with me."

I cast a glance behind me, ready to die from mortification. A whole restaurant just witnessed me lose my mind.

But the place is empty, save Ricardo and Antonio.

I blink. "You... you cleared them out? For me?"

"For family? Yes." She touches my cheek, and her thumb sweeps over my scar. It reminds me of how Gemma reacted. A bit surprised, but mostly sad. "You didn't have this the last time we met."

"No, I didn't." I reach in my pocket and extract her ring. "We have a lot to talk about."

She nods once, then says something in rapid Italian. It sounds like an order. Antonio and Ricardo nod, and both leave us. The first goes to the front, and Ricardo goes into the kitchen.

I flinch when the door swings behind him.

"Sit." She picks up my wine glass from the bar and sets it in front of me. She returns a moment later with a glass of her own, sighing as she joins me. "My aching bones. I've been on my feet all day."

I nod and glance around the place again. I can't imagine working so hard for something your whole life. To feel fulfilled. It's foreign. I assumed I would settle into my role of wife, but I didn't imagine *enjoying* it.

"Please tell me what happened," Paloma says. "You've lost weight. You have a new scar. You're without Luca and you have a gun."

I jerk, then realize she might've felt it when she hugged me. Or maybe they're just used to people running around with firearms strapped to them, and she knows what a shirt looks like when it falls over it.

"I don't know where to start," I hedge.

She motions to the ring—*her* ring—on the table next to my glass. "How about you start with how you came to be married?"

I take a deep breath and nod, and then I tell her everything. From my sixteenth birthday, meeting Wilder and his brothers, to seeing them every so often, to my parents' pushing. The wedding, Wilder's death. Here I pause and take a large gulp of the wine, because up until that point, my life was guided exactly where it was supposed to go.

Her face remains impassive until I describe Luca's reaction to not actually being married. The held-up death certificate. I close my eyes and grip the edge of the table when I reach the point of Luca locking me away. More tears slip down my cheeks.

"I thought escaping would fix me," I say. "But I feel more broken than ever."

She pries my fingers from the table, clasping them in her hands.

I focus on that as I tell her how I reached out to the only person I thought might help me: the West girl, Gemma. An enemy of the DeSantises. I'd only met her once on the street, but it was enough. Like calls to like, in a way.

"You made it." Her voice is gentle. "You're okay."

I sniffle and retract a hand to wipe my nose. "I don't feel okay."

"Yes, well. Maybe you're not *okay* in the head, but you're physically okay." She raises an eyebrow. "And the scar?"

"The plane on the way home had turbulence. And then..." I don't want to tell her, but I do. "I ripped out my stitches after he locked me away. I'd never felt such terror, and I needed it to go away. To focus on *anything* else."

"Pain is a good distraction." She pats my wrist. "But let's not do that again."

I choke on a laugh. "No, I don't think I will." I sigh. "I don't know how to be okay in my head again."

She leans back and raises her glass to her lips. Once it's back on the table, she says, "That's up to you. You can forgive him or hold on to your anger. You can right the wrongs in your life or let them remain in your past. What do you want to do?"

I pull my leg up and hook my arms around it. "I want to see Mariella Costa."

She sighs. "This is a dangerous path you will walk."

"She and Wilder had something. I was supposed to have something with him, and I saw him die in front of me. What if a conversation with her gives both of us closure?"

"Tomorrow," she says. "For now, you look like you could use a hot meal."

My stomach growls, and she laughs. "See? Paloma always knows."

We rise. I pocket the ring and follow her into the kitchen. Ricardo, who is standing at the back door, nods at us. But he doesn't move from his spot.

Before I can question why he's acting as a guard, Paloma motions for me to come to the island. She puts an apron over my head, tying it at the small of my back. Then she puts me to work chopping cucumbers for a salad. She tosses and manipulates dough into a flat circle. I keep one eye on her smooth movements, the way she rolls out sauce, the flat circles of mozzarella. Basil, ricotta, lemon. My mouth waters.

She slides it into the oven and comes over to help me. Together, we assemble the salad with a lemon dressing. It takes my mind off everything, although I can really only focus on how my stomach cramps.

The pizza comes out steaming hot, smelling *amazing*. We don't go back to the table, just cut it and dig in standing around the island. Antonio joins us with water glasses for the four of us, and Ricardo steps away from the door.

"This is the best pizza I've ever eaten," I confess, catching sauce from the corner of my mouth on my finger. "I'm in awe."

Antonio grins. "The only reason I'm in shape is because this town is so damn hilly."

"In shape might be a loose description," Ricardo retorts.

We laugh, and soon the food is all gone.

"I'm sorry," I say to them. "I know it wasn't really my fault, but I just feel guilty about what happened here."

"This thing between the DeSantis boys and the Costas has been going on for years," Antonio says. "We live in this neighborhood. We see firsthand what they do to each other. It's been a long time since they've acted in such a way. *We* feel bad that it was your first experience in Sanremo."

I scowl at the table.

"Don't blame yourself," Ricardo adds. "I don't know what's going on with you and Luca—"

"There is no me and Luca," I inform him. "I came here because he can't. Or won't."

Paloma frowns. "You don't miss him?"

I do, I almost say. I missed him every damn day he kept me in that room. But I don't know how to deal with it, because it feels like I'm betraying myself. I can't love someone who uses my worst fear against me.

"No," I say. "I wish I could take it all back. Agreeing to marry him, coming here. Returning to New York. He messed up, and I can't forgive him for that."

The corners of Paloma's lips pull farther down. This is her nephew we're talking about, after all. I take the ring out of my pocket again and set it down in front of her.

"You gave this to him for me. But he was never my husband, even if we thought that while we were here. You should take it back and maybe give it to him when he finds someone he'll treat with respect." I step away from the counter. "I should go."

Ricardo follows me out the back door, up a narrow alley of stairs, and onto the street. The same way I came here, I return. I stick to the shadows, creeping along the houses. Ricardo is just as silent behind me, and I sense him stop when I reach the house. *My* house.

"Goodnight," I say over my shoulder. "And thanks."

He doesn't respond, and I lock myself in. Now that I'm alone, in the dark, my heartbeat kicks up again. I withdraw the gun and sneak through the house, checking every nook and cranny. There's no one here. I lock all the doors as I go, silently berating myself for not doing it sooner.

But once I clear the bathroom and closet, I relax.

I set the gun on the dresser, aimed for the door, and shed my clothes. I crawl into bed, utterly exhausted, and close my eyes. And I only hope I don't dream at all.

CHAPTER 29
Luca

I step off the elevator and stride down the hall. The door to Amelie's room is shut, but I doubt it's locked. It's not holding her captive anymore, so what's the point?

All day yesterday after the funeral, Aiden and I played the role of dutiful sons, haunting our father's footsteps. We've been spending time with the family that came in for the ceremony. I tried to drink, to drown out my sorrows, and I went overboard. I woke up buzzed, showing me I'm well and truly fucked.

Amelie left, and I can't even blame her.

I could say I was going to free her after the funeral, once the world knew Wilder was dead. Once we could file *our* marriage license. His death certificate is the only thing that can release her from Wilder, and then she could be mine again.

But that would be a lie.

I pause in front of her door, taking a deep breath. This might be what Cat felt like every day, two or three times a day. Unable to help Amelie. Not in a way that counted.

There's a window at the end of this hallway. It's dark out now, just one day after the funeral. It feels like a dream—or maybe a nightmare. Wilder is gone, Amelie is gone. I did my duty today, as Dad ordered, and now it's late. I've been released, and I came here.

I need to know what I did to her. To face it with my eyes open.

Finally, I force myself to move. I push the door open and step inside.

Horror goes off in my body like little bombs detonating. There's a trail of smeared blood on the walls. She took the sheets off the bed, rolling them up in the center. The comforter is on the floor with a pillow.

Did she sleep on the floor?

I ignore that thought and go closer, inspecting the nest she made. There's a charger plugged into the wall, and a pad of paper. More than half of it is missing. In the bathroom, I find different sheets soaked with dark-brown blood. I can't even fathom how... what she did to herself.

The guilt twists like a knife in my gut. *I* did this to her.

Her words from the plane, after I discovered her in the bathroom, slam into me full force.

I'm afraid of a cage. Of being shut away.

I turn and punch the wall as hard as I can. It dents under my knuckles, and the pain that reverberates up my arm does nothing to dull the storm in my chest. My actions hurt her, and I didn't even listen.

Why?

Because I was so caught up in my own anger to listen?

I shake out my hand, furious with myself. It's like I drove her away myself. I practically shoved her onto the plane.

"Luca," Aiden calls. "Cat said you... holy fuck."

I step out of the bathroom and find him staring around.

"Scale of one to ten, this is like a thirteen on the fucked-up scale," he says. "I mean, damn. I didn't know you had it in you."

I grimace. "I wanted to keep her safe."

And I completely, utterly failed.

He shakes his head. "What are you going to do?"

What is there to do? Dad ordered me to stick around until our visitors leave. He said I had to support my brother so they don't try to steal his inheritance out from under him. Family first, right?

He glares at me. "What's going through your head?"

I blow out a breath. "I don't know. Dad said I needed to stick with you to not show weakness to everyone else."

Aiden rolls his eyes. "Fuck what Dad says. You clearly don't agree."

"No," I argue. "I *do* agree, and that's why I haven't gone after her yet."

He shoves me. "You're an idiot. What was your first reaction? Before Dad jumped in."

I scowl. "I was going to find her. I figured she'd go to the airport, so I wanted to stop her."

"To..."

"Bring her back." I glare at the floor. "But that's stupid now, clearly. I just... God, she's all I can think about. I had her in here for two weeks, and I didn't once go see her. Did you know Cat said she was crying every day?"

Aiden smacks my chest again. "Your instinct is to put her first."

"Yes," I say hoarsely. I rub where he hit, wondering if Amelie stole my heart when she left.

"Above everything. Me, Dad, the rest of the family. If you had to pick, you'd choose her."

God, yes. But I didn't realize that's what I wanted until I lost her. And that makes me the biggest kind of asshole.

"You better go grovel, brother." He looks at me with sympathy. "Dad didn't marry for love, so he's clueless. He raised us with one thing in mind: the family business. My advice? Disregard everything and follow your heart. Wherever she is in the world, you have to find her and make it right. Something tells me you'd never forgive yourself otherwise."

He's right, but I can't vocalize it. I just nod, until he claps my shoulder and leaves me standing in Amelie's prison.

It makes me wonder if he would do the same: if he would pick Gemma over the family. If the family is just getting shuffled further down in both of our priorities. The merger between my family and Amelie's, my duties to Aiden and my father, the future... None of it fucking matters. My thoughts orbit around Amelie.

I will find you, I promise her.

CHAPTER 30
Amelie

There's not one piece of paper in my denim jacket—there are *two*. And all at once, I remember Gemma slipping me the note.

I scramble to unfold it, then stare down at the phone number. Butterflies erupt in my belly. It's a New York area code, but the number is different from the one I had been calling. I dial it and wait, holding my breath.

It's early here, though. Six o'clock in the morning. I woke earlier than I would've anticipated, but the sun reached the bed and bathed me in light. And now, I pull out one of the stools at the breakfast bar, waiting for someone on the other end to answer.

"Hello?" a groggy female voice answers.

I do the quick math and realize it's midnight in New York.

"Hi, um—"

"Amelie." The voice is clearer now.

"Gemma?"

"Yeah," she says.

"Why did you give me your number?" I sit up straight. "I mean, I don't mind it. I just... am confused."

"I hoped you would call and tell me you got wherever you were going all right."

"Oh." I glance around the space. "I did."

"And are you happy?"

No. The answer comes out of the recesses of my mind without hesitation. So instead of admitting that, I say, "I would like your opinion on something."

She pauses, and something shuffles around. "Hang on one sec." Running water fills in behind her breathing, and then she says, "Okay. Sorry, my brother is nosy. If he hears me talking, he'll barge in and start asking questions..."

"Ah." I swallow. "Between you and me, Wilder did some shady stuff to a family where I'm staying, and they tried to take it out on me last time."

"So you're in danger?"

"No," I hurry to say. "Well, I don't know. I just want to make things right."

She hums. "Women are more receptive to change."

"Ain't that the truth," I mutter.

She chuckles. "Okay, so I'm assuming it's a girl he screwed over... or maybe just screwed? Either way, start with her and go from there."

"That was my plan. I have her address. But I just wanted to make sure I wasn't going to get shot... in your humble opinion."

I smooth the second paper out. Ricardo's handwriting is a sharp staccato, all pointed lines and little flow. It's easy to read, although I don't know exactly where this is.

"Be prepared," she says.

I hesitate to ask the question on the tip of my tongue. It's not really anything I expect she can answer, but I woke up with this on my mind, and I haven't been able to shake it. "You spend most of your teenage life being told you have to fit a mold, and suddenly that mold is smashed to bits. Do you break with it?"

She thinks about it. "No, I don't think so. I'd like to think I'm flexible enough to form something new. Maybe my own shape entirely."

"I like that," I reply. I like the idea of deciding for myself.

"And now I have a question of my own."

"Shoot." I owe her a lot more than a question.

And a favor.

"They're still looking for Wilder's killer?"

I tilt my head. "I think so. Last I heard, Aiden was in charge of that." I think back to the menial chatter at the funeral. People who thought he wasn't doing the best job digging out information on the Wests. "They know it was one of your family."

"Know," she scoffs. "They're guessing. And we're in danger because of it."

"Are you saying everyone in your family is innocent?" That seems... unlikely. Especially given their feud.

"No," she replies. "I just don't know who did it, and it's my family that's under the gun. How are they supposed to know when I can't even figure it out? I suspect, but..."

"Don't want to ask?" I snort. "I get it. But to answer your question, I'm pretty sure Aiden is on the hunt."

She doesn't reply.

"Do you... know him?"

"Once. A long time ago." There's another short silence, then the water cuts off. "I've got to go. Good luck with the girl. I don't need to tell you not to underestimate her, do I?"

"Not at all." She might be the most dangerous of the Costa siblings.

After I make a cup of coffee and eat the last of the frozen waffles, I go upstairs to get ready. I try not to think about it like going to war. Really, I'm going to bargain for my own right to stay here. I shower quickly, then strap the knife in its sheath to my leg. It's warm out today, and I have a feeling I'll be taking off the jacket eventually. I slide the gun holster's clip onto the waistband of my light-wash jeans. It goes well with the dark color of the jacket.

I shake out my wet hair and put a hair tie on my wrist.

And then I'm ready.

My phone plots out the best route for me, and I commit it to memory before stowing my phone away. It would be just my luck to wander down the streets of Sanremo and run into someone who wanted to hurt me.

Again, rather.

This time, I'm prepared. I've steeled myself for potential violence. There's no one to rely on. No one I can ask for help. That, in itself, is a lesson in bravery.

Along the way, I explore. I stop in some shops, smiling at the store owners. I didn't bring a lot of money—in fact, my budget will be running out soon, and I need to save for food. But I smile at the people I come across.

That untethered feeling comes back, stronger now. If I just jumped, my feet might never touch earth again.

I've never *not* had money. It's the most ridiculous thing in the world. My parents always provided financial stability. And not just that—but excess, sometimes, too. I plan to stay here as long as possible, casting off the nets that wanted to anchor me to New York. And that means I should probably get a job.

Eventually, I make my way to Mariella's street. She lives in an apartment above a storefront, squashed close to two others. It's tall and narrow, befitting of the narrow street. It seems like the buildings are leaning in closer as I go. I ring her doorbell and take a step back.

My nerves are shot. The gun and knife don't make me feel any safer, and I glance over my shoulder in both directions. The street is quiet.

The door opens, and Mariella appears. She stares at me for a second, as if trying to place me, then scowls. She begins to shut the door in my face, and my stomach knots.

"Please, wait," I blurt out.

She pauses, and somehow I know she won't ask me why I'm here. To ask would be admitting curiosity, and right now only disdain fills her expression. Her curly dark hair is pinned partially back away from her face. Her skin glows against the white dress, tanner than I had assumed when we met before. She's all bronze and gold.

"I lied to you. About Wilder. And, if you'd let me, I want to explain what happened."

She lifts her chin. "I know you lied about Wilder."

"Because you didn't find him at the villa in France, or because you saw our news and know he's dead?"

She flinches slightly.

"Let me in, Mariella. I just want to talk."

Her dark eyes appraise me, then she steps aside. We climb a set of steep, narrow stairs to her apartment, and the hairs on the back of my neck stand up straight until we're on even ground, and she's not behind me anymore.

"Tea?" she offers.

I nod, following her into the kitchen. The walls are light yellow, the counters all white tile. It feels like a place she could be happy in.

"Here," she says, offering me a mug. "Let's sit."

She has a tiny dining table against the wall, two chairs that face each other. A small vase sits in the center with wildflowers in it.

"Talk," she says.

I stir milk and honey into the tea, sucking my lower lip between my teeth. I contemplate my words, then say, "Wilder and I were arranged to be married. For the past three years, I lived knowing I was going to marry a stranger. I only had hope that I could love him eventually."

She inclines her chin. "That's what you meant when you said he hurt you? Because you were arranged to be married? That's a load of shit, Amelie. You can marry someone and be happy."

"Or you can marry someone and it can be the worst thing in the world," I reply quietly. "I was prepared to walk down the aisle and accept the consequences. It was a duty. I think you understand that."

She narrows her eyes.

I'm not making any friends here.

"Listen." I exhale. "He died, and I married Luca. I thought I could love him, but I was wrong." That hurts to say. It's like I've turned my knife in on me, impaled it into my stomach. All those jagged edges inside me shift again, and I can't help but wonder when they'll eventually slice through my skin. "I'm so sorry for lying, but your brothers didn't give me a choice."

She looks away. "He's really gone, then?"

"Yes. We just had the funeral two days ago."

Her gaze comes back to me. "Where's your ring?"

"What?"

"You're married to Luca, so you say. Where's the ring you were wearing last time I saw you?"

I grimace. "Ah, well, so *technically* I was married to Wilder, and Luca and I thought we were married, but the license for Wilder and me had been filed and processed. A clerical error... So I took off the ring. And he held me captive for two weeks, so there's that."

Her mouth drops open. "I didn't expect that."

I offer her a brittle smile. "Life hasn't been all sunshine and roses. Trust me."

"I..." She can't meet my eyes. "You were seen coming here. My brothers are on their way."

I lean back. "Cristian?"

"And Matteo, I think," she whispers. "They called me and told me you were in the area. If it were up to me, I'd just call it moot. Wilder is gone. Our grievance isn't with you, if we can believe that you're not married to Luca."

The panic of knowing Matteo is on his way here claws up my throat. I can't speak for a moment, terrified of a repeat of last time.

It won't be. I'd shoot him in the face before I let him touch me again.

But then it's too late—her apartment door opens, and footsteps pound on the stairs. They emerge a moment later, first Cristian, then Matteo.

My eyes go to the second brother. His jaw is swollen, even now, but there's no other sign of damage. His eyes are angry, landing on mine.

Like *I'm* the one who broke his jaw.

I glare right back.

Mariella stands and goes to Cristian. "Don't," she pleads. "Amelie and I have talked. I don't blame her for what happened, and I don't think you should hold it against her, either."

Matteo sneers, although his mouth moves funny. And when he speaks, his voice comes out a bit muffled. "Is that right? The DeSantis bride was sent here—"

"No." I set down my mug but keep my fingers wrapped around it. I lean back in my chair and cross my legs. "I'm not a DeSantis bride. Not anymore. And I'm no one's lackey."

"Ah." He saunters closer, stopping just in front of me.

He seems to have an issue with women. I refuse to believe it's just a *me* thing.

"Don't fucking touch me," I warn him. I'm surprised at how furious I am, immediately. "You already violated me. Do you expect me to let it happen again?"

He puts his hand on the table and walks his fingers to my arm. "I don't think you're in control here."

I force myself to remain relaxed, while terror and indignation battle for the top spot in my brain. I'm so sick of people thinking they can take advantage of me.

He touches my arm, and I move fast. I channel the attacking power of a snake, ripping the knife from its sheath on my ankle and swinging it in a small arc. I stab the blade down into the top of his hand, through the tendons and bones.

He screams, dropping to his knees beside me. The knife's tip buries into the wood, keeping him pinned.

"Sooner or later, you'll realize I don't fuck around," I say in his ear. I twist the hilt.

He screams again.

I hold on to the blade the same way I held on to the knife in Ricardo's stomach. A bit of wild desperation clings to me. I wonder if they see how far gone I really am. The blood pooling on the table is nothing. Not compared to my head, or Ricardo's injuries. Not compared to the fury churning my gut.

"We're even," I say to Cristian, rising from my chair. "Whatever bad blood was between your family and Wilder should've ended with his death. Luca killed two men who attacked me, but he spared your brother. *I* am sparing your brother." My attention goes to Mariella. "They might be your brothers, but where is the respect for women?"

She avoids my gaze.

"Agreed?" I snap.

"Fine," Cristian grits out.

I yank the knife free from Matteo's hand and shove him aside. I might even feel bad if he wasn't such a dickbag.

I storm downstairs and onto the street, sucking in a huge breath. That might not have been as productive as I'd hoped...

"Wait," Mariella yells. She chases after me.

She stops a few feet away, eyeing the bloody knife still in my grip.

"What?" I glance around. "No offense, but I don't really want to hang around and wait for their retaliation."

She exhales. "You're right. That's all. I should be more accountable and stand up when they do something bad. I'll talk to Cristian, make sure nothing comes back on you."

"Or Luca's family," I add.

She nods. "I'm the one who should've apologized for that night. It made me sick to see it, but he's..."

"I don't want to hear about how he is," I say gently. I offer her a slip of paper with my number written on it. "If you ever want to talk, that's how to reach me."

Her smile is tentative, and she slowly backs away from me.

I mirror her smile. I won't say hope has come back to me —not yet. But this is a step in the right direction. A truce... a friendship. I mull that over and head for the water.

CHAPTER 31
Amelie

When I was a senior in high school, I was miserable. I was the head cheerleader, I had boys interested in me, I had all the popularity I could win. My name was the first one entered for prom queen, and it was my face everyone glanced at to see how they should react. They followed my lead like little sheep.

I was seventeen. I started my year in Paris as an exchange student. My parents wanted a cultured lady for a daughter, and where else to learn sophistication than the heart of France? And it was nice. Pleasant, even. I learned French, I had a nice host family. But I couldn't seem to make friends. My popularity had remained in the States, and I didn't know what to do without it.

I wore it like a cloak, keeping people back. It was the haughtiness in which I approached situations that did it.

But now, as I stride down the street with that familiar expression, I feel more than ever like I'm putting on a show. That person isn't me anymore. France wasn't able to tear the mask from my face, but Luca did.

"Amelie!" Paloma steps out of a doorway and beckons to me.

I raise my eyebrows, then follow her. She leads me up a steep set of stairs to a wide terrace that overlooks the street. Her house is set back, small and neat. There are flowers planted along the walkway, the soil around them seeming well-tended to. I smile to myself.

"I didn't realize you lived out this way." After my chat with Mariella, I decided to wander. There was no one to stop me, and I was feeling better about confronting Cristian and Matteo. I'd sort of poked the hornet's nest with my knife, but some guys only respond to a display of power. Being weak or relying on Luca did nothing for me.

"We're quite close to the restaurant," she says. "Only two streets over."

"Oh. Oops." My cheeks heat. I was a bit lost—not enough to ask for directions or consult my phone, though—but now I can see how the city connects together. It's enlightening, almost like puzzle pieces clicking into place. It's not enough, though.

We enter the house. The first room has floor-to-ceiling bookshelves, everything a rich, warm wood. The bookshelves are crammed full. The front window lets in a stream of light, and the leather armchairs make it seem like a den area, of sorts. We keep moving to the living room, which has massive sliding glass doors that show a fenced-in backyard and a breathtaking view of the ocean.

I gravitate toward it.

"What did you do today?" she asks.

"I saw Mariella Costa and straightened some things out," I say, unable to tear my eyes away from the view. "I think I'm going to stay a while. Do you know if anyone is hiring around here? I don't speak Italian, but I catch on fast."

She steps up beside me and sighs. "Sometimes it's nice to

be reminded of youth. What do you mean you straightened things out?"

I shrug. "I just corrected their perception. And warned Matteo to never come near me again."

She tsks. "Did you threaten them?"

"Only slightly." I'll keep the hand-stabbing to myself, then.

"I can use an extra pair of hands in the restaurant, if you're willing," she says. "You're practically family."

That gets my full attention. I stare at her. "What? Really?"

Never mind that she just called me family—that's a marvel for another time—she's offering me a job. A job I could very well suck at.

"I'm getting tired," she says. "Standing all day, preparation, cutting. I love the restaurant, but someone to share the work would be nice. I've been telling Antonio for a year now that we should look for someone."

She steps away, and I follow her to the kitchen. She's picking up her keys and purse, slinging it over her shoulder.

"Besides, I am an excellent Italian teacher."

My heart swells. "You'd do that for me?"

"We're going to be late." Without further ado, she heads outside and down the street.

I close the door behind me and race after her. She's surprisingly fast, and my legs are burning by the time we arrive at the restaurant.

We circle around back, and Paloma stops short behind me. I bump into her back.

"Have you seen Amelie?"

I step around her, eyeing Ricardo. "She has. I'm right here."

He comes forward with his hands out, like he's going to grab me, and I jump backward.

"Ricardo," Paloma snaps.

He freezes and slowly lowers his arms. "Sorry. I just, I went to the house, and it's been empty. I was worried, especially after I gave you her address."

I shake my head and move to the side. Paloma unlocks the door and eyes us, then disappears inside.

"I'm fine." I spread my arms wide. "I went to speak with Mariella... and her brothers. I think things will be okay."

"Because you tried to smooth things over?" His expression is skeptical.

"Because I told her the truth, and also because this has gone on long enough. They all stood by while Matteo assaulted me. I don't really give a fuck about what happened before I arrived. Yes, it's heartbreaking that Wilder was a colossal asshole to Mariella. But that is *not* my fault."

He raises his hands. "You're right."

I huff. "I know I'm right. Mariella agreed with me."

"Well, good."

"Yes."

He stares at me. "Okay."

I sigh and go forward, wrapping my arms around his shoulders. This is new for me. Blatant affection. But it's also nice to hug him after worrying about his health. He freezes for a second, then hugs me back. We stand like that for a solid thirty seconds, until I release him and step back.

"Thank you for worrying about me," I say. "It's kind of a foreign concept."

He rolls his eyes. "You're like family."

Paloma said that, too. I squint. "I was never married to Luca."

"Yeah, but the feeling was there."

No, it wasn't. It's so automatic to reject it, because that's what will keep me safe. I take in a ragged breath, shoving down that damn loneliness again. I'm standing in front of a friend. I am in a city full of people. Paloma is waiting for me just inside. I don't have any excuse for loneliness.

But I can't stop the wave of it that crests above me.

I spin away before he sees anything on my face. "I'm sure you'll turn up for dinner?"

"Or to walk you home," he says to my back.

"Okay."

And then I go inside, and Paloma keeps me blessedly busy for the rest of the evening.

It's late by the time the dinner rush slows to a stop. My feet are sore, my legs burn, my eyes have been replaced with sandpaper. I'm pretty sure I have flour in my hair, although no one has pointed that out.

For the first half of dinner, I stayed in the back. I made the pizzas, which were luckily just a set few specials for the evening. Most of their business is the liquor, beer, and wine, but their pizza is just too good to resist. I tossed more dough than I ever have in my life—which, let's be honest, I haven't tossed dough before—and got the hang of the wide wooden paddle used to slip the pizzas into the ovens.

The second half, she sent me out to shadow Antonio on the art of pouring a glass of wine. I became efficient on using a bottle opener and locating particular bottles from the shelf. Antonio laughed and joked with his customers in Italian, and I kept falling in love with the melody of it. Over and over, different words, different people. It rings as music in my ears.

"Amelie," Paloma calls now, beckoning me to the kitchen.

I leave Antonio with his few regulars, those who've just started on their meals, and step into the kitchen. I wipe the back of my hand along my forehead, about to ask what she needs. But then I freeze—and I mean that in the worst possible way.

It isn't just my muscles that freeze. My brain stops working.

Luca stands in the middle of the kitchen, hands stuffed in his pockets.

My heart stutters and skips, and suddenly it's racing. I can't be near him. All I can hear when I see his face is an echo of my begging. I begged him and cried and pleaded, and *that* shame is what drops on me now. The shame I thought I'd shrugged off, left behind, fills me from top to bottom.

I never thought I'd be my own worst enemy, but here I am.

I hate you, I try to say. The words won't come out. I fear I'm gaping like a fish, because I can't *speak*. Can't do anything except stare and hope my emotions translate.

He winces slightly. He has a shadow of a beard on his cheeks. Dark circles under his eyes.

I don't care. I force my observations away. I'm lying to myself—that much is clear. My first reaction wasn't the loathing that crawls through me like spiders. It's the traitorous part of my brain that just wants the loneliness to go away.

Paloma is the one to grip my hand and shake off my ice.

I don't break eye contact with Luca as I step backward. My heel hits the door.

"Amelie—"

"Do not say my name," I whisper.

Hurt flashes across his expression.

"You do not have a reason to be upset." I lift my chin to hide my tremor. "You don't have a reason to say my name, or be here. You don't have the *right* to look at me. Not after what you did." Tears burn my eyes. "I hate you, Luca DeSantis. With every ounce of my being."

Paloma squeezes my hand, and I can't tell if she wants me to stop, or leave, or—

"I'm sorry." His voice is hoarse. "I'm so sorry."

I back out into the dining room. My hand slides free from Paloma's. I don't know where I'll go, but I'm certainly not entertaining a conversation with him.

Never again.

Antonio tilts his head when I return to his side. I try to be subtle about catching my unshed tears, blinking them away.

"I'm fine," I say.

He grunts and names a beer, and just like that, I'm back to work.

Except sooner or later, the night will end. And it does, almost sooner than I expect. I peek into the kitchen and find it empty except for Paloma, and I creep in. My cheeks are already hot with embarrassment.

She comes over and wraps me in a hug.

This time, I'm ready for it and don't fall apart. I spent the last hour stewing over Luca's arrival, worrying over whether Cristian and Matteo will leave him alone, furious with myself for giving him the time of day.

"I'm sorry," I say into her shoulder.

"Don't be. He deserves a reckoning for what he did, don't you think?"

I do.

"Go home. Sleep. Come back tomorrow for noon, all right?" She pats my back.

"Yes, ma'am." I force a smile.

There's only a slim chance Luca waits for me at his house, right?

"He's staying with me," she adds.

I exhale my relief and grab my denim jacket. I slide it on and step outside. Ricardo leans against the wall next to the door, a cigarette in his hand. He blows smoke at the sky and straightens, following me to the street.

"Amelie."

I turn sharply toward Luca, who emerges from the shadows at the front of the building. His gaze flicks to Ricardo, then back to me.

"Can I talk to you? Please."

There's a little voice in my brain that wants to hear him beg, but I'm exhausted. I tip my head in the direction of the house—his, mine, I'm not sure what to classify it as anymore. "I just want to go."

"I'll make it quick. On the way."

I stare at him and wrestle with my emotions. "Okay."

He falls into step beside me. Not close enough to touch, but... too close.

We walk down the center of the street, and it isn't until we've put some distance between us and Ricardo that he says, "I want to apologize."

I grit my teeth. "For?"

"For everything."

"You can't just say sorry and expect forgiveness. If that's why you came here—"

"It's not. God, I just..." He kicks at a loose stone, sending it clattering ahead of us. "I've been replaying it."

"Why did you do it then, Luca?" I'm breathing through the broken pieces of me all over again. I don't want to say his name or think about what he did. The mold is shattered, but I'm terrified he's going to shove me back into one. "Why did you lock me away when I *told* you that was the thing I was most afraid of?"

He's silent for a moment, and then he nods. It's almost to himself, like he's deciding how much to tell me.

I don't bother saying it better be the whole truth, because I need him to come to that conclusion on his own.

"I've been thinking a lot about the reasons behind my actions," he starts. "Trying to make sense of everything after the fact. I couldn't see it when we were in the thick of it—when I was actively hurting you. I did it because you were mine, and then suddenly not. I thought it was because I wanted to keep you safe, but I was selfish. I was cruel. I *thought* if you were in my control, I had you. But that's not right. That's not remotely true. You were my prisoner."

He takes a deep breath and faces me. We've both stopped now, squaring off with only three houses left to go before mine.

"I'm so sorry for that, Amelie. For not listening to your fears. For not letting you make your own decision about us. I'm sorry for taking away your freedom and hurting you." He steps forward, his gaze intent on mine.

Just as fast, I take a step back.

I don't know how I'm feeling. I had weeks to build up my hatred, and now I'm confused. How can I be confused? He threw me in a room and forgot about me—because his father told him I wasn't his?

I rub my eyes. "I can't, Luca. I need to think about this—away from you. That's why I came here."

His expression falls. "I know. I'm staying with Paloma, so you have your space. Just... let someone know if the Costas give you any trouble, okay?"

I laugh. "Why? You didn't stop Matteo from touching me the first time."

"I fucked up," he murmurs. "I was breaking your trust before we'd even been married for twenty-four hours. You're right—I should've stopped him. I should've killed him."

Uncertainty is a snake coiling in my chest. I stop myself from moving back again and square my shoulders. "Thank you for your apology. I'm going to go."

He nods once and watches me pass him. Ricardo doesn't follow me, either, and I wonder if both of them will just watch from their current positions. I make it inside and lock the door, then set a chair under the handle. It won't stop someone determined to get in, but even if Luca has a key... I'll hear the chair be knocked aside, hopefully.

I climb the stairs and shed my jacket. Moonlight comes in through the sliding doors. It reflects off the small pool. I move through the dark house, hooking my purse on one of the chairs, pulling the gun and holster out. I set them down, then kick off my boots and remove the knife and sheath. I'll need to clean it properly, better than just wiping it on a patch of grass.

My hand lands on a piece of paper.

I squint, trying to decipher the paper in the dark, and finally turn on my phone's flashlight.

Not just one, but two papers.

The first is a copy of Wilder's death certificate. It lists his cause of death as a gunshot wound to the chest, dated our wedding day. I set that aside and lift the second one.

This is...

The marriage certificate I signed with Luca.

'Til death do us part, I distinctly remember thinking as I signed it. If only it were that simple. Death *did* part us, but it was living that really came between us.

There's a folded paper clipped to it, taped shut. I gently tear the seal to discover a page of Luca's cramped handwriting. My heart gives an extra hard *thud*, reminding me it has a say in this. My heart and my brain aren't in agreeance.

Amelie,

I've returned this original copy of our marriage license to you to do with what you will. Destroy it, if you'd like. Dad never filed it, obviously. You fulfilled your duty by marrying Wilder, and through no fault of yours was he taken away. I think Dad knew your father had sent in the license with Wilder's signature, and then... it took too long to get everything straightened out.

But with Wilder's death certificate, you're a free woman.

I considered, for a brief moment in time, just sending in our marriage license. I thought it might erase the wounds between us. But... that's not what either of us want. You don't deserve the bars of a forced marriage containing you. I don't want to tie you to me if you don't love me.

I once told you I married you because I was happy to finally have someone of my own. Someone to love, to cherish. I don't regret telling you that—and I don't regret marrying you the first time. You changed me, and I'm so thankful for that. Even if it was painful.

The house is yours.

Your life is yours—forever.

I promise.

With love,

Luca

I COVER my mouth and reread the note.

I'm Amelie Page, not DeSantis. And I'm... free?

A laugh bubbles out of me. I sink to my knees and hold my head in my hands, unable to contain the lightness. I can't stop, even when tears blur my eyesight. He thought about filing our marriage license, but he didn't. He wants my freedom.

My parents aren't here to order me around. Luca... he won't. I do trust his word on that. I never thought I'd be ecstatic to *not* be married. Never thought undoing it was a possibility. I rise and stare at the gun on the counter, the knife next to it. I set down the note, the certificates, and peel off my shirt. I unhook my bra and step out of my jeans and socks.

Outside, the cool night air pricks at my flesh. My nipples harden. I cross to the pool and test the temperature with my foot. It's colder than I was expecting, but not unbearable.

I slide in fully, going under for a long few moments.

When I break the surface, I roll onto my back and open my eyes. My limbs are weightless. The sky is full of stars above me.

And I can finally breathe easy.

CHAPTER 32
Luca

Paloma and Antonio are out of the house bright and early this morning, leaving me to sulk. Maybe not sulk, exactly. I didn't expect Amelie to accept my apology. The whole flight over, I was tormented with the *why* behind my actions.

Part of letting her go—really and truly—is allowing her space to heal.

Whether that takes her a day, a month, a year, is up to her. Maybe she'll never forgive me. I have to be okay with that.

I lean on the fence in their backyard, staring out at the view of the ocean. The rust-colored rooftops line up like dominos all the way down, built practically into the side of the hill. Antonio asked me to accompany him into town later to pick up more liquor, and he'll be expecting me soon.

But the sun creeps higher in the sky, and still I don't move.

My mind is stuck on Amelie. If she found my note, what she thinks of it. If she's okay. I try to recall every detail about her, but I can't. All that comes back to me is the fire in her gaze. If looks could kill, I'd be dead three times over.

"Hello," Ricardo calls, stepping out of the house. He joins me at the fence.

"You seem better," I say.

"I feel better. Still stiff, but the doctors say my muscles are repairing nicely." He shades his eyes. "What are you doing?"

I tilt my head. "Enjoying the morning breeze. What are you doing?"

"*I'm* wondering why you aren't at the restaurant."

"Because they don't need me until later."

He rolls his eyes. "You're daft. Amelie is there, so you should be there."

That sounds like a bad idea.

"You love her," he states. "Only men in love do crazy things."

I shift.

"Besides, if you don't act soon, she'll start dating one of the locals. Word of a pretty foreigner working at Paloma's travels fast, and all the men are thinking of swinging by for a drink tonight." He wiggles his eyebrows at me.

Anger kicks up dust in my blood, and my heart pounds faster. It's impressive how swift a reaction I have to that news. She's free... but that doesn't mean I can let Italian assholes moon over her or sway her with pretty words.

"Ah," he says. "See?"

"I hurt her," I state. "I don't trust my love."

I've never done it before. I love my mother, and I love Paloma and Antonio. I love my father and brothers. But those aren't romantic. They don't fill me with the desire to protect like I feel around Amelie. That platonic love doesn't drive me to the point of madness.

He shrugs. "Has she been in love? Did she fall in love with you?"

"I don't know. High school, maybe. Or Wilder. We didn't talk about it."

He laughs and pushes off the railing. "You're less fun than a wet basket of laundry. Go to the restaurant. Show the girl you're not leaving, hmm?"

I grunt, and he departs. It takes me all of five seconds to realize I can't *not* go, not when I know people are aware Amelie is there. What if Matteo or Cristian pay her a visit?

I change quickly into a fresh shirt and get to the restaurant in record time. I go in the front, walking down between the bar and tables. The last time we were here was bad, and I meant what I told Amelie: I should've fucking killed him for touching her.

If he so much as looks at her, I will. I'll pull the trigger without remorse.

The kitchen door swings open, and Amelie appears with a box. She stops dead.

"Luca?"

I scan her. I didn't last night, but now I take in all of her. The way her clothes fall on her frame, like they're a bit too loose. Her hair has grown more wild, pinned back away from her face. There's a raised scar cut across her forehead that stands out more now than it did in the darkness.

I step forward, then pause. When she doesn't retreat, I take the box from her and set it on one of the tables. It's filled with utensils and napkins to roll together.

"I'll help," I say.

She nods once and slides into a chair, and I choose the one diagonal from her. I used to have this job when I was a boy, back when my mother and Paloma ran this place. We'd fold so many, only for them to be used each night.

I didn't like it as a kid, but now the action is soothing. Our silence isn't awkward.

"Thank you," she says quietly. "I don't... I don't know how to navigate this thing between us."

I lift my gaze and meet hers. "I don't, either. But until you know, I'll be here."

She nods once, expression unsure.

My gesture was a double-edged sword. Because I know, just as I didn't have anyone except my aunt and uncle to look up to, she hasn't had anyone provide a good example of love. She didn't have anyone on her side through her arranged marriage to Wilder, then to me. Her parents literally shoved her into the Mafia without remorse.

So by giving her freedom, I also cut our tether.

And only time will prove that I'm not going to leave her.

CHAPTER 33
Amelie

Every day, I show up to the restaurant and Luca is there. My skin tingles when his gaze lingers on me. The avoidance game doesn't work on him. He's *there*, everywhere I am.

I'm on the verge of a breakdown.

I feel the broken edges inside me now more than ever. They rasp against my lungs, my heart, my skin. I'm being sliced open from the inside, and I don't know how to fix myself. How to deal with trauma.

Paloma watches us with a close eye, but she doesn't say anything. She hired me so she could rest more. She leaves me to my tasks in the afternoons, when they're closed between lunch and dinner.

He walks me home at the end of the night, sometimes striking up conversations. Other times we're quiet, lost in our own thoughts. He's effectively taken the job from Ricardo.

But every day, I feel myself tip closer and closer to the edge.

"Amelie," he greets me today, the same as always.

I don't see Paloma, so I don't answer. I'm tired. The nightmares have been creeping back without warning, showing me Wilder's death over and over. Sometimes it's Luca who gets shot instead of his brother.

"How did you sleep?" he asks.

Maybe he knows I don't sleep much. There are dark circles under my eyes, I'm always tired. I came here to live, and I'm barely existing.

"Don't." I push past him.

He follows me into the dining room with a tray of silverware and sets it down. He's too close to me. My skin is on fire.

"Amelie, talk to me, please." He reaches out and touches my shoulder.

It's my fault that I snap. At least, that's what I'll tell myself later. It's my fault for not dealing with my problems head-on, because when *he* touches me, all I see is Matteo, and the gun he presses into my side.

I snatch one of the butter knives from the tray and have it at his throat faster than either of us can blink. It digs into his skin under his jaw.

We watch each other for a moment, and then he takes control.

Haven't I been waiting for that to happen?

He knocks my hand away and twists my wrist until my fingers loosen. The knife clatters to the floor, and something raw opens up inside me. I shove at him, pounding my fists against his chest. He takes the hits, then suddenly grabs my wrists. He spins me around, encasing me in a bear hug from behind. His arms crisscross in front of me, still gripping my wrists.

I let out an awful sound. My voice screeches, echoing and rattling in my brain, but he doesn't release me. It's been a while since I've had a full-on panic attack, and this one seems to have roared out of nowhere. My skin is cool and clammy, although my face is still on fire. A weight settles on my chest. My shriek dies off into something of a whimper.

"It's okay, it's okay," he says in my ear. Over and over. We sink to the floor, and he cradles me on his lap. He tucks my hair behind my ear, smooths it down. "I'm sorry. I'm so sorry, Amelie. It's going to be okay."

"I'm not okay," I whisper. "I have nightmares. I'm always on edge. And I keep waiting for you to leave."

His grip tightens. "I'm not leaving."

I nod.

Paloma bursts through the door. "What on earth?"

"She just needs a minute," Luca says above my head.

After a moment, I climb off Luca and scramble to my feet. Paloma is in the kitchen, and I slink in to apologize.

She waves me off, telling me I deserve a break. To see the city, eat food other than pizza from her oven.

I've been paid. My fridge is full—actually, I think I can thank Luca for that. The morning after he arrived, I opened the refrigerator door and found the shelves full of my favorites.

"Where are you going?" Luca calls, rushing out behind me.

"Exploring." I don't stop, and he watches me go. I need... something. Space. To move my feet. I'm undecided about it, but I'll figure it out.

A minute later, he bounds up beside me.

Last week, I told him about my truce with Mariella. I felt guilty that he might feel the need to keep a low profile, but he only grinned at me, shaking his head. I didn't want to decipher what he meant by that, so I didn't ask.

Now, he nudges me. "I have an idea."

I raise my eyebrows. "What's that?"

"There's a great row of shops, but it's far. Come with me." His steps are light. His arms swing at his sides.

I pause and really look at him. His dark hair has been

freshly cut. He has on a denim shirt similar to the jacket I usually wear. It's too hot now, with summer raging around us. I've been opting more and more for the flowing, loose dresses Mom packed for me. I hated them originally, but maybe she was onto something.

We stop in front of my house.

His house.

I shake my head, still undecided about how to refer to it. I follow him into the garage, but he doesn't go inside. He cuts across the space usually reserved for a car and hits a button.

The door's mechanical engine whirs, opening it and letting light and air inside.

"What are you doing?"

He grins. I haven't seen him like this in a long time. He's practically back to the Luca I experienced here the first time.

Until he unveils a motorcycle and smirks at me.

I cross my arms, scowling. "I'm in a dress."

"I think you'll survive. You're the one who keeps talking about living life to the fullest."

He rolls it out and strides closer. I expect a smirk, but his face is carefully blank. He gets closer than he's gotten in a long time. I hold my breath as a surge of heat sweeps through me. He brushes my hair off my shoulders and pulls a helmet over my head. His finger on my chin, tilting my head back, gives me unnecessary tingles.

I'm betrayed by my own body.

And his grudging hotness.

"You okay?" he asks me. He doesn't follow that with what I might expect. No *you can trust me* bullshit. He doesn't offer an opportunity for me to back out, though, either.

I narrow my eyes, seeing the challenge for what it is.

Finally, his smile appears. It's just a slight upward tip of the corner of his mouth, but I see it before it disappears. He sits on the bike and pats the seat behind him.

I grimace, but... I can't say no.

I lift my dress high enough to swing my leg over. He steadies my arm, another point of contact. My body is at war with itself trying to figure out if this is a good or bad thing.

Bad, my brain screams.

My heart thinks the opposite.

It isn't too bad sitting like this. There's a good six inches between Luca and me.

"Put your hands around me," he orders.

"Isn't there a handle or something—"

He tugs my wrist.

I slide down the seat until I'm flush against him. My cheeks burst into flames. I carefully wrap my arms around him, digging my fingers into his shirt. My chest aches, and my cheerful mood slips away. Sadness takes its place, but it's hidden behind my helmet and visor.

He starts the motorcycle, and the sudden roar surprises me. I clutch him tighter, and that ache grows. I want so many things, but I don't know how to reconcile them with my life.

I could be with Luca.

I could give him the power to break me again.

Or I could protect myself.

He hits the throttle, and we roll forward onto the street. Soon enough we're flying along the streets. We head east, the landscape changing as we move farther into Italy. I take in the changing landscape and dare to release him, holding on only with my thighs. I throw my arms wide, letting the wind snatch at me.

The sadness melts from my body, carried away behind us. I tip my head back and suck in a deep breath. It feels like the deepest breath I've ever taken, eradicating my worries.

Luca slows the bike, and I wrap my arms back around his torso. He turns up a steep driveway and slows to a halt in front of an ancient building. It has rows of narrow, stained-glass windows along the side. A church, then.

He offers his arm, and I use it for balance to get off the bike. My legs are jelly, and I pause for a moment. He meets my gaze, and my cheeks heat. I quickly step back. He swings his leg over and follows me until I stop moving. My heart is beating out of my chest.

His fingers undo the buckle under my chin, grazing my skin.

"Luca," I whisper.

"Yes?" His voice is as strangled as mine.

"If I ask you to kiss me again, will you refuse?"

He helps remove my helmet and drops it at our feet. His hands come back up and cup my cheeks. "I won't refuse you. Ever."

I fist the front of his shirt and drag him closer. Maybe it's the adrenaline, or I just want something to ease my soul for a moment, but I say, "Kiss me, then."

His eyes widen a fraction, and then he obliges me. His lips touch mine softly. Once. Twice. He's dipping back down again, and I press myself up. I tangle my hands in his hair, tugging on his dark locks, and our lips meet again.

My body molds to his, and one hand leaves my face to lift me by my ass. I lock my legs around his hips. Something eases in my chest, and I know I'll replay this moment in my head later. It's the moment when my fears dissipate into thin air.

I wonder if, deep down, physical touch has always been my love language. If this kiss will undo me one step further than the sex.

His hand coasts up my back, and he freezes.

He pulls away slightly, meeting my gaze. "Are you carrying?"

I grin. "I am."

His expression heats. But he sets me down carefully and

steps back. "I need to stop touching you, or else I'll ruin this whole thing."

There's a strange buzzing in my ears.

The sound of another rejection.

He tilts his head, analyzing whatever emotions are playing through on my face. Does he know I know? He could think he's subtle about it. I let out a ragged sigh.

"Amelie."

"What?"

"This isn't what you think." He comes up behind me and puts his mouth to my ear. "If I keep touching you, I'll want to fuck you. But you're not ready for that."

Shivers encase my body. "I'm not?"

"No." He trails his finger down my arm. "But I think you might be ready for something else."

I spin around and squint at him.

He laughs and offers his hand. "Come with me."

I take it, and he tugs me toward the old church. We wind through the tall grass, and I crane my head back to take in the architecture. The bricks are tightly packed in even rows, like this place has been well-preserved. A bell tower casts a long, narrow shadow over the grass.

We circle around the church, emerging in the back.

I gasp.

The whole city lies before us, with the ocean beyond. It's more stunning than a photograph. The lawn back here is more well-maintained, trimmed down, and there's a gravel path that leads down a slight slope to a gazebo.

"Come on," he says. "It gets better."

"This is beautiful," I murmur.

He stops beside the gazebo stairs and helps me up. I cross to the railing and stare down. We're at the edge of a steep hill. I hadn't even realized we were riding along such a severe incline to be brought this high.

"Do you like it?" he asks.

I glance back. He's standing in the center of the space, fiddling with his hands. I watch him for a moment and try to figure out why he's fidgeting. He's not the nervous type. My stomach knots, and I quickly face the view again.

What if he brought me up here to tell me he couldn't do this anymore?

"Do you still have nightmares?" I ask.

We spent a grand total of one night together, in the same bed. A single night in a month and a half's time. It was one of the only peaceful nights I can remember, before everything imploded. Of course, I had a head injury that night...

"Sometimes." He comes up behind me, stopping without touching me. "Other times I dream of you."

"Me?" I turn now, my tone incredulous. "That's..."

Ridiculous?

Impossible?

"I dream of what you'd look like as a proper bride," he confesses. "In a dress you actually like, at a wedding surrounded by people who love us. And then I think about what it would be like to have a home with you, and come home to you. And grow old with you. That's what I dream about most often."

He cups my cheek.

"I just hope you'll be open to that future someday."

There's that hope again. I once thought it would crush me. That hope was the root of my heartache. It dropped me, didn't it? It carried me too high and let me slip through its fingers. I fell, and no one caught me. Not Luca, not my family.

I hadn't dared hope for *anything*. Not since I escaped.

But it's the bird inside my chest now, fluttering its wings against my ribcage. It's the steady drum of my heart. Funny, how much I tried to suffocate it, it comes roaring back into me.

"I'm afraid." I'm terrified to think what might happen—so many possibilities, and Luca is giving me a choice. To love him or not. To be happy... or not.

He kisses my forehead, and I close my eyes when he lingers. "That's okay. I'm not going anywhere."

I believe him.

CHAPTER 34
Luca

Amelie drifts behind me, lost in thought. We have an evening off from the restaurant. Paloma has been giving us whole days off lately, as if sensing we spend more time together outside of work than at it. Which is simultaneously true and not. *At* the restaurant, I can keep my eye on Amelie as she works, and I half-ass my jobs. When we're off, we talk. We explore. So maybe my aunt is onto something, but this evening carries a more somber tone.

She has a bouquet of wildflowers in her arms—something she insisted on bringing when I told her where we were going.

My heart is in my throat—it has been since I proposed this idea to her. I wasn't ready for her to agree or be eager about it. But we wind through the cemetery now, and I can't help but feel a deep disappointment that Mom never met Amelie.

She would've loved her.

My aunt insists as much, both in front of Amelie and when it's just us. My conniving aunt seems convinced we're going to end up together. I'm convinced, too... but Amelie isn't there yet.

The best way to prove to Amelie that I'm not leaving her is

by being consistent. No matter how long it takes.

"Here she is," I call.

It takes Amelie a moment to reach us, and she stares down at the marble headstone for a moment. Then she drops to her knees and reaches out, pressing two fingers to the curling numbers of Mom's death year. She did the same thing to Wilder's portrait at his funeral—a sincere action. Her brows are drawn together now, lips pursed.

"Nice to meet you," she whispers.

She sets the flowers down and clears away some of the brush. It might be a nervous habit on her part, but I find my inner turmoil settling.

I join her on the ground. Unbidden, a lost memory floats back to me. When this happens, I think of it as a gift. There's so much about a person, so much life Mom lived. The random bright moments illuminate in the dark for a reason. So I don't forget her.

"We went to Venice one time. Just as a little week-long trip, her and me. We didn't get a lot of time to bond, and I think it was one of those moments where Dad felt guilty about it. So he paid for the whole thing. We got to ride the gondolas, visit museums, try out wine." My lungs ache thinking about it. "I was sixteen."

"And she passed on your eighteenth birthday?" Amelie confirms.

I nod.

She reaches out and threads her fingers with mine. "You got to know her the best way you could, and I'm sure that memory will stay with you." She shuffles closer and hugs me, pressing the side of my face into her chest. She rests her chin on top of my head. "I would've liked to meet her."

I let out a ragged sigh. "Sometimes I wish she knew that I found my person."

Amelie winces. "You mean me."

"I do."

She's immobile above me, then slowly relaxes. I scoop her up and set her in my lap, changing our dynamic. Now she's the one in my embrace.

"You're my person," I repeat. "You understand me when no one else does."

She exhales. "You know why I came here, of all places?"

I go still. "I don't. I wondered, but I don't."

"Because you were so upset when I made the deal to get us away from the Costas. So I came back to barter. I met with Mariella and Cristian and told them their problem was with Wilder. It wasn't your fault, Luca, just like it wasn't mine. And them taking it out on us, and us taking out our grievances on them—it just wouldn't work anymore."

I'm pretty sure my mouth is hanging open. I grip her chin and tip her head back so she meets my gaze. "You met with them. I knew you had sought out Mariella, you said as much, but—"

"Her brothers showed up," she mumbles.

I narrow my eyes. "Brothers—not Matteo." It's a wish, but I can see it's in vain by her guilty expression. "What did you do? And why didn't you tell me?"

She shrugs. I haven't released my hold on her chin, and at this rate, I don't think I will.

"He tried to touch me, so I stabbed him in the hand. And I yelled at Mariella for letting it happen. She needs to hold the men in her family accountable. How would they like it if someone touched her and got away with it?"

I almost kiss her. *Almost*. I have to bat down the pride that threatens to erupt in my chest, and now I do release her. She doesn't move from my lap, though.

"I'm so fucking proud of you," I say, choking on my laugh. "Goddamn, I would've liked to have seen that."

She beams. "I was scared shitless, but it worked out. It was either that or shoot him..."

"Oh, well, glad you didn't do that." Honestly, it would make the surprise I have for her next week that much more difficult to obtain.

She glances at the headstone again. "I think your mom would've done something about it, if it had been her family. She stood up to Jameson, didn't she? She didn't keel over and have an abortion, like Wilder made Mariella. She had the strength to have you—and lose you, over and over again."

"I never thought of it like that," I murmur. "Thank you for that new perspective. And... you've made me realize something."

She cocks her head. "What's that?"

"I don't want to be like my father. Hell, I'd love nothing more than to stay out of New York City for the rest of my life. My mother was the strong one. She was happy when she was surrounded by family." *And you're my family*, I almost say. I can't quite voice it.

What if she isn't ready to hear it?

All I need is Amelie, and a life that will fill both of us. Freedom. Joy. I can see it, but it isn't enough. I want to reach out and take it with both hands.

She puts her hands on my shoulders and uses me to force herself up, then offers her hands to me. "I think we should come back here," she says suddenly. "It's peaceful."

I take her hands but don't pull on her to stand. I just like touching her and watching the tiny shivers run up her spine at the contact.

"I'd like that," I say. "Are you hungry?"

She grins. "You don't even have to ask."

And that's that. I mentally go through the checklist in my head, wondering if I've missed anything. I'm sure I'm missing a whole hell of a lot, but I'll take what I can work with.

Everything is falling into place.

CHAPTER 35

Amelie

Today is a big day.

There's nothing distinctly pointing to its grandness, except a nervous fluttering in my belly. And Luca's mysterious absence, up until this morning. I woke to a note on my pillow, folded into the shape of a swan. Its wing said, *Open me*. Inside was instructions to meet him at the harbor.

I suppress the emotions that threaten to block my throat. If I think about him in my room, watching me sleep, my heart skips. The origami note is uncharacteristically cute, but I can't help but think it *means* something bigger than just... meeting him at the harbor.

We've been talking about taking Paloma's boat out on the water for a few days.

So... it could just be that.

Still, I take extra long in the shower, shaving and scrubbing myself raw. My routine seems to double in length, but finally, I slip on a strapless dress. It's white, form-fitting against my breasts and down to my waist, then it flares out and falls to my knees. It's one of my favorite new purchases. The fabric is silky to the touch and flows out around me if I spin.

Anyway, today seems fitting for it.

He hasn't tried to kiss me since taking me to the church gazebo, but we're closer. He finds reasons to touch me at the restaurant. His hand trailing across my shoulder or waist when he passes, our fingers brushing any time he hands me a glass or plate.

Little moments that elicit goosebumps over my skin.

The summer has crept up on us, and tourist season seemed to spring out of nowhere. The restaurant has been busier than ever, with our fair share of English speakers. It seems that the hole-in-the-wall anonymity has faded. And rightly so: they deserve the success.

Someone rings the bell at my garage door.

I swipe on a pale-pink lipstick and slip it into my purse, then hurry downstairs. Parked against the curb is a small white car. Ricardo rolls down the window and waves to me. "We're going to be late!"

I shake my head. "What, Luca didn't want to pick me up on his bike?"

We've taken a few rides on it, thankfully when I was better prepared with my clothing. Nothing crazy, though, and the nights always ended idling at the curb, just as Ricardo's car is now.

"Are you joining us?" I climb in and slam the door shut. He's dressed nicely—another indication that *I'm right*. I enjoy being right, but today... I don't know. It's a bit like an impending storm. There's electricity in the air.

He smiles. "You want me to?"

I shift. "It depends on what we're doing."

He chokes on his laugh, then pulls away from the curb. "Do you want to hear how I met Luca?"

My curiosity kicks into gear. They've never volunteered

more information than was necessary. Ricardo rarely talked about his family, so I just assumed he was sort of roped into this by circumstance. "Absolutely."

He lets his arm hang out of the window. "I was twelve. Luca thirteen. My family was quite poor, desperate for any sort of job. It got so bad that my parents told my siblings and me that we needed to work, too. My mother brought me to Paloma's restaurant and asked if they would take me on." He goes quiet for a moment, maybe reliving it. "I'm pretty sure Antonio and Paloma were going to say no, but then Luca comes out of the back. He came right up to them and said if we needed the money, it was their duty to help us."

I cross my arms to keep from reaching out. I can't imagine what it would've been like to grow up like that, unsure of anything—a meal, electricity, the roof over their head.

"He convinced them. Once they managed to get me to talk about what was going on at home, they took care of us. But I still feel that loyalty to him, you know? He saved my life without even realizing it, and then he stuck with me."

"You mean a lot to each other." Their friendship isn't clear-cut, but I've been putting the pieces together over the last few weeks.

"Yes."

I smile. "I don't think I ever had a conversation with Luca until my wedding day. He and Aiden were kept away—it wasn't really necessary for me to have a relationship with him when I was supposed to marry Wilder."

Ricardo shakes his head. "You got lucky."

I'm surprised to agree with him. Even after everything we've gone through... I think I've forgiven him. That was one of the choices I could've imagined myself railing against. There was *no way* I could forgive him after what he did.

But he apologized. He's here. He set me free.

I've been lighter than I've ever felt in my life, but that

untethered, free-floating sensation has gradually disappeared. I'm not lost anymore.

"Here we are," Ricardo says, coasting to a stop at the marina gate. "Go on now."

I glance at him, but he just shoos me out. The gate swings open under my fingertips, and I go by memory across the docks. It's a bit of a maze, but I smile at a white balloon tied to the corner, a paper with an arrow leading me to the right final dock.

Luca stands beside *La Bellezo*, waiting for me.

I tilt my head, trying to figure out what's different. It isn't the white linen shirt, or his tan pants. It isn't his fresh haircut.

It's the look in his eyes.

Love.

I see it so plainly, my heart breaks. I almost stop walking, trip over my feet, and fall into the water. I didn't think I would recognize it, but my heart beats harder, and I know—*I know* that this is it. It swirls in my chest like its own little lightning storm, waiting to burst out.

A reciprocation.

"Hi," I say, immediately shy. I tip my head back and meet his gaze. "This seems fancy."

"I want today to be special."

I narrow my eyes. "Why?"

"Because I have something for you." He grins and takes my hand, and for a moment I think, *this is it.*

But he doesn't get down on one knee—he doesn't present a ring.

Instead, he lays an envelope on my open palm.

"What's this?" My fingers close around the paper, and I tear it open carefully. For a split second, I wonder if he lied and had filed the marriage certificate. But it's not—it's a letter from the Italian government, approving my long-term visa application. I hurry to read the rest of it, not quite understanding. I don't know how he managed to do this without my knowledge, although I suppose all it would've taken was my passport and an application. At the bottom of the form, it says that Paloma and Antonio have vouched for me.

"I wanted to give you the option of staying here," he says. "There's a lot of Italy left to explore, since you're here on a tourist visa right now... But after it's done, I thought you might like to stay. I was born here, so I have dual citizenship, but you..."

I glance around. The boat, the water, Luca. He wants to live here.

The dreams he said he had, of me and our future, suddenly come to life in my mind. My chest tightens, and I reach for him. Because I think I'd be perfectly happy living here. Paloma and Antonio are more affectionate parental figures than my own, and Luca...

Luca is family.

"Thank you," I whisper.

He clasps my outstretched hand.

"One more thing."

Now Luca lowers himself down on one knee and shows me a familiar ring. He fiddles with it, then looks up at me. "You told my aunt, when you gave this back to her, that I should save it for someone who I'll treat with respect. I can't emphasize how right you were to give it back."

"Luca—" My heart.

"I've apologized for my grievous misconduct," he continues. "I will continue to apologize. And learn. You've given me so much of yourself. You're unfailingly brave, even in the face of terrible odds. You're kind. You know how to push my buttons, and I think you've figured out my family's, too. *You* are the woman I will cherish for the rest of my life, because I'm in love with you."

Tears fill my eyes.

"Will you marry me, Amelie?"

My breath hitches. This is an honest question. The most important question of my life, and it's *my* decision. As soon as I realize that, everything snaps together. There are no more bars holding me hostage. No more rules about what to say or how to behave. We're free of the DeSantis obligation here, and Luca's created a future for us where we don't have to return.

His expression wobbles.

I do love him. It's lodged deep in my soul, this warmth that spreads across my skin. It's an armor all of its own.

"I love you, too," I answer. "And absolutely, I want to marry you. Yes."

I hold out my hand, and he catches my fingers. He kisses each one, then slides the ring on. It… it's a perfect fit. I stare at it, amazed. It was loose last time—which means this has been planned well in advance.

He rises and kisses me soundly, tipping me back. I wrap my arms around his shoulders, opening my mouth. This kiss sends shoots of pleasure down to my toes.

"To the newly engaged couple!"

We part just before the kiss gets deeper, and my cheeks heat. Luca's eyes are dark, trained on my face. I glance around us.

The boats surrounding Paloma's are covered in people that seemed to come out of nowhere. I spot Mariella on one, sitting beside Ricardo. She raises a champagne glass to me. The people around us are all familiar faces from the restaurant, from the shops we frequent.

"Come aboard?" Luca asks me, offering his hand once again.

I take it, and he steadies me. We step on at the back and follow a walkway to the front deck. There is a bottle of champagne with two glasses. It's already poured, the white foam of a freshly poured glass just kissing the rim. I consider that odd until someone appears from inside, a glass in her hand.

Paloma.

Antonio is right behind her, grinning. They both clink their flutes against mine and Luca's, and then Paloma wraps me in a hug.

"He was a fool, but boys often are before they shed their youth and transform into men," she says in my ear. "It takes a strong woman to see before, and still want the after."

I chuckle, hugging her tightly with one hand. "Thank you for everything."

"Nonsense." She withdraws and pats my cheek. "You brought hope back into my world. And for that, I'm immensely thankful. You always have a home in Sanremo."

"And Italian lessons," Antonio adds. He hugs me.

My grin widens. Any more, and my face might split in two. "Looking forward to it."

"Okay, okay," Luca urges. "We're taking her out."

"Me?"

"The boat." Paloma chuckles. "And we're going. Should I assume you won't be back tonight, Luca?"

"Right." I take a large swallow of the champagne and try not to think about the fact that she *knows* what Luca and I will probably get up to. I mean, unless he plans on remaining celibate. That's a possibility.

He meets my gaze, and the fieriness of it sends heat straight to my core. "I don't think I will," he says to her, although he doesn't look away from me.

We're caught in a staring contest as Paloma and Antonio disembark, their laughter floating back to us.

"Just us," he says to me, tipping his head toward the stern. "Come and sit while I take you out to sea."

"You know, um, how to drive?"

He grins. "Of course."

I follow him to the top deck where he took me the first time. I take a seat, then watch as he pulls ropes loose down below, freeing us from the dock. He returns and fires up the motor. The air is unusually still, and he navigates us out of the marina with no trouble.

The water out here is a stunning turquoise. I stand and go back down, creeping to the front to kneel at the most forward spot. We're not going fast, and it seems like this area is still protected from harsh waves. But what little wind we generate sweeps my hair back, and I relax into it. The firm netting beneath me lets water spray up, and I retreat just a bit.

We leave the protected alcove and follow the shoreline east. Eventually, Luca kills the engine. He calls to me, and I climb the stairs back to where he sits. There's a series of clanks as the anchor drops.

"Now what?" Sudden anticipation twists my stomach into knots.

"Come here." He spins slowly in the captain's chair.

He probably means his lap... but I have a different idea.

I sink to my knees between his legs and bite my lip. His fingers tighten on the arms of the chair, but he says nothing to stop me. I unbuckle his pants, finagle the zipper, and slide my hand in. I grasp him, and his cock hardens in my grip. I free it, running my hand lightly up and down.

"God," he groans.

I smirk and lean forward, letting my hair fall over one shoulder. I take him in my mouth and suck, bobbing up and down. He doesn't grab the back of my head. His hands stay glued to the leather chair. I cup his balls, and his hips jerk up.

"Come here," he says, firmer. He drags me up.

I release him and wipe my mouth with the back of my hand, but that's all I have time for before his lips are on mine. His tongue sweeps into mine, and that electrical storm in my chest doubles in intensity. He catches my lower lip in his teeth, tugging, and I moan. I climb on his lap, flinging the skirt of my dress out of the way, and press against him.

He moves down my neck, sucking and biting my throat. My body burns for him. His erection brushes my damp panties, *so close*. I reach between us, feeling him again, and move the thin fabric aside.

He grasps my hips as I rise slightly, positioning him. His teeth latch on to the space between my neck and shoulder, and I lower myself. His length enters me, and we both exhale. I stay there for a moment, letting the feel of him inside me just be enough.

But it isn't for long.

He slides the top of my dress down, exposing my pale breasts. I roll my hips forward and lift. He pinches my nipple.

"God, you feel good." He jerks his hips up.

"I need this off." I yank at his shirt until he leans forward slightly. It allows me to pull it off, and I toss it behind us.

"This, too, then," he says.

I raise my arms, and he sweeps the dress off in one motion.

He places me on my feet, then stands, as well. He kicks off his pants and boxers, then kneels before me. He lowers my panties off my hips, kissing just above my small strip of hair.

I use his shoulder for balance to step out of my underwear, and then he rises. He catches my thighs in his grip, propelling me over his shoulder. I squawk when he stands upright, and his palm lands on my ass. He kneads it for a moment, then carries me down the stairs, through the kitchen area, and to the bedroom below deck.

He sets me down on the bed.

I glare up at him. "What was that for?"

He smirks. "I think you like this side."

"What side is that?"

"The side where I manhandle you." He lifts his chin. "Crawl backward."

I eye him, but I can't deny the excitement that flushes my body. I scoot back on my hands and feet until my shoulders bump the back wall.

"Put your wrists through the loops, Amelie. Tighten it with your teeth."

I glance over my shoulder. There's a rope hanging there, anchored just above my head. I can't deny that this is turning me on, and I trust him not to hurt me. I slip my hands in and bite the rope, yanking it until it's tight against my skin.

He climbs over me, checking it. It loosens a fraction.

I stare up at him. He's straddling me, his heavy erection resting between my breasts. I lick my lips, gaze moving from it to his face.

"Ready?" he asks.

I nod.

He scoots backward, all the way off the bed. I watch with my brows furrowed.

"Spread your legs," he says softly.

I do it without hesitation.

He grips one of my ankles, then yanks. I flatten on the mattress, my arms straightening. He kisses my ankle. My calf. The sweetest slow torture.

"Luca," I pant. How can his lips on my leg twist me up inside?

"I haven't touched you in weeks," he says to the corner of my knee. "I'm making up for lost time."

I whimper when his teeth scrape the inside of my thigh.

"Do you know what I see when I look at your scar?" He thrusts his finger into me, curling slightly.

I arch off the bed. My skin is overly sensitive. His breath on my thigh is almost enough to unravel me completely.

"Ames."

I smile. I can't help it. And it prompts me to answer, "I don't know what you see."

"I see your strength. Your resilience." He kisses higher, almost to the apex of my thighs. And still his finger moves in and out, playing me like a damn fiddle.

He's going to bring me to the edge and shove me off it.

"I need to feel you," I whimper. "Please. Luca."

"I quite liked calling you wife," he mumbles. "Fiancée is nice, though. Betrothed. Beloved." His tongue swipes through my slick folds, and I barely bite back a scream. I wiggle, trying to get away, but he latches on to my clit and sucks.

I see stars.

"Which do you like?"

He sucks again, then his tongue plunges inside me. I buck against him, ready to break apart, but he pauses.

"Wife," I blurt out. "I like wife best."

He returns his attention to my pussy, his tongue thrusting in me as his thumb presses to my clit. I come violently, tipping my head back and yelling his name. I try to bat him away and yank my wrists, but the rope holds fast.

"Luca," I demand. My chest heaves.

He rises, crawling over me. "Wife."

My smile is huge. "I love you."

He slides into me without warning, and we both groan.

"I love you, too." His pace is slow, moving in and out of me in centimeters. Every withdrawal causes tremors to rack through my legs. My thighs quiver.

I heave on the ropes again. "I want to touch you."

He obliges with a nod, undoing the binds. I bring my arms around his neck, pulling him flush against me. His weight is grounding, but I've let go of any connotations of being trapped. This is solid comfort. I hold him tighter and wrap my legs around his hips, and we move like that, completely connected.

His hand slips between us, flicking my clit again. He rolls his hips in a new angle. My eyelids flutter at the heady sensation, and then his lips are on mine again. Our tongues tangle, and he swallows every noise I make. His chest vibrates in a silent hum, and he picks up the speed. He leans back slightly to meet my gaze.

Another orgasm takes me by surprise, and I dig my fingernails into his shoulders. But I can't look away from him. It's rawer for him to see it. To see *me*. It crashes through me over and over, and he groans and stills.

We stay locked together for a few long moments, our hearts pounding in near-synchronization.

A small fear claws its way into my heart, but I think he sees it the moment it ensnares me. He cups my face, concern etched in his brows.

"Can he force us to go back?"

He being Luca's father. What's to stop him from coming here and dragging us back by our ears?

"It's not in his best interests," he says. "But if we go back, he might stop us from leaving."

I nod, and a tear slides down my cheek. He leans forward and kisses it, his tongue catching the salty drop.

"I just wish Lucy had been here, you know? She has her own life, but she's still my sister."

Luca nods. "The wedding," he suggests. "We'll fly her out."

I hug him tightly, burying my face in his neck. It means more than I can say, so I don't. I just hold on to him a moment longer.

The sun creeps far enough across the sky that it shines in through the side window, and it's only then that we head back onto the deck. We collect our clothes, and I hunt around the kitchen for food. Luca reels the anchor back up, and I pause on the lower deck to enjoy the sunshine.

When the engine rumbles to life, I go upstairs with the

champagne in its ice bucket, the two glasses, and a brick of cheese and sleeve of crackers.

He grins at me as I set everything down to adjust my dress.

"I like you naked," he calls.

I shake my head, scooping my hair back into a ponytail. "You would."

"Come join me, Ames."

There's the nickname again. It brings another smile to my lips, and I hand him a glass. He guides me onto his lap, and I switch my hold on the cheese and crackers to loop my arm around his neck.

We ride the rest of the way back to the marina like this, close enough that the urge to climb into his skin isn't quite as strong. We eat, we kiss. I rest my chin on his shoulder and watch the view of the mountains behind us fade into the distance.

"This would be a good forever," I murmur in his ear.

He smiles. "I agree."

Epilogue

AIDEN

I slide into my car.

It's been eight weeks since Wilder died, and my leads have all but dried up.

Until tonight.

On my phone is a voice recording of two men discussing my brother's murder. They mention Colin West, the heir of the West empire. They talk about the house in Rose Hill where he hides.

Anger burns through me. It's one thing to sow my brother's blood across the chapel floor—it's another to hide from the truth.

From *me*.

I step on the gas pedal, eyeing the speedometer as it creeps higher. Driving in itself is an adrenaline rush, but this urgency that's captured me is something else entirely.

For the first time in weeks, I'm fucking eager.

My phone beeps at me, alerting me of the upcoming destination. I kill the headlights and roll to a stop a bit down the street. I've got a killer instinct, honed from years of training, and something feels... off.

Over the past few weeks, the Wests have been slowly and methodically evacuating their women from New York City. I'll hand it to them, it took me a long time to realize it. They moved slowly, one or two at a time, until nearly all of them were gone.

The contact who sent me the voice memo suggested Gemma West would be next on the list of women to leave.

The only reason you get the women out of town is when things turn vicious. I didn't realize they assumed we were at that point—I certainly didn't escalate it. Neither did my father. No, we've been riding low while we looked for confirmation of which West killed my brother. And Dad let me take the reins.

This has been my pet project, and I hope to finally close it.

Manhattan in the summer is stifling, and I've been trapped in the public eye for too long. That's my role now—the imposter heir.

That's stifling, too.

I keep my gaze on the house Colin is supposed to be hiding in. It's fancy, a light-colored stucco with the front covered in ivy. A fence adjoins the house on the side I can see. All the windows are dark, and I can't spot any movement. No sign of life.

It seems the universe is determined to prove me wrong, because immediately following that assessment, a dim light illuminates one of the upstairs windows. A shadow crosses in front of it, the light stuttering, and then it all goes still again.

I climb out of the car and release my gun from its holster. I approach the front of the house and keep my weapon at my side. In my other hand, my thumb hovers on the *on* button of a pen light. The front door is unlocked, and I push it open by my fingertips.

A loud clatter rings in my ears, and I drop into a crouch. If that was a surprise attack, I'd probably be dead. I curse my laziness and shine the flashlight in. I hold it aloft with the gun, snapping myself into precision technique to clear the downstairs.

Nothing moves.

I click the light off again and move to the stairs. My foot lands on something, triggering a *snap-snap-snap* in rapid succession.

My anger surges higher when I discover *this* setup: mouse traps.

I grunt and nudge the snapped ones aside, leaving enough space for my foot. I launch up the steps, on full alert. If he's not here, then this whole house is a trap—and my contact is a dead man.

A slight glint of reflected light ankle-high catches my eye, and I freeze. I bend down, touching the fish wire stretched across the hallway. It's attached to a bucket of water balanced precariously on the edge of a side table. Shaking my head, I step over it and continue on.

The lamp is lit in the first bedroom I come to, and I peer into the room. I do a quick inventory, then step fully into the doorway.

And when I see who waits for me, my heart stutters to a stop.

"Gemma."

Her name is out past my lips before I can stop it. My whole world has screeched to a halt, mirroring my heart. *She* can't be here. *She* can't be the one waiting for me. I prepared for anything except this.

The wild, uncaring part of me wants to stomp forward and drag her by her hair out of here. How *dare* she? Does she not care about her life?

Her brother is responsible.

Her brother will pay.

But it's Gemma who squares off to me now, her expression trying hard to be indifferent. There's a little fear in her eyes, though. Like she can't possibly predict what's going to happen next, even though she's here on purpose.

She knows she's the sacrifice. It might have even been her idea to plead for Colin's life.

But she doesn't know that this sacrifice doesn't matter. That the feud between our families doesn't even matter when it comes to her.

I'd never kill her, because she's been mine for years.

That possessiveness strikes a chord in my chest. Her family has given her to me. The girl I claimed when she was sixteen, the one I've watched hungrily since then.

She stares back at me, waiting for me to say something. Anything.

And I will, as soon as I know what the fuck I'm going to do with her.

No one knows the depths that I will go to keep her.

Not even me.

TO BE CONTINUED

in *Savage Prince*, Aiden & Gemma's story.

Acknowledgments

2021 is ushering in so many fabulous things. New friends, new series & characters, new adventures.

I am SO thankful to be able to write for a living. It's been my dream for... well, it feels like forever. But I never thought I'd get here before I turned 30. (By the skin of my teeth, though!)

And you know what? I get to do what I love because of you.

I absolutely adored Luca and Amelie's story. It was so much fun to write and dive into the Mafia world (two worlds, I suppose, if we're being technical). And I had two fantastic cheerleading alpha readers along the way—Rebecca (AKA *my ride or die*) and my lovely PA, Ari. To my other early readers, Tara, Erica, Amber, and Jo: the fact that you take time out of your day to read my stories and give me feedback truly means so much to me.

To my team: Ari, Emmy at Studio ENP for editing, Cassie's beautiful cover design, and Paige for the proofread—you guys are worth everything. I'm so lucky to have found you all. And sorry, I'm never letting you go.

Thank you for reading. For your kind notes and reviews and interacting with me. Onward to the next story!

Also by S. Massery

Dark Bully Romance

College Hockey

Brutal Obsession

Devious Obsession

Fallen Royals

#1 Wicked Dreams

#2 Wicked Games

#3 Wicked Promises

#4 Vicious Desire

#5 Cruel Abandon

#6 Wild Fury

Reverse Harem Romance

Sterling Falls

#1 Thief

#2 Fighter

#3 Rebel

#4 Queen

About the Author

S. Massery is a dark romance author who loves injecting a good dose of suspense into her stories. She lives in Western Massachusetts with her dog, Alice.

Before adventuring into the world of writing, she went to college in Boston and held a wide variety of jobs—including working on a dude ranch in Wyoming (a personal highlight). She has a love affair with coffee and chocolate. When S. Massery isn't writing, she can be found devouring books, playing outside with her dog, or trying to make people smile.

Join her newsletter to stay up to date on new releases: http://smassery.com/newsletter

Made in United States
Troutdale, OR
01/10/2024